THE SHEPHERD AND THE REAPER

THE SHEPHERD AND THE REAPER

BREANNA BRIGHT

CHAPTER 1

THE GIRL GROWS HER HORNS

There was no storm, but the thrashing of the ocean was violent, on par with the pain in Ruby's head.

Two points on her skull had throbbed and ached unyieldingly for the past week. She couldn't sleep at night, so she went to the beach in the early morning hours. She sat there in the sand, the pounding waves peaceful compared to the pounding of her head. She waited for the time to be right to knock on Marlene's door.

Ruby balanced on her haunches, staring at the water crashing over the sand. It clawed forward, hesitated at her shoes, and then crept back to the ocean. The waves were frightening and had prevented any fishing for the past few weeks.

It was a bad omen, but she didn't know what it meant.

She thought she heard the whisper of bells, but when she turned her head, nothing was there.

It was so early her eyes hurt and her mind swam groggily. Dawn slowly snuck in, climbing over the horizon like a child scaling their neighbor's fence. Ruby knew it was still too early to go knocking on doors, but she stood up anyway and approached the small house built on the grass where sturdy farmland bordered the uncertain shore.

When she knocked, it was answered right away by Marlene, who was fully dressed and had her hair done, as if she'd been up for hours.

"I thought you might be visiting soon," she said, stepping aside so Ruby could enter. The girl took a deep breath as she stepped into the cottage, filling her lungs with the scent of dried herbs, sea-battered wood, and tea. She continued to breathe through her nose as she sat down, focusing on the smells of Marlene's home.

The sea witch poured hot water into mugs where tea bags were already waiting. She handed one off to Ruby, who drank deeply, not waiting for it to cool.

"Where is Aster?" Marlene asked.

"I left him at home. Didn't want to worry about losing him in the dark."

"You should keep him with you; he will keep you safe."

Ruby nodded noncommittally. "What do you hear from the sea?"

Marlene set her cup aside and stood up, going to a shelf where a row of glass vials stood at attention. She selected one and popped the cork.

"Trouble," she said.

The witch stood behind Ruby and poured the oil inside the vial onto her fingertips. She handed it to Ruby to hold, and the girl occupied herself with pushing the cork in and out of its home.

Pop. Pop.

Marlene messaged her fingertips into Ruby's skull, and the girl moaned with relief, her body slumping back into the chair. The old woman's fingers moved smoothly through her orange strands, shining from the oil. Her fingertips expertly found the sources of pain and focused on them, making small circles.

"They haven't been able to fish for weeks," Ruby said. "The town will die if the ocean doesn't calm. What is it?"

"Flies come for rotting meat. I don't know what the corpse of a god will attract."

Ruby gritted her teeth at that. She didn't like the idea of more *things* on the water, on her shore, hurting her people. "What can we do?"

"Wait for it to pass," Marlene said. "How does that feel?"

"Better." Ruby straightened up and curved her back until it popped like the cork she played with. "It's been bugging me all week. I don't know if I can wait it out."

"Try." The witch took the bottle back to the shelf. "Come back whenever you need help with the pain."

"Do you want help shell hunting today?"

"No, it's chore day for me. Laundry and cleaning."

"Ugh." Ruby sighed and stood up. "Summer vacation is so boring. There's nothing to do."

"I bet your mom can find some chores for *you*," Marlene said pointedly. The girl rolled her eyes and slumped toward the door.

"See you tomorrow, Marly."

"Better put a stop to that nickname before you do."

Ruby smiled mischievously and left the cottage, leaving only a vague threat of nicknames-to-come.

The sun was up, and though it was still early—about six a.m.—it was already hot. Ruby groaned through her nose and took her shoes off so that she could walk in the water and balance out the temperature. Usually, summers weren't so bad in Loch Lamond, but this one was wilting the plants and forcing everyone to turn on their fans. Autumn never seemed so far away.

Sweat rolled down her stomach as Ruby walked home,

rubbing moisture out of her eyes. She wondered if she should actually start wearing a bra to prevent all the sweat build-up. She hadn't been in need of one, but her body was quickly catching up with her age. The decorations from her sixteenth birthday still hadn't been thrown away.

When she reached the front door, Aster was there, jumping up to glimpse her through the window. The other side of the door was covered in his claw marks.

Ruby had worked tirelessly to train him, but the young Berger Blanc Suisse wasn't taking to it. Not yet a year old, he had undying energy, the attention span of a toddler, and was curious to a fault.

When she opened the door, she saw that the trashcan lid was stuck around his neck.

"Aster, *sit*," she practically begged. He did, but only for a moment. She barely had enough time to get the lid off before his wagging tail propelled him forward and he tried to jump on Ruby's knees.

"*No*," she hissed, nudging him off.

At least he hadn't knocked over the trash can. Ruby replaced the lid and glared at him. "How are you your mother's pup?"

Speaking of mothers, Ruby's would be waking up soon to get ready for work. In preparation, Ruby made some coffee, filling the house with its warm scent. It soon drew out Hannah, sleepy-eyed and dressed for work.

"Hey, sweetheart," she said breathlessly, taking the cup Ruby had readied for her. "Still having trouble sleeping?"

"Yeah," Ruby muttered.

"I guess we can try some sleep medicine. I'd hate for you to deal with insomnia when school starts again."

"Okay."

"So, what are your plans for the day?"

"I dunno. It's so hot, but the ocean is still too choppy to swim in."

"Here, take some money and get an ice cream this afternoon. You cleaned the house for me all week, so I think you've earned an allowance."

"Aw, thanks, Mom. Want me to bring you one for lunch?"

"Tempting, but no. Betsy brought cupcakes yesterday and I don't need any more sugar."

"What were the cupcakes for?"

"Leftovers from her son's birthday— Aster, down!" Hannah pushed the dog, who had been eyeing the table for food, away from her.

"Maybe I'll just work on his training some more," Ruby said, exasperated.

"He doesn't need training—he needs Adderall." Hannah drained the rest of her mug and set it in the sink. "Alright, baby, I'll see you tonight. You making dinner or me?"

"I'll make it. Got nothing else to do."

Hannah kissed her head, right between the two points of pain. They exchanged "I love yous" and parted ways.

Ruby went to the couch and managed to fall asleep for a couple of hours. When she woke up, it was nearing noon and she was feeling hungry. Ruby put a leash on Aster and led the unwieldy dog through the door. Ruby walked everywhere since everything was so close.

Aster pulled hard against his harness. When he first started with a collar, he would strain so hard that it choked him and made him wheeze. Ruby's shoulder ached from trying to hold him in place. Sometimes, she was tempted to take the leash off and just let him run through the countryside until he finally tired out.

She felt guilty thinking it. Aster had been a gift, after all.

The village was busy, or as busy as such a small town could be. Shop owners swept their porches, tourists drank beers on restaurant patios, and kids passed her on their bikes. She passed the library, tempted by the air conditioning and books, but she didn't want to leave Aster outside, so she continued on to the ice cream shop. She bought herself a cone and a cup of vanilla and peanut butter for Aster. The pup gulped it down in seconds and they continued their walk, Ruby focusing on licking up the melting treat.

Eventually, she found herself at the docks, hardly meaning to go there.

They were empty, of course. No one was able to boat or fish safely in these waters. The waves crashed up over the dock, soaking the wood. The large boats bobbed haphazardly, as if they were nothing more than toys.

Ruby relaxed her jaw, realizing that she was gritting her teeth.

Her head hurt like two knives piercing her skull.

If Tess were still here, she would take her out on the waters, but the sailor had left Loch Lamond months ago. Last Ruby had heard she was teaching sailing in a larger town upshore. She had sent her a birthday card.

Ruby sighed deeply. Her head hurt so much. She kept hearing bells. Aster wouldn't stop *tugging*—

She dropped the leash and Aster ran across the street to sniff whatever had his attention. Ruby locked her eyes on one of the dock storage sheds, heart hammering.

Aster needs you...

There were kayaks in that shed.

Mom will be so worried.

She just had to look, see what was happening. This was her town. She had earned it by saving it once, and it was her job to continue to do so.

She went to the shed and forced the door open. It was locked, but Ruby was feeling strong. The plastic door bent, the locking mechanism snapping as she pushed it inward. The canoes and kayaks were lined against the far wall. She grabbed an oar and a life vest. Aster appeared at her feet, drawn by the sound of violence. Ruby ignored him and heaved a boat out of the tiny room.

Aster followed as she dragged the kayak over the dock. She put the life vest on and prepared to board. Aster jumped on her, as if asking what was going on.

"Go home," she said fruitlessly. Aster removed his paws from her thigh but didn't stop staring. Ruby put the boat on the water and lowered herself into it. The waves threw her up and down, but it was an ocean-grade kayak and hard to tip.

Aster started barking and whining, dancing along the edge of the dock as if getting ready to jump in.

"Go away!" Ruby snapped. When she spoke, it didn't sound entirely like her voice. There was a heavy pressure on her head. Aster yipped and ran away.

Ruby gripped the oar and started to paddle. The ocean gave her no help, tossing the boat up and down. But as she rowed further from shore, she felt a strength rise in her arms. The headache disappeared, replaced with a comfortable pressure. Ruby felt in control as she navigated the waves that threatened to capsize her.

Nothing could touch her like this.

She rowed for hours. Each stroke through the raging water was a battle, only pushing her forward a little. She knew where she was going, though. It pulled her, even as it fought against her.

The waters turned black and the sky became featureless and white. Ocean water pounded against her, leaving the taste of salt in her mouth. Her clothes were soaked, and she felt a little nauseous from the rough ride, but she saw it through, finding her way to the place where The Dead God had fallen.

In the water, there was a whirlpool of decay. The smell made her gag so hard she almost threw up. The waters churned and rose from its surface, revealing creatures in its depths, their reflections warbling on the sheets of water. Ruby glared and dropped her oar, standing in the boat.

They all snapped to attention, turning their hungry gazes on her. Some were white like sea foam, while others had translucent skin and glowing bones. Others seemed to be just shadows—until they moved.

She sees...

The horns...

God killer...

Ruby saw a flash of her own reflection, a dark silhouette in the water that shined with yellow where her eyes were and revealed the large antlers on her head.

"Leave this place!" she screamed.

They stared, and she caught a strange smell through the rot. There on the breeze, then gone again.

Fear.

"You dare impede us, human?" They couldn't speak, so they borrowed her voice, speaking as one out of her throat.

"I dare!" she screamed, cutting them off. The water fell and the monsters charged.

Ruby jumped from the boat, meeting them head-on. Her feet hit the water, but she did not sink. The demons fell upon her, and she fought back with her claws, fangs, and horns. Blood stained the water and turned bitter on her tongue.

She felt the thuds as she hit her horns against the creatures, sending vibrations through her entire body. She shuddered and smiled at the sensation. She felt intact and strong. One of the monsters became impaled on the antlers and she laughed at the additional weight on her head.

Jaws snapped onto her limbs, teeth sinking down to the bone. Ruby held them there, trapping the creatures with her own body so that they couldn't pull their mouths free.

Let them starve.

She hooked her elbows around their necks, feeling them thrash against her hold.

Let them choke.

They couldn't break out of her hold, couldn't free their teeth and claws. Ruby felt the tickle of blood run down her antlers and stream in thin rivulets down her face and the back of her neck.

She breathed deeply, even as the monsters continued to squirm. She had them, and would never let go, couldn't afford to let go. The water around them continued to churn, but had calmed down considerably now that Ruby had the monsters contained.

She focused on her breathing, deep and steady.

Don't let go.

She couldn't afford to get tired. She needed to take things slow.

Never let go.

~

"**H**annah?"

The receptionist looked up in surprise to see Sheriff Jack enter the medical center. She gave him a bright smile. He didn't have an appointment, but they had plenty of room for walk-ins.

Jack walked forward, looking nervous. "Are you busy?"

Hannah shrugged. "I'm working."

"Umm, someone found Ruby's dog, Aspen?"

"Aster?"

"Yeah, that all-white puppy with the triangle ears. I have

him in the car, but when I stopped by your place no one was there."

Hannah frowned. "Oh, he must have run away from her. I'll call the house real quick." Picking up the office phone, Hannah dialed their house, but after a few rings, it went to voicemail.

She heaved a heavy sigh. "Of course, no answer. Here, I'll take Aster. I'm about to go on lunch anyway."

Jack nodded and they stepped outside together. Aster had covered the back window in paw prints and saliva, and he looked at Hannah as if he couldn't wait to tell her about his trip in a police car.

"Thanks for grabbing him, Jack."

"No problem. I'll keep an eye out for Ruby, too. How's she been doing, by the way?"

"Fine, I think. Hard to tell with teenagers. Mostly she stays up late and complains about how bored she is."

"Well, if that's all she has to complain about, I'd count it as lucky."

Hannah grabbed Aster's leash—still connected to his harness—and pulled him toward her car. Once the door was open, he eagerly jumped in and Hannah shut it with a sigh. "Mostly she's just been trying to train this dog. Ivas gave her some advice, but he's just so…much."

"How is Ivas?" Jack asked. "Haven't heard from him lately."

"Fine as far as I know. Still dog training with that farming family."

Jack lingered a moment, seeming like he wanted to keep the conversation going but had nothing else to say. "Well, I'll leave you to it."

"Thanks again." Hannah started her car, having to actually turn on the AC, and headed back home. She usually ate her lunch at the picnic table outside the medical office, but it looked like it would be a desk lunch today since her break would be spent wrangling dog and daughter. She gave Aster the stink eye as he obliviously stared out the window.

"You're a real handful, you know that? I can't believe you ran away from Ruby."

Aster didn't answer, but in the rearview mirror, she saw his tail cease wagging and his tongue slip back into his mouth.

He whined.

Hannah glanced toward where he was staring and saw the docks down the hill.

Changing course, Hannah turned and headed back into town, driving to the docks where she gave everything a scan. Aster whined again, digging at the door as if to get out.

Through her window, Hannah saw that one of the storage sheds was open and some canoes had fallen out.

Parking the car, Hannah hopped out and ran into the nearest shop, not bothering to ask permission before she grabbed their phone and tried the house again. The shop-keeper frowned at her with concern.

No answer.

She immediately dialed the sheriff's office. After Ruby had disappeared last year, she had it memorized.

Hannah's stomach twisted.

"Jack, can you come down to the docks? I think something's wrong."

~

Ruby was tired.

It didn't matter. How she felt wasn't impor-tant—only holding these things back was important. They had caused the ocean to become turbulent and had to be held back. The blood of the creature on her horns ran into the corners of her mouth. She licked it to clench her thirst.

She focused on her breathing.

She promised that she would never let go.

But she couldn't do it forever.

The soft sound of bells echoed over the vast ocean. Ruby gasped and looked up, knowing that she was really hearing it this time.

As if knowing it was needed, the Messenger appeared. Its spider-like legs walked gracefully over the water, as if there were an invisible film. Each point of its legs bent the water but did not break it. Ruby looked up at the darkness of its hood, and it looked back at her silently.

"I need to send a message," she said. Each word physically hurt.

The Messenger only stared, and it took her a few moments to remember that everything had a price.

She often had nightmares about the price her father paid to send his message.

She sighed. "I don't know what to give you."

The Messenger studied her a moment, then reached forward with a single spindle leg. The bells tied to it whispered at the movement. It touched her chest.

Ruby gasped and clenched her teeth in surprise. The Messenger pulled something away from her, an orb so gorgeous and bright she couldn't believe it had been inside her. As beautiful as it was, it was excruciating. She winced, unable to look at it as the rays of light struck her eyes.

The Messenger tucked it into its cloak. Payment received, it then produced a scroll tied in green ribbon from a bag hanging off its body.

"This message needs to go to Ivas S'barge," Ruby panted. Sweat rolled down her temples. "Tell him to please come. Tell him I need his help."

The Messenger went as far as the legends would allow. Its story wasn't spoken of beyond that point, no longer known as the coast transformed into hills and the hills became mountains.

When its story faded, it was forced to stop.

But it had help.

From its cloak, a little butterfly appeared, its black wings highlighted by red spots and yellow stripes. It fluttered into the air and continued the journey, using the strange instincts migrating animals have to find its way.

If all went well, it would arrive safely.

The Messenger waited.

CHAPTER 2

THE POSTMAN COMES

*I*vas stared down the coyote.

Blanc was behind him, growling, her hair standing straight up. Ivas used his harshest voice to command her to stay back. She didn't want to obey, but it was imperative that she did so.

The coyote was aggressive and foaming at the mouth. It had wandered into the paddock during the day, which was alarming enough, but when Ivas spotted the creature, it was clear it was very sick.

No, it was passed sick. At this point, it was already dead —only the body still moved.

Blanc had smelled the intruder before the sheep even started to cry out. She darted into the field so fast that Ivas barely registered it. He barely reached her in time, calling her off before she could engage the predator in battle.

Now, the sick beast stood only a few yards away, and all Ivas had was a shepherd's staff, held out in both hands so that if the animal launched, he could catch it in the mouth. He could keep the coyote at bay, but if it attacked, he wouldn't be able to stop Blanc, and if she got even one cut or bite…

He needed to think fast.

Ivas took a few careful steps forward. The coyote swayed, its head bobbing nauseatingly. Ivas shouted and slammed his staff on the ground, hoping the noise would frighten the creature off. Spurred by his intimidation tactic, Blanc snarled and barked.

The coyote took a couple of shaky steps back. Ivas felt sorry for it. Blanc inched closer and he snapped at her to stay back. Her entire body trembled, fighting an internal battle between listening to him and protecting him.

With no other choice, Ivas made his move. With just a few feet between him and the coyote, he leaped forward, first whacking his staff at Blanc so she wouldn't jump as well, then going for the coyote. The animal stumbled in surprise and Ivas was able to get behind it, putting the staff against its neck and pushing down on its throat.

Ivas fell onto his back, pulling the coyote down with him. It laid on him, back to chest, flailing and yelping. Blanc made circles around them, barking and screaming. Ivas just focused on his task.

"It'll be better this way," he said into the coyote's ear, "it'll stop hurting soon."

He pulled the staff down. It wasn't strangling the coyote, but crushing its windpipe. The animal jerked and twisted. Ivas used his knees to hold it in place and keep the coyote from rolling off of him.

They remained in that position for a long time. Ivas wanted to be sick, his heart aching at the sound of the coyote's strangled death yelps, foamy saliva running from its open mouth as it struggled to pull in air. The whole while, Ivas kept whispering his sorrows.

Eventually, the coyote stopped moving.

Blanc continued to growl, watching the coyote's body become limp and heavy on top of Ivas's. He released the staff and let the coyote slide off of him. His arms and hands ached from holding the strangling position for so long. He stood up and hooked the crook of his shepherd's staff around the neck of the animal so that he could drag it into the woods.

Blanc was shaking, her fur still spiked up, following with her head down low as if she expected the coyote to attack again. Ivas went into the woods and buried the coyote as best he could under rocks and leaves.

He would have to burn it later, but the shadows had grown long while he worked. With a deep, tired sigh, he turned away from the grave and called for Blanc to follow him. The body would wait until the morning.

The sheep grazed without any care in their fenced enclosure. He ordered Blanc to gather them up and she did so. The sheep obeyed, knowing it was time to go into the barn with little prompting. Ivas double-checked that everything was sound, counting the sheep as they filed inside. When it was done, he eagerly headed for his cabin next to the farmhouse.

His place was separated from the main home of the family that owned the farm, giving him plenty of privacy. It was only one room with a kitchenette—a farmhand's residence, rustic and simple, which suited Ivas just fine.

Inside, he took a long, hot shower, getting the smell of wild dog off his skin. Blanc settled down on her dog bed next to the wood oven, no doubt tired from their stressful encounter. When he finished, he heard a bell ringing, the sign that dinner was ready and he was welcome to join. But Ivas didn't feel like eating that night. Normally, he enjoyed spending time with his host family, but the coyote had rattled him. Instead, he warmed up a can of pasta, watched some television, then went to bed. His hands ached from where he had gripped the staff, and his breath came out in a rueful shudder.

"Had to be done, yeah, Blanc?" he asked, looking down at his pretty white dog. She smiled at him and gave her tale a tap. She was safe, he was safe, so were the sheep.

But it still hurt.

He rolled over and shut his eyes as if he could scold himself to sleep. After a while, the aches and tiredness caught up with him—there was no insomnia on a farm—and he went to a blissful sleep.

That's when the postman arrived. His red and yellow-striped wings fluttered through the air as he made the journey into Ivas's cabin. He was a slow but strong traveler, and physical walls posed no problem. He slipped into Ivas's home and made a safe landing on the sleeping man's fore-head, settling in as if he had found a good flower.

It was time to rest. Time to dream.

Ivas dreamed of Ruby.

She stared at him with those hard brown eyes, blood running in thin lines down her face. She had the look of someone holding up a great weight, sweating, struggling to breathe.

Monsters.

They had latched themselves onto her limbs, digging their fangs in deep. To Ivas, they looked like the coyote he had killed, foaming at the mouth and making that terrible dying sound. That scared, pain-filled animal scream that wracked his very soul.

He could hear the ocean, smell decay.

"Come back," Ruby said, "I need your help."

Ivas woke with a jerk, startling the little postman. He felt the flutter of its wings and swiped at it in panic, but the butterfly moved to the foot of the bed, sitting on a post instead. Blanc looked up and whined.

Come back.

Was it just a dream?

Ruby needs you.

No, of course not. As much as he wanted it to be, he knew better. He looked at the postman and sighed.

It was a message.

The Messenger.

Ivas sat up and pushed the covers away. He didn't know what time it was, but it didn't matter. He wouldn't be sleeping tonight. Instead, he found his bag and started to pack.

~

In the morning, before the sun was fully up, he met Bram outside at the barn. The old man was always up first, and usually the last to bed.

Bram saw the bag on Ivas's shoulder and took a deep breath as if readying himself. "I thought you weren't leaving until winter."

"Something has come up. I received word from home and I need to return."

"Not much notice."

"Sorry, Bram. I'm going to return as soon as I'm able."

"You sure you have to go?"

"I'm afraid so."

"Alright. At least Eli is back from school."

Ivas nodded in agreement. "I'll contact you as soon as I know when I can come back."

"Need a ride to town?"

"If you can provide it."

"Yeah, yeah," Bram grumbled as they walked to his truck and got in. Blanc hopped into the back, used to their rides into town. The well-cared-for vehicle started up right away and Bram steered them toward the gravel road, which turned into a highway, which took them down the mountain, almost an hour's drive into town. From there, Ivas would have to take a bus to the nearest port town, another couple of hours.

"Here," Bram practically punched Ivas in the chest with a fist of cash. "For lunch."

"Oh, that's okay. I have some," Ivas said.

"Take it. It's payment for the last week plus a little more so you'll be guilted into coming back." Bram glared out the window, grumpy.

"Thanks, Bram." Ivas accepted the cash and shoved it in his pocket.

"Shut up."

"Okay."

"We still have to finish training the pups," he insisted.

"Of course."

Blanc's pups were growing fast and were undergoing strict training so they could be sold as herding dogs. Ivas was the only one who knew how to properly train the dogs, and that was the reason Bram really wanted him back.

"Connie will be pissed."

"Tell her I'm sorry."

"No, you tell her when you get back. I'm not your damned messenger. What are you still doing here? You want to miss your bus?"

"Nope." Ivas smiled, gave Bram a friendly pat on the shoulder, and slipped out of the car as the older man swiped him away. Blanc jumped out of the bed and joined him, tail wagging eagerly.

Ivas bought himself a coffee and pastry for breakfast and ate it on the bus once it arrived. He had to put a leash on Blanc to appease the bus driver, and she sat quietly at his feet. A woman across the aisle noticed her and smiled.

Snowcapped mountains lined the horizon, and the sky was a special shade of blue—clean and clear. He took it all in as the bus carried them down the mountain toward the shore. When they arrived, Ivas alighted, and a little boy squealed upon realizing that there was a dog on board. Ivas allowed him to pet Blanc, then quickly headed for the port.

The port master was set up in an office with a window half-open to talk to passersby. He nodded to Ivas politely and gave Blanc a smile.

"Are there any passenger boats available?" Ivas asked.

"Where ya heading?"

"Loch Lamond."

"Hmm, no boats going that way, I'm afraid. Water's been too dangerous."

"What do you mean? Storms?"

"No, just choppy water, no good fishing, everyone just been staying away."

Ivas frowned. The image of Ruby surrounded by monsters flashed in his head, and his stomach jerked nauseously.

"What would be the best way to get there?"

"I'd say take the train to Balliecroy and see if they have a bus."

Ivas sighed. It wouldn't be as fast as a boat, and time was of the essence.

"Is there *anyone* willing to sail to Loch Lamond?"

"It'd be cheaper to take the train than bribe one of the sailors."

One of the sailors.

Ivas thought back to his letters to Tess and the postcards she had sent to him. She was working along the bay, hopping from port to port, and last he heard, she had been in a place called Cape Pale.

"How far is Cape Pale from here?" Ivas asked. The port

master turned away into his office then spun back around with a map in his hand. He pressed it to the window so that Ivas could see.

"Little ways north of here."

Ivas studied the map, finding his location on the shore, then following the coast up until he found the label for the cape. It wasn't too far.

"Anyone going *that* way?" He asked.

The port master lowered the map and smiled. "Got a boat just about to ship out."

~

It was a short trip to Cape Pale, which Ivas was grateful for. He and Blanc stood at the railing the whole time, watching the coast crawl past. Sands turned to cliffsides painted white by the sun, and these soon gave way to heather fields. Houses and buildings cropped up, becoming more abundant as they reached Cape Pale. At the dock, Ivas quickly made landfall and headed to the next port master.

"I'm looking for a woman who goes by Tess. She's a sailor."

"Just missed her. She was set to head out about fifteen minutes ago."

Ivas huffed in frustration. "Do you know when she'll be back?"

"Maybe an hour?" the port master shrugged unhelpfully.

With a quiet swear, Ivas turned away and began walking down the port, letting his legs move so his brain could think. Blanc trotted alongside him, indifferent to their schedule.

Head down, hand clutching his pack, Ivas listed his other options, not sure which one would be the most efficient.

Wait for Tess? Get on a train? He was terrified that Ruby couldn't wait for either of them.

And then he heard her voice.

Ivas froze and shot his head up, looking toward the boat from where the voice echoed. It was rare enough to hear women working the port, but Tess's voice rang out at him clearly. He ran down the dock.

There she was. *The Ocean's Scorn* floated patiently, and standing on the ramp to board her was Tess, who was talking to another man loaded down with various luggage.

"Sir, please…" Tess was trying to cut off the man's conversation, but he didn't seem to hear her.

"…frozen mud laid on the other side, which was said to be twice as large as the ocean. This alone made travelers weary, for even if you got past the monsters, who could pack provisioning enough to make it over such a vast—"

"Tess!" Ivas yelled her name, and she turned her head to him, expression going from exasperated to elated.

"Ivas!" Pushing past the other gentleman, she jumped onto the dock and took a running tackle into the shepherd. Ivas braced himself and put his arms around her, using the momentum to spin her around. Tess laughed, lifting her goulashes into the air.

"You're here! What are you doing here?"

"I need a ride and I'm told you're the best sailor in the bay."

"Best sailor in the country," Tess corrected him, looking smug. "You're timing is right. I was just trying to tell *this* gentleman that I'm not giving passenger rides today —but now that you're here…"

Ivas smiled apologetically.

"Guess I have no choice if I want to spend some time with you. Hope you don't mind some company." She pointed at the other man, who was watching them from behind a pair of round glasses. He wrung his hands nervously.

"I don't."

"You will. I was supposed to leave fifteen minutes ago. He won't stop talking."

Tess turned back to the other man and threw her hands up. "You're in luck. Looks like I'm a passenger voyage today."

The man beamed and immediately began gathering his luggage, dragging it up the ramp as if worried Tess might change her mind.

Tess put an arm around Ivas's waist and held on to him as they boarded. "So where am I taking you?"

"I need to get to Loch Lamond."

Tess stopped halfway up the ramp. Ivas stepped out of her arm and looked back. "What is it?"

"…I can't take you there, Ivas."

"I know the seas have been rough, but you're truly the best sailor I know, and—"

"It's not that." Tess looked down at her feet shamefully, grabbing her arm with the opposite hand. "I wasn't planning on ever going back there. Not after what happened."

"Ruby's in danger," Ivas said quietly. "I wouldn't ask this of you if it wasn't important."

He could see the divot where Tess was biting the inside of her lip.

"I *can't.*"

"You're the only—"

"I can't!" Tess snapped, head shooting up. "How can *you?* After what happened, I could barely get myself back on a boat. I can only give lessons now because if I lose sight of the shore, I start to go mad." Her hands went to her face, covering her eyes. "I'm not… I…"

Ivas stepped forward and put his arms around her,

pressing her head to his chest. "I'm sorry. I didn't mean to put that on you."

"I'm sorry." Tess hung limply, not returning the hug. "I'm not…who I was. I've been trying to get there, been trying to get past the fear, but it's so…"

She heaved a deep sigh and finally returned the hug. She lifted her face to meet Ivas's eyes. "Ruby's in danger?"

He nodded.

She shuddered. "Then I guess it's time I get past the fear."

"Get me as close as you can. That's all I ask."

They released each other and boarded the boat, a heavy tension replacing the happiness of their reunion.

"Life vests on!" Tess called out. "We're leaving in one minute!"

Ivas found an orange floatation device and strapped it over his chest. The extra passenger was having trouble with his, so Ivas helped get it situated and tightened.

"Thank you, sir. You seem to be familiar with our captain."

"We're old friends," Ivas confirmed.

"Then I owe you. She wasn't going to grant passage until you came along." He held out his hand. "My name is Archibald Cobstone."

"Ivas S'barge."

Archibald was a small, thin man with spectacles and a corduroy jacket. He looked particularly out of place on the small vessel.

"And where are you going, Mr. S'barge?"

"Just Ivas. I'm trying to get to Loch Lamond."

"I've never been out that way, but I hear it's lovely country." The man's spectacles slid down his sweaty nose and he pushed them back into place.

Ivas nodded in agreement. "It is. Where are you heading then?"

"My day is full of station hopping, but I missed my last train to Balliecroy. That's why I was attempting to commander our fine captain here."

They both looked over to Tess, who was finishing checks on the boat. In the driver's seat, she started the engine. Blanc had decided to assist her with boat driving, following her around the deck.

"From Balliecroy I need to get on a train to the capital. I'm attending university there," Archibald explained.

Ivas studied the man for a moment, trying to determine how old he was, but his droopy complexion and wide eyes made it impossible to tell. "Student or professor?"

"Assistant professor, and lucky to get it too. Not so many jobs for folklore history these days."

"That's your degree?"

"History is my degree, with a minor in literature, but I specialized in mythology and f-folk- folklore. I managed to find a professor at university teaching such a class who agreed to take me on. I'm very e-excited."

"Congratulations."

"Thank you! But what do you do?"

"Sheep farmer."

"No kidding? You know, most people I interviewed for my thesis regarding oral storytelling were farmers and the elderly. I assume you have tales passed down to you as well."

"Oh yeah, lots of that in Loch Lamond. Lots of superstition, actually. A man down there, Mr. Poppermill, is sort of the town's local historian. He has all kinds of stories." Ivas was happy to share his fondness of the story-collector.

"You don't say? That is quite interesting. Would you say these are rather commonplace? Or unique?" Archibald leaned forward, going past sincerity to overeager.

Before Ivas could answer, the boat began to move, and

Archibald's complexion went from clammy and pale to sickly green.

"Excuse me," he said quietly before turning quickly to the boat rail and leaning his head over the side. Ivas winced in sympathy and walked over to Tess instead.

"It's good to see you again."

"You too, despite the circumstances."

"I really am sorry. If it weren't an emergency, I would have found another way."

Tess sighed. "Then I hope you'll understand if I don't stay. After I drop you off, I need to head back."

"Then I'd better make the most of the time we have." Ivas sat down next to her. "Tell me everything."

Tess smiled. "Pretty much what I tell you in my letters. I've been giving lessons to potential boat drivers, helping them earn their licenses. On my off days I've been heading inland, doing kayaking and canoeing in rivers instead. Oh, and hiking, too. Getting my land lubber legs. I was seeing someone for a bit, but it didn't work out. Since then, I've been avoiding dates like the plague. I know it's cliché, but I'm taking the time to just work on myself. Started taking some art classes."

"What kind?"

"Recently did pottery. I'll send you a lopsided mug."

"Please do," Ivas smiled. "You like it? Your life right now?"

"I do. Part of me thinks about leaving the water entirely. Guess we'll see."

"Hard to imagine you not on a boat."

Tess shrugged. "We all go through phases, you know? Maybe someday you won't want to herd sheep anymore."

"What? And let Blanc retire? She'd never forgive me."

The Berger Blanc Suisse looked up at her name, resting her head on Ivas's knee as if in agreement.

Tess laughed. "And you? Still enjoying training the dogs?"

"Absolutely. Blanc's pups are doing great. They should all be able to be adopted out as herding dogs in another year or two. The family is good to me. It's been a long time since I didn't live by myself."

"And they have kids, too, right?"

"Yeah, but they're both grown up. Don't have to deal with any brats."

"Aw, come on, don't like kids?" Tess teased.

"I was barely one myself."

"Yeah, your grandpa grew you up pretty quickly. Hey, you mind checking on our friend? I've never seen someone get seasick that fast. There's some drinks in the cooler."

Ivas obliged, returning to Archibald after fetching a bottle of water from the in-boat cooler. Archibald accepted it gratefully. They stepped away from the rail and took a seat in the passenger chairs.

"T-tell me one of your stories, if you don't mind. Such things are my passion and I would be- b-beside myself if there were one I had missed." He burped. "I might help take my mind off the...sea."

"Well..." Ivas considered it, and of course the story most foremost to his recollection was the fog and the Messenger. So Ivas told him the legend of the strange spider-like creature that visited people in the night, delivering messages from the dead.

The historian was enthralled, elbows on his knees as he leaned forward to listen. "I've never heard this b-before. A messenger? That's fantastic. And you say this Mr. Pop-po-Poperwill...?"

"Poppermill."

"He has texts of these stories?"

"He has a lot of books, but most of them he just remembers."

"How old is he?"

"Couldn't tell you. He was old when I was a kid. Some people are just like that, I guess." Ivas shrugged.

Before the man could ask another question, the boat gave a pitch, and Archibald was on his feet, rushing to the edge.

Ivas looked over at Tess worriedly. The ocean was getting rougher, and her hands were tight on the wheel.

"Are you okay?" he asked.

Her eyes were wide, staring ahead. "I... I don't know..."

"Are we close?"

"Still one town over."

"Stop there then. I'll find my way."

Tears built up in Tess's eyes, shining as she looked up at him. "I'm sorry, Ivas."

He pressed his forehead to the top of her head and gave a reassuring squeeze to her shoulder. "You did more than enough."

They ported at the next town. Tess wouldn't make eye contact with him as they set the ramp down and disembarked. Archibald had to lie down on the dock.

"Hey," Ivas took Tess's hand. "Thank you for everything."

She shook her head. "Don't thank me. I couldn't even get you to—"

"It's okay, really. I left too, remember?"

"Do you still have nightmares?" Tess whispered, her hand tight on his.

"Every night."

She exhaled, letting herself tremble. "Be careful, Ivas. And... don't tell Ruby. You may not be disappointed in me, but she would be."

"You know, maybe it is time to find a new phase in your life. It's too short to live it scared, right?"

Tess smirked. "Maybe, but I have no idea what I would do. Sailing is all I've ever really known."

"You'll find it," Ivas said confidently. "And if you do find yourself landlocked, come find me, okay? We'll learn some pottery together."

"I will, and that's a threat."

Happy to leave on a laugh, Ivas whistled to Blanc and left the boat, heading toward the nearest patch of grass so the dog could have a bathroom break.

He turned back one last time, giving Tess a farewell wave.

"Write to me!" she shouted at him, cupping her hands around her mouth.

"I will!" Ivas called back before turning away and leaving the docks.

As he headed down the street, looking for the nearest bus or train station, a voice suddenly rang out.

"Sir! Sir!"

Ivas recognized the assistant professor's voice and turned his head. Archibald was running toward him, suitcase in hand and a duffle bag under his arm. His free hand was holding down his hat as he attempted to catch up.

"Ah-ha! I caught you! Thank goodness. I've decided—and pardon me if I'm being too forward—to go to Loch Lamond with you!"

"You did?"

"Yes. I can r-rent a car and it will be much more comfy—comfortable and fast— faster than the bus, don't you think? Of course, you don't have to, but the university is covering my traveling costs, and I owe you for getting me on the boat."

Ivas blinked at him, perplexed. "But why? The stories?"

"Of course the stories! That's what it's all about, isn't it? If this Mr. Poppermill has original folktales, then imagine what that'll do for my reputation. I'll be prom... pre... promoted in no time. What do you say?"

Archibald released his bag and held out his hand. Ivas took it.

"I won't turn it down. Is it alright if my dog comes, though? This is Blanc, my sheepdog. She travels everywhere with me."

"I see. Well, let's keep that hush-hush. I'll go rent the car and meet you at the front."

"Alright, if you're sure?"

"Absolutely. This will be a great adventure!" With a wide grin, Archibald headed toward the rental services and Ivas exchanged a look with Blanc.

"Well, can't turn down a free ride, yeah?"

Blanc wagged her tail.

Ivas drove since he knew the way. Archibald excitedly tapped his knees in the passenger seat. Blanc sat in the middle seat in the back so that she could peer over the console through the windshield. Soon, Ivas could see the grey ocean on the horizon. He noticed how the trees moved in the wind. The tall waves in the sea.

"Are there any places to stay around here?" Archibald asked, seeming to realize that this place might be too small to host an inn.

"We can find you a room to rent," Ivas said. "Though I'm not sure how long we'll be staying."

The cobblestone streets of the town weren't friendly to vehicles, so Ivas parked in a public lot and they left their bags in the trunk as they walked through the village. Archibald commented on the charming architecture, but Ivas wasn't paying attention, focused solely on his next move.

The town felt quiet and heavy.

Where was Ruby?

Should he go to Ruby's house? Would she be there? Maybe he should go see Jack first. Would Poppermill know? Archibald was talking, but Ivas didn't hear him. He was remembering his dream—the smell of salt water, the vision of monsters with their teeth clamped onto Ruby's body.

He jumped when Archibald poked his arm. "Mr. S'barge?"

"Sorry, what?"

"I asked where this storyteller was."

Ivas cleared his throat. "Umm, there's something I need to do first. Sorry, but I'm going to have to abandon you for a moment."

Archibald laughed. "Not to worry. I commandeered *your* trip, remember? No, no, don't worry about me. I'll wander to this nice cafe over here and you come find me when you're done."

Ivas was grateful for Archibald's compliance. He gave him a thankful nod and started off toward the docks while the assistant professor split from him to go to the restaurant.

At the port, Ivas found that all the boats were docked and covered against the choppy sea. Blanc pulled her ears back and squinted her eyes against the spray of gray water that rained on them as the waves hit the dock. Ivas turned up his collar and stuck his hands in his pockets, shoulders pressed against his ears as they walked down the dock away from the boats, out where it jutted into the ocean. Normally, this area would be filled with fisherpeople and their reels, but the shores were empty.

Ivas walked until the soaked wood of the dock ended and he could only stare out into the misty sea, not sure what he was looking for.

Was Ruby out there? Did Hannah know? Why did she call for him? Why did she go *out there*?

Blanc barked sharply, startling Ivas. He swung his head to and fro to see what the herding dog barked at, and finally spotted a tall, dark figure walking out from the horizon.

It was the Messenger.

Ivas gripped the railing of the dock, his stomach turning in anxiety at the sight of the creature. Even though he knew it meant no harm, there was an instinctual part of his brain that saw the ragged cloak and long spider-like legs and told him to *run*.

But he stayed still, watching the Messenger approach. It did so calmly, the points of its strange legs walking on top of the water, not bothered by the frequent waves. When it arrived, Ivas tilted his head up, seeing a glimmer in the darkness of its hood, but no other details.

"Where is Ruby?" He asked.

The Messenger lifted a spindly leg and reached into a pouch hanging from its body. It produced a single slip of paper and presented it to Ivas, who took it, careful not to accidently brush his fingers against the creature.

Touching it just seemed…wrong.

Its job done, the Messenger turned away and began walking back across the sea.

Ivas looked down at the paper and read two words: *The Harvestmen.*

That was it. With a frown, Ivas shoved the paper in his pocket and quickly turned away from the icy cold water. Blanc eagerly followed, giving herself a shake to dismiss the droplets of water that had gathered in her white fur.

Ivas returned to the restaurant where Archibald had gone and found the scholar sitting at a table with a cup of tea, talking to the server. Ivas approached and, without a word, took the man's tea and gulped it down, trying to get rid of the cold that had overtaken his body and soul.

"Everything alright?" Archibald blinked at him in surprise.

"Not sure. Let's go see Poppermill."

The scholar became excited, forgetting about his stolen tea. He hopped up and followed Ivas out the door as he led the way to Poppermill's private library, squeezing the little piece of paper in his pocket.

CHAPTER 3

THE SHEPHERD LEARNS A NEW TALE

*I*vas took the lead again and headed toward the tall, crooked building where Mr. Poppermill lived. He had no worries about whether the door would be answered when he knocked, and rightfully so, as it was opened right away.

"Ho, ho! Ivas! Good to see you back!" The old man was all wrinkles and smiles. He had a cane that wasn't there the last time Ivas had seen him. His small frame was hidden under a heavy cardigan despite the warm air.

"Good to see you too. May I present Archibald…" Ivas trailed off, forgetting the other man's full name.

"Cobstone," the scholar finished, reaching out his hand to shake. "I hear you are a collector of stories?"

"Didja now?"

"What?"

"I told Mr. Cobstone here about your collection," Ivas said. "He studies such things and was very keen on seeing it."

"Well, I'm always happy to receive visitors." Poppermill stepped back and allowed the two men and the dog to enter.

Ivas was immediately wrapped in the smell of aged paper. Books lined the floor, staircase, and any available gaps in the bookshelves. He heard Archibald gasp with wonder behind him.

"This is amazing. I've never seen such a large personal collection," the smaller man said, running his fingers over some spines. "How did you acquire them all?"

"A long life," Poppermill answered simply. He made his way through the maze of book piles into a kitchen, where he filled a kettle with water. "Have a seat anywhere."

Luckily, Poppermill's sitting room was more easily accessible, and the two guests sat down on a couple of chairs. Blanc obediently laid down at Ivas's feet, crossing her paws in an amusingly lady-like way. Archibald snatched up one of the books on the coffee table and began leafing through it.

Soon, the kettle whistled, tea was steeped, and Poppermill joined them. "So then, you've come for some stories, eh?"

"Yes! Stories!" Archibald looked up from his book. "The backbone of one's culture. I'm sure you would agree."

Ivas interrupted quickly, realizing that Archibald was the kind of man who would have long conversations about his favorite subject. "There is a specific story I'm looking for."

"What's that, sheep farmer?"

"Do you know any stories about things called the Harvestmen?"

"Like the spider?" Archibald asked. "Where I'm from, they're called Grandfather Long Legs. Isn't it interesting how a few hundred miles will change the name of something, even if it's the same language?"

Poppermill wiggled a finger in his ear. "I do have some spider stories."

"No... Well, maybe," Ivas said. "I think these are creatures of myth. Have you heard of them from any story?"

"Eh, not specifically any stories *about* them," Poppermill said offhandedly. "They're these creatures that are said to come out and scavenge on dead things."

"Just like the sp-spider!" Archibald said, shooting a finger into the air.

Blanc's head shot up worriedly as she felt Ivas stiffen.

"Like…dead bodies?" he asked.

"Nah, nah, not people. *Supernatural* things that have died. Hang on a sec." Poppermill pushed himself up, using his cane for support as he went into the hallway. Ivas listened as books and papers were shuffled around. The old man returned holding a thick volume in black leather. "Got a story that mentions them in here."

"How…how did you do that?" Archibald asked. "Do you have a catalog?"

"Just the 'ol noggin'," Poppermill said, tapping his temple. He sat down again, opened the book in his lap, and flipped through until he found the story he wanted.

"This story tells us about the death of a fae queen. She stole a child from its home but forgot to leave a changeling in its place. The child's mother, who I'm sure you can imagine was in a horrible frenzy, entered the winter court to challenge the fae queen and get her baby back. The queen tried everything to stop the mother. She tried to put her to sleep with a fae song, so the mother stabbed her own ears with iron nails. Next, the queen gave her impossible riddles written on parchment paper, but the mother used the same nails to hang the riddles in trees so the fae could not reach them.

"The queen tried to tempt her with amazing food, but the mother did not eat, drinking her own breast milk instead so that she would not starve. The queen sent terrible creatures after her, but the mother killed each ghoul and goblin that tried to thwart her. Her last defense was an illusion around her castle, but the cries of the babe lead the mother right to her child.

"To put a stop to the fae queen of the winter court, the mother offered her own blood in exchange for the child's freedom. The fae queen said she would need a lot of blood to satisfy the contract, and she kept demanding more and more from the mother until, almost completely drained, she passed out on the floor, surrounded by buckets and teacups and goblets of her own blood.

"Thinking she had won, the queen toasted to her victory and drank from one of the goblets. The iron in the mother's blood poisoned her and she died. When the mother regained consciousness, she took her baby and left the winter court, but her triumph came at a price.

"The fae queen's death brought a terrible imbalance to the seasons. The ice and snow melted, leading to unusually warm weather, terrible thunderstorms, and hurricanes. The Harvestmen swarmed the court, who sought to imbibe themselves on the essence of the queen—swallowing the souls she had stolen over the years. They ravaged the court so that no fae could enter, and winter did not return for many years."

"They came for the dead queen," Ivas murmured to himself.

"I have never heard this story before. This is fantastic!" Archibald clapped his hands together. Blanc's triangle ears perked up at the sound. "Do you have others? Could I make copies?"

"How did they make the Harvestmen go away?" Ivas interrupted again. "You said the fae couldn't get into the court because of them, so how did they make them go away?"

"I don't know." Poppermill shrugged. "The story ends there. You're a farmer, how do you get rid of scavengers?"

Ivas thought back to the coyote, choking it to death with his staff. Scavenger animals were usually shy, almost cowardly, but sometimes they were desperate enough to fight back. Sometimes, the meal they wanted was worth it.

"I need to go." Ivas stood up.

"O-oh…" Archibald stood up as well, unsure of the proper measures for decorum to take in such a situation.

"You're welcome to stay, professor," Poppermill said. "Seemed like you still had some questions for me."

Archibald grinned in gratitude and sat back down. "Will you be coming back, Ivas?" he asked. "We did share the car, after all."

Ivas hesitated. "I'm not sure. If I'm not back by tonight, you can take the car back to the train station. Leave my bag with Mr. Poppermill."

"Are you sure?" Archibald seemed genuinely concerned, and Ivas appreciated the small man's sincerity.

"Yes, don't worry about me. Good luck with your new job." With a sharp whistle, Ivas called Blanc to follow him, and the two of them left Poppermill's house. It was time to visit another old friend.

~

Ivas walked across the sand toward Marlene's house, his boots struggling on the uneven surface. Blanc jogged ahead and met Marlene as the woman came out of the house. The sea witch gave Blanc a thorough ear rub, making the dog fall over on her side in bliss.

"What's wrong?" she asked, looking up at Ivas. The wind tossed hundreds of strands of her greying hair around her face and tried to pull away her shawl.

"Something has happened to Ruby," Ivas said. "I had a dream about it."

Marlene sighed. "I've been trying to keep an eye on her, but the summer has been tough."

"I think she's out there." Ivas pointed to the ocean, where the murky waves were tossed and flung about. "There are these things called the Harvestmen. Do you know anything about them?"

Marlene's brow furrowed and she shook her head. As Ivas told her the story of the doomed fae queen, she led him inside and began making tea. Ivas explored her collection of jars and drying herbs with his eyes. Bundles hung from the ceiling, and different containers lined the wall shelves of the kitchen, old pasta sauce and peanut butter jars filled with a variety of concoctions.

"There wasn't any information on how to get rid of them," Ivas finished. He sat at the heavy wooden table, fiddling with a small yellow flower that had been left there. "I thought you might have an idea."

Marlene set down a cup covered in painted mushrooms in front of him. Ivas sipped the tea within. She drummed her fingers rapidly on the table, then blew raspberries through her lips as she thought. "Some ideas, but nothing solid. I guess we're going to the cards." With a swirl, Marlene snatched up a deck of tarot cards from a bookshelf and sat down across from Ivas, shuffling them as she stared.

"You plan on going after her?"

"If I can."

"You'd better take my boat then."

"You have a boat?"

"Just a small one. It was Henry's. Haven't had to use it in near a decade, but she'll handle the water just fine. Now..." She set the pack down and fanned the cards out. "How do we handle these Harvestmen?" She motioned to Ivas to draw a card. He did so, grabbing at a random one from the middle.

Two got caught in his fingers, the second fluttering away as he drew them out. Marlene snatched that one and regarded it with a frown. Ivas hesitated with his card. "I didn't mean to grab two."

"No, sometimes the deck feels that you *need* two." She looked up at him. "What's that one?"

Ivas turned it over. On the card was a drawing of a person in medieval garb surrounded by six swords. Three pierced the person's body, while two others were stabbed into the ground. The final sword was held in the person's hand, pointing outward.

"What does this mean? Do I need a sword?"

Marlene pressed her lips thoughtfully, staring down the card as if mad at it for being so cryptic. Her eyes focused on the sword in the drawing's hand and followed it to where it was pointing. She followed it to Ivas's cup, the one covered in painted mushrooms.

She smiled. "Of course."

"What?"

"Harvestmen come to feed off what has died, so you need to get rid of what has drawn them. And what loves dead things?" She lifted up the mug.

"Mushrooms?"

"I've got some dried ones," Marlene said, going to one of her shelves and shifting through the many jars there. She plucked up an old pasta sauce jar full of dried morels and presented it to Ivas.

"What am I supposed to do with these? How does this help Ruby?"

"How do your dumb questions help Ruby?" Marlene challenged. "You have your mushrooms, now take the boat and go find our girl."

Ivas sighed but stood up. Blanc, who had been obediently

lying under the table, perked up and followed him back outside.

Marlene led them to the side of the house where a large tarp covered a small dinghy. She whipped the tarp off with a flourish, presenting the sand-covered, paint-chipped disappointment.

"You want me to go off onto the ocean in a dingy with a jar of mushrooms." Ivas glared at the witch. "You're out of your mind."

"That is true, but it doesn't mean I'm wrong." Marlene picked up an oar and tossed it to Ivas. He fumbled but caught it. "Ruby's running out of time, shepherd boy."

Ivas knew this was true, but he didn't know how to drive a boat, and there was no one around willing to go out in the rough sea.

Tess...

"You're keeping Blanc here with you," he ordered, trying to find some semblance of control in the situation. Marlene nodded, so he grabbed the bow of the boat and started dragging it toward the water. It struggled against him, rocking back and forth, leaving a long divot in the sand. Ivas forced it into the bumpy water, soaking his calves and boots before he could jump in and hook the oars in place.

Blanc yelped and barked, making circles to indicate that she desperately wanted to go with her master.

"Stay," Ivas ordered.

Blanc laid her ears back but sat down.

Marlene braced herself against the boat's stern and gave him a push until he was floating freely. Ivas grabbed the oars and fought against the current that wanted to push him back to shore, forcing the boat farther out.

"Good luck, shepherd!" Marlene called. She stood in the shallow edge of the water, the bottom of her skirts soaking as she watched Ivas go. When he became a distant silhouette, she pulled the tarot card—the second one he had pulled by accident—from her pocket.

The Tower card stared back at her.

CHAPTER 4

THE SHEPHERD PAYS A PRICE

The splashing sea was cold despite the summer months, and the salt was overwhelming as it gathered at the corners of his lips. Ivas grunted with the effort of paddling the little dinghy. The waves raised him up, then brought him back down, making his head spin.

He didn't know where to go, but after an hour of stroking, the Messenger appeared. He walked atop the water, tattered cloak waving like a flag. Thin, spider-like legs braced against the crashing waves. It appeared from the grey mist and began walking next to his boat. Ivas steadied himself.

"Can you show me the way to Ruby?" he called out.

The Messenger turned to him, empty, cloaked head unanswering, but it started walking ahead, peering over his shoulder to make sure Ivas followed.

Further they traveled. Ivas's shoulders cried out in pain with each stroke, and the pain was slowly making its way down his back. He had to stop several times, but the Messenger was ever patient, stopping and waiting alongside him until Ivas's energy returned.

And then he smelled it—something dead. The water became an unnatural color, and he heard the deep rumble of many throaty growls. Turning his head, Ivas saw the Harvestmen—strange, twisted creatures with fangs like a spider's teeth and small nubs for horns. Long, twig-thin legs balanced them on the waves. Their bodies held no real shape. Rather, they were made of rope-like muscles that shifted and curled over themselves. They looked like they had been pulled inside-out. Wide, blood-shot eyes stared out from the coils of twisting brawn, twitching in panic, unable to blink.

They were latched onto Ruby, their claws and fangs sinking into her flesh, lines of blood running in thin rivulets down her limbs.

Her horns were huge, muscles bulging as she held the creatures to her, squeezing their necks with her arms and legs. Many were impaled on her antlers, still weakly squirming.

Ivas swore out loud and the sound drew Ruby's attention. She turned her gaze—eyes golden—up from behind her tangled hair.

"Ivas…" she rasped.

"Ruby, I'm here. I'm here to help." Ivas rowed closer. The creatures struggled and Ruby tightened her grip. Ivas fumbled in his pockets for the mushrooms.

"You got…my message…"

"Yes." Ivas found the jar and spun the lid off, letting it fall into the boat. He pulled out a shriveled mushroom and stared at it, not knowing what to do. He tossed it into the water. When noting happened he pulled out another.

Marlene should be here…

Need magic…

"Cleanse this place, please," Ivas said. It wasn't a magic spell, but he didn't know what else to say. He put more mushrooms into the ocean, throwing them around Ruby, across the grotesque waters.

When the jar was empty, he picked up an oar and hit one of the Harvestmen with it. Its body twisted, physically wincing at the blow. The creature snarled, its fangs shifting inside Ruby. She winced.

"Just let them go," Ivas said.

"Can't... They're killing the village... We can't fish..."

"Ruby, *stop*, please."

Still a child... Just a child...

Ruby relinquished one arm, setting one of the Harvestmen free. Ivas hit it as hard as he could, remembering the coyote that had wandered into the farm. The creature backed away fearfully, it's many eyes darting about, looking in different directions.

Whatever they were, they were just scavengers. They wouldn't take on a fight they could avoid.

Eyes on the monsters, Ivas didn't notice the growth stirring beneath the water until it surfaced. He startled, looking down as a strange fungus began to crawl through the water. Anywhere there was discoloration, the fungus grew. The mushrooms appeared, rehydrated, creating a circle around Ruby.

The Harvestmen whimpered and struggled at the sight, and Ruby began releasing them, one at a time. Ivas swiped at them, but they were already on the retreat, weakened and frightened of the magic.

With their food source being taken over, there was no reason to fight.

Ruby shook her head, casting the half-dead Harvestmen from her horns. She sank to her knees.

"Ruby." Ivas held his hand out to her. The girl looked at him with tired eyes. Everything else about her seemed so wild—her red hair tangled in her horns, the claws growing from her fingers, the mixture of red and black blood tainting her skin.

"It's okay. Let's go," Ivas said. Ruby took a deep breath and raised her clawed hand. It trembled. Ivas clasped it tightly and pulled her up, off the water's surface and into the boat.

Ruby immediately collapsed. Ivas went to her, checking her pulse, which was quick and erratic, then tried to wipe the muck from her face.

The Messenger appeared next to the boat, looking down at them.

"What was the price?" Ivas asked, looking up. He saw only a faint twinkle of light in the shadows of the Messenger's cloak. "She had to pay something to send the message to me, right? Whatever it was, will you give it back to her and take something from me instead?"

The Messenger stared at him for a moment, as if considering the offer, then it lifted one of its legs and reached into a pouch hanging from a strap on its body. It brought out something small and bright, like a glowing bulb, and passed it over to Ruby. The light flickered, then faded, sinking into her heaving chest.

Then, the Messenger looked at Ivas and plucked something from his forehead. Ivas gasped and flinched as a long white strand was pulled from his head. It took a moment for the Messenger to pull the whole thing free. The discomfort made Ivas cringe. It felt like unraveling a loose string from a sweater, but *he* was the sweater.

The Messenger tugged the thing free and tucked it away into one of its many bags. It gave them a final nod and turned away.

When it did, Ivas suddenly realized that the ocean had calmed down.

Looking around, he saw that the area that contained The

Dead God was now coated in various mushrooms and fungi. Colorful caps had replaced the bad color, and the smell was fading. The circle of mushrooms where Ruby had stood still remained.

Ivas wrapped Ruby up in his jacket and made sure she was comfortable before turning his back and taking up the oars.

With the waves down and the sea sated, the trip home was much easier.

~

Jack sighed heavily, setting the phone down and leaning back in his office chair, which creaked from the movement. It was old and tiny, and Jack had put on some weight over the winter. He hadn't meant to. Usually, he was able to keep his plate portioned and get some exercise, but over the holidays he had indulged a bit too much. Pies and cakes and homemade candies would be brought out, and at first Jack would shake his head and wave them away, but then he would remember what a stressful fall it had been, how a girl had disappeared, the town had become a mob.

A monster tried to eat him.

His deputy had been caught attacking poor Tess. He would remember all those things and say, "Oh why not, it's been a stressful year," and a mouthful of chocolate and sugared fruit and a glass of booze would help him forget.

Now it was summertime, and he kept telling himself that he really needed to work it off, but he'd been busy babysitting sailors without work.

The ocean. What's wrong with the ocean?

Sailors who drank too much until he had to haul them in to sleep it off.

And then, yesterday, he had found Aster, Ruby's dog, wandering around town with his leash dragging along behind him. He took the pup to Hannah, and they both felt that fear again, the one that had taken over last autumn.

Where was Ruby?

She didn't come home that night, and Hannah called him. She had driven around town all day, asking every neighbor if they had seen her daughter. She even drove up the road to Balliecroy and back.

Ruby was gone again.

Again. Again...

Jack went out that night, expecting a fog to roll in, but the evening was clear and dark. There hadn't been any fog for months, except for the early morning winter mists, but nothing like the village was used to, so thick you could walk right of a cliff.

He walked through the town and the farmlands, calling Ruby's name. Men came out and joined him, howling the girl's name like wolves in the night. He fell asleep in his car and woke in the darkness. He checked on Hannah, but Ruby had not returned.

So, he returned to his office.

The day dragged on. A search party was organized.

Again. Again...

Jack helped as much as he could but had gotten a cold from walking around and yelling all night, so he returned to the office to drink some tea and listen to the phones.

The call from Hannah came in late afternoon.

Ruby was found.

Ivas was back.

Again... Again...

~

"*H*ow are you, Jack?" Ivas asked his old friend. It was close to evening, and Ivas was standing on Hannah's front porch. The village sheriff looked tired and old and overweight. Some of the buttons of his flannel were strained. Jack grabbed Ivas's hand and pulled him in for a brief hug, fiercely patting his back.

"I could complain, but who'd the hell'd listen?" Jack said.

They were at Hannah's house. The farmland stretched long and green and was dotted with flowers. The sky was blue. The sea was calm.

"Heh, that's a good—"

"What the fuck are you doing here, Ivas?" Jack snapped. The circles under his eyes were deep. "You're supposed to be in the mountains, right? Why'd you come back? How'd you know where Ruby was?"

Ivas looked down at his boots. Blanc laid her ears back, not liking Jack's tone.

"You going to tell me it was a coincidence?"

"What else could it be?" Ivas asked. Jack's shoulders tensed. He opened his mouth to yell, but Ivas held up a hand to stop him. "Ruby called me."

Jack froze, still glaring.

"She got my number from Tess. They've been writing each other. She called and told me she was having a hard time with Aster, that she missed her dad, she doesn't have any friends…stuff like that."

Jack sighed, a long deflating exhale. Things were making sense again. "So, you came to see her?"

"I offered to come back. She said she didn't want me too, but I did anyway. It's only a few hours by train, so why not?"

"You guys are close," Jack said. "I know she trusts you. Why didn't she tell Hannah?"

"Didn't want to worry her."

Jack snorted.

"Teenage logic."

"So, what was she doing out on the ocean?" Jack asked.

"Being stupid," Ivas said sincerely. "She told me she was going to camp out on the beach. That she stole a kayak."

"Was she…" Jack hesitated. He was an officer of the law; it shouldn't hurt to ask questions like these. "Was she trying to die?"

"I don't think so. Just being reckless. Looking for a thrill."

Jack looked at the door to the house. "I'm about to go in there and whip her."

"I actually had a different idea," Ivas said. "I was hoping you might help me out."

"Anything to keep this damn kid from kill— Getting herself killed."

"Here's my idea…"

~

Ivas's little story had paid off. He had talked it over with Ruby when they had gotten back to shore. He had woken her up and forced her to walk the shoreline back to Marlene's house, on the way telling her exactly what she was going to tell her mom.

Ruby barely heard him, dragging her feet and accidently bumping his shoulder with her antlers. Ivas took pity and put the girl over his shoulder once the sea cottage was in sight. Marlene took them in, tea was brewed, soup was made, and a bath was drawn. The tea revitalized the girl enough to eat her soup, and some life finally came back to her. Ivas stayed outside with Blanc while Ruby washed the blood from her body in Marlene's bathtub.

"I will cast a glamor on you to hide the horns," Marlene said when Ruby came out of the bathroom, dressed again.

The water in the tub was brown and salty. Marlene told her to leave her hair and clothes dirty so that her cleanliness wouldn't be too suspicious. Only when Ruby was close to herself again did she call Hannah and tell her to come get her daughter.

Hannah was silent.

She took Ruby home and brought Ivas as well. She washed her daughter's hair and changed her clothes, not seeing the large antlers that adorned her head. She gave Ruby food and they sat together at the table.

"Why?" she finally asked.

Ruby stared at her sandwich and sincere tears dripped from her eyes. "I miss my dad."

~

"I think Ruby should come with me," Ivas said. The subject of their conversation had been put to bed and the three adults sat at Hannah's table drinking coffee. Jack had practically begged for some.

"Go with you where?" Hannah asked.

"To the farm I'm working at in the mountains. I work for a family there who have a daughter of their own, and I could ask if Ruby could come stay for the summer."

Hannah frowned. "I'm not sending her away to live with strangers."

"Maybe you should consider it," Jack said. "She hasn't been doing well since her dad passed away. This is the second time she's run off. Maybe getting away from this town would do her good."

"You seriously think it's a good idea?" Hannah scoffed.

"Why not?" Jack asked sincerely.

"Because! I take care of her. She's my daughter."

"That's not what's being contested," Ivas said. "It just

seems like…with everything that's happened, maybe Ruby needs a change of scenery."

Hannah's brow furrowed at that, remembering her daughter's words.

I miss my dad, and everything reminds me of him. I keep looking at the ocean, looking for his ship, expecting him to come home. Aster won't listen to me. I don't have any friends. Everything hurts.

"Who is this family you work for?" Hannah asked.

"They're names are Connie and Abraham Carns. Their son Eli is going to college, but he's home for the summer. And their daughter, Traverse, is around Ruby's age. There's also a farmhand named Cherry, but she doesn't live there."

"Sheep farmers?" Hannah asked.

Ivas nodded. "We could bring Aster with us and I can help her train him. That's what I've been doing with the rest of Blanc's pups."

"He has been quite the handful," Hannah relented. "Poor Ruby has read every dog training book at the library, but nothing seems to stick."

"It's a mountain ranch, so there'd be plenty of work for her," Jack added. "Keep her busy, keep her mind off things."

"What if she runs away again while she's up there?"

"That would be pretty hard for her to do with all the dogs," Ivas said. "They bark at everything, and I would make sure everyone helped keep an eye on her."

Hannah tapped her fingers on the table. "I guess we can ask, see if it's okay with the Carns, and if Ruby even wants to go."

"I think it would be a really good idea," Jack said, reassuringly. "Change of scenery, some new friends, and hard work."

Hannah sighed. "I don't know about the whole summer though…"

"She'd be back in time for school, or sooner, if need be," Ivas said. "I'll bring her back myself."

Hannah gave Ivas a sharp look. "I know Ruby trusts you, that she called you instead of me."

Ivas flinched at the hurt in her voice.

"That's the only reason I'm considering this."

"Sleep on it," Jack said. "Talk to Ruby. Ivas will call the Carns and we'll go from there."

"Mom?" Ruby's voiced called out from the bedroom. Hannah turned sharply and went to her, trying not to seem like she was rushing.

She returned a moment later, arms crossed, lips pursed.

"She wants to see you," she said, jerking her head toward Ivas.

The shepherd looked down apologetically and stepped past Hannah, moving down the hall to Ruby's bedroom. She was seated on her bed, wrapped in a quilt. Despite the glamor, Ivas could see her antlers, so large they bumped against the wall when she turned her head to him. Her face was swollen, covered in red splotches. The aftermath of tears.

Ivas sat on the bed next to her. "What is it?" he asked gently.

Ruby looked down at her hands. "I couldn't find him, Ivas."

"Who?"

"My dad." She sniffed. Her lips disappeared between her teeth. "I thought I would find him out there. Maybe he got away from the Dead God."

Fresh tears, large ones that made soft pinprick sounds when they landed on the blanket.

Ivas reached forward and cupped her hands. "I'm sorry."

"He's really gone now," she whimpered. "I thought he— I'm so stupid…"

Ivas's stomach clenched painfully. He squeezed her hand tighter. "It's not stupid to try and save someone you love."

She looked at him, brown eyes shining behind a film of water. "Your parents died."

He nodded.

"At the same time?"

"Yes."

She looked down at their hands. Tears calming. "What do I do, Ivas? How do I make it stop hurting?"

Ivas winced. He didn't have the heart to tell her that she couldn't. Saying "it takes time," while true, rang empty in times like these.

Instead, he pulled her forward into his arms, ducking his head away from her horns. "Just cry. And try to get some sleep."

~

The two men who wanted to take her daughter away thanked Hannah for the coffee and bid her goodnight. The sun had sunk, but Hannah wasn't tired, despite a full night of not sleeping. She kept going through the proposal in her head, trying different wording to see if it sounded better. She hated the idea. She hated that it was a good idea, that Ruby would probably say yes, and the Carns would say "the more, the merrier." She hated that she kind of liked the idea too, of having some time to herself to just…

Just what?

Ruby had lost her father, but Hannah had lost her husband, and she had barely had time to mourn, putting it aside so that Ruby could grieve instead.

Maybe this would give her a chance to make some hard decisions she had been putting aside for too long.

Sometime in the night, Ruby woke and wandered into

the kitchen, seeking junk food. Hannah sat her down and served her a midnight snack. Her eyes kept darting up to her daughter's head. She felt like she kept seeing something there, like a hat, but it was only in the corner of her vision, then gone.

"Baby," she said, taking Ruby's hand, "there's something I need to ask you…"

~

When Ivas was ushered into Jack's house, he allowed himself to collapse. He went straight to the couch and laid down on it, exhaustion deep in his bones. Blanc came up to him worriedly, pressing her nose into his cheek.

"Yeah, been a hell of a day," Jack agreed, shedding off his shoes.

"Thanks for letting me stay." Ivas's voice was muffled by the couch cushion.

"I should be thanking *you*. It's really good to see you, Ivas." Jack sat down in a chair cattycorner to the couch. The two pieces of furniture did not match. "I always thought the three of us would be here forever, but both you and Tess are off living your lives. I'm just sitting around here getting fat."

Ivas turned his head and lifted his eyes to look at Jack. His old friend gave him a smile that was too weak to hide his pain behind an I'm-just-joking façade.

"You're not fat," Ivas offered.

Jack laughed. It had the same cadence as his smile.

"Have you heard from Tess?" Ivas asked.

"Got a letter a few months ago. I'm bad at letters, though. I read a book once where this couple wrote to each other all the time, made it seem so easy and romantic. I can never remember to write back."

Ivas forced himself up, trying to think of his friend instead of how tired he was. "If you can't write her, why don't you go find her?"

"I haven't really thought about a visit," Jack confessed. "It seems like she needed to get away from this town. What if I'm part of the thing she needed to get away from?"

"Maybe *you* need to get away from this town."

Jack shrugged.

"Go visit Tess, Jack. I just saw her myself. She brought me here on her boat."

Jack startled. "She was here?"

"No, she could only get as close as the next town over. The waters were too rough. But I know she would really like to see you. She's been struggling with things too, and a friend is what she needs. You're the one person she would never need to get away from."

"She's struggling?" Jack asked worriedly.

"She's trying to figure out what to do next with her life. Maybe that's what you both need. Maybe you can help each other."

Jack sighed. "I hadn't even considered leaving Loch Lamond. I'm the sheriff."

Ivas shrugged.

"Sometimes I have nightmares…" Jack's eyes darted out of contact.

"So do I."

Jack's gaze returned to Ivas. "How does she look?"

"Tess? She's been hiking. Looks really good."

Finally, a smile peeked out in the corner of Jack's mouth, small but true. "Will you have time for breakfast in the morning?"

"Absolutely. I am nothing if not a demanding guest."

His smile widened. "Good. I'll let you get some sleep, then. You look like you're going to pass out."

"Looks can be deceiving, but this time they're on the nose."

"I've missed you, Ivas."

Ivas held out his arms and Jack came in for a hug, brief but tight. With a firm pat on the back, they released each other, and Ivas fell back onto the couch, sighing with relief as Jack shut off the lights.

In the quiet and the dark, fear pushed through his exhaustion to put forth the question Ivas had been hiding from since they had returned from the ocean.

What had the Messenger taken from him?

~

Archibald stared at Ivas, a vague kind of terror in his eyes, a slight tremor to his hands, which were loaded down with books.

"Uh, w-what day is it?"

Ivas told him.

The little scholar untensed, sighing in relief. "It's only been a night then, thank goodness. This has happened before you know. Once, my mother had filed me as a missing person and the authorities found me in the library after three days. I hadn't even realized that much time had passed because I was so wrapped up in my project."

"Didn't you sleep?" Ivas asked, raising an eyebrow.

"There were moments when I would fall into a brief doze, but I didn't really realize it."

"Aye, he's a strange one." Poppermill stepped into the room next to Ivas and nudged his ribs. "Didn't hear me when I spoke and didn't eat."

Archibald blushed and rubbed the back of his head. "I'm sorry. It really is a problem."

"No problem for me." Poppermill shrugged. "Glad

someone appreciates all the work I've put into this collection. Most of the village thinks I'm crazy."

"Oh no!" Archibald jumped to his feet, disturbing some loose-leaf paper. "What you have here is incredible, Mr. Poppermill! Histories and stories I've never even heard of! Not derivative of other traditional oral storytelling. It's like some of these were written in a vacuum!"

"That'd be hard to do, all that sucking."

"I-it's absolutely incredible! Mr. Poppermill, will you allow me to study your collection further? This could revolutionize the history of oral storytelling."

"I'm a little old for revolutions," Mr. Poppermill said. Ivas rolled his eyes.

Archibald couldn't contain his excitement. "Mr. Poppermill, do you have any background information on these stories? Origins, cultures, anything?"

Poppermill scratched his beard thoughtfully. "Well, some of 'em have been in my family for generations. Passed down from storyteller to storyteller. Others, I stumbled upon in dusty old bookstores and obscure auctions. I can give you what I know, but part of the charm is the mystery, don't you think?"

"W-will you allow me to borrow them, then? I swear, on the university's reputation..."

"Eh, don't want to risk anything happening to them. It's probably best if you just stay here and read 'em, yeah?"

Archibald gave a happy hop. "Yes, thank you. I've got my camera, so I can take copies. I'll need to get more pens. Oh! And I must contact the university. I'm sure they won't like me being late, but surely they'll understand when I tell them..."

"You don't have to host him here," Ivas told Mr. Poppermill. He spoke quietly, but it was unnecessary as Archibald was in a whirlwind, talking to himself.

"He ain't no harm. I like the company," Poppermill said. "Besides, I don't think we'll be able to get him out unless we knock him unconscious."

Ivas chuckled at that. "Well, I'm returning to the mountains, so you'll be stuck with him."

"You sort out your little Harvestmen problem, then?" Poppermill gave him a teasing smirk.

"Ruby needed my help," Ivas said. "She's actually coming back with me."

"You and that girl have been getting into strange happenings, haven't you?"

"I don't know what you mean."

Poppermill studied him for a minute, then walked over to where Archibald was rummaging around, trying to get his things in order. He stole a scrap of paper and scribbled something down. He handed it to Ivas.

"This is my phone number. I unplugged the damn thing years ago because it was just people wanting money, but I'll plug it back in. That way you can give me a call if you need any more stories up there in the mountains."

"Hopefully I won't need it," Ivas said, pocketing the paper.

"Everyone needs stories."

CHAPTER 5

THE SHEPHERD AND THE HORNED GIRL
TAKE THE TRAIN

The train whistle sounded and the metal wheels began to groan. Ruby stared out the window, waving to her mom as the train pulled away. They had already hugged and kissed for the full half-hour they had waited on the platform. Now Ruby was close to tears again.

"Come on, now," Ivas pleaded, handing her a tissue. "I thought you were excited about this."

"I don't know," Ruby admitted, sitting back since her mom was now out of sight. "It sounds interesting and terrifying at the same time. Every time I think about going away, I just want to jump off the train and run home. But then I think of home and don't want to ever go back. It's annoying."

"Hmm."

"I still can't believe Mom even agreed to it. I think she's still kind of suspicious of you, like you're a pervert or something."

Ivas shifted uncomfortably, clearing his throat.

"Have you ever been married?" Ruby asked.

"No."

"But you've had girlfriends? Did you and Tess go out?"

"No."

"What? Are you serious?"

Ivas sighed.

"How have you *never* had a girlfriend?"

Ivas gave her a look, but Ruby only shifted forward, genuinely interested. At least she wasn't pining anymore.

"Just wasn't interested, I guess." Ivas shrugged.

"Oh, are you into boys instead?"

"No. Not boys either."

"Really? Wow." Ruby leaned back, studying him. Ivas drummed his fingers and stared out the window, trying to ignore her.

"Can we go check on the dogs?"

"We just started."

"But we're allowed to, right?"

"Yes, but if you go back there, you're going to get them all worked up. We'll check on them in a little bit."

Ruby rolled her eyes and sat back. She grabbed her backpack and began digging through it, pulling out some candy. Ivas thought about telling her to wait so she didn't run out too quickly, but then she offered him some and he accepted.

"I've never had a boyfriend—or a girlfriend—either," Ruby admitted. "Maybe I'm like you. Although…do you even want a girlfriend?"

"Never really had the inclination," Ivas said.

"See, I kind of want one." Ruby spoke around a mouthful of candy. "But maybe a girlfriend because boys are annoying. But sometimes they're cute too. Like, this one time, this boy in my class, Tommy, was paired up with me when we were playing sports in gym, and he was actually pretty nice and funny. I might have gone out with him if he didn't move away. But then sometimes, when I've had sleepovers with my friends, I'll look at them, like, too much, you know? Like, I just think they're kind of pretty. Is that weird? Maybe *I'm* the pervert."

"How about we go check on the dogs?"

Ruby beamed and nodded.

They walked down the narrow aisle, then through the doors to the next car. Ruby was disappointed that the space wasn't open to the outside, thinking they would have to jump between cars.

They made their way to the back of the baggage car, where the dogs began to bark and whine. Ruby rushed forward to the kennels they were being kept in. Blanc and Aster wagged their tails so hard that the thin bars shook and rattled. Aster danced and whined.

"It's okay, guys. Don't be scared," Ruby cooed. "Do you think we put you in jail? We didn't. It's just temporary." She pouted at Ivas. "I wish they could sit with us. They're probably so scared."

"They're fine," Ivas assured her. "They're spoiled mutts is what they are."

Ruby chuckled and gave them each a dog treat from her pocket. With one hand in each kennel, she gave them pets and ear rubs until they calmed down. Ivas was happy to let her dote on them. It was a good distraction from the strange teenage conversation he wasn't accustomed to.

More rubs and a couple more treats, though, and Ruby was ready to go back. She apologized to the dogs profusely, promising them they would be out soon. The dogs cried as they left, making Ruby groan.

"Don't let them make you feel guilty. They're manipulators," Ivas joked.

Back in their seats, Ruby pulled out a word puzzle and Ivas stared out the window for a while before closing his eyes and leaning his head back.

"Ivas?" Ruby asked tentatively.

He didn't answer, pretending to sleep.

She shook his knee. "Ivas."

"*Yes?*" He gave her a one-eyed glare.

"Can we call my mom at the train stop?"

"It's not far from the station to the farm," Ivas said.

"I want to call her, though."

"Alright, you can if you want to. Got change?"

"Some."

Ivas dug through his pockets and gave Ruby all the coins he had. Ruby went back to her puzzle, though it appeared she had given up on the words and was doodling instead. Ivas recognized the face of Aster, as well as a house on a cliffside—Ruby's house. She was now drawing a sailboat.

"That your dad's?"

She nodded.

"It's really good."

She smiled bashfully.

The rest of the ride passed quietly. Ruby asked if they could see the dogs again, but Ivas insisted they were probably sleeping by now and it would be best not to wake them up. Ruby snacked some more, stared out the window, finished her puzzle, and walked the train car back and forth when she got too bored.

She was on her feet and getting the bags down before the train came to a full stop at the station. Ivas took her heavier suitcase while she carried her smaller backpack and they departed. Ruby stared about the station, doing a twirl to take it all in.

"I've never been to a train station before," she said. "I feel like I'm in one of those old black-and-white movies!"

While Ivas retrieved Aster and Blanc, Ruby stayed on the platform to watch the train leave, waving as it departed. Some strangers waved back.

"People waved at me!" she told Ivas happily. She picked

up her suitcase and did another spin. "I feel like I'm in a musical."

Her excitement died down as they had to do yet another round of waiting. Ivas found them a bench and sat with the dogs and bags while Ruby went to the payphone and called her mother. They talked until the change was gone. Ruby sat down, much less spirited.

"What's wrong?" Ivas asked.

"Nothing," she said, trying not to pout, head resting in her hands.

"Your mom doing okay?"

"I guess. She's all worried. Told me to call when we get to the farm."

"Don't need change for that one. You can talk to her as long as you want."

"They won't mind?" Ruby asked.

"Nah."

The bus arrived and Ruby perked up, marveling at how their bags were stored under the vehicle, then at the bus's interior. The driver was a bigger woman who was all smiles and accent. Ruby sat in a front-row seat so that she could talk to her. Ivas preferred some quiet and sat a few rows back.

The bus took them as close to the mountain as it could, and when they disembarked, Bram's pickup truck was already waiting for them. The old vehicle visibly shuddered as it idled.

Bags were grabbed and dogs were leashed. The bus driver stepped off to lend a hand.

"You take care now, sugar," she told Ruby. Ivas watched in surprise as the two women hugged, the driver whispering something that made Ruby laugh. With a final wave, she got back on the bus and pulled away.

Then, it was like a switch flipped. Ruby looked at her feet

and sidled up to Ivas as Bram got out of the car and gave them a nod.

"You guys have any trouble?" The farmer asked.

"Nope, smooth sailing," Ivas said. "Abraham, this is Ruby. Ruby, this is Abraham."

"Call me Bram," the old man said, shaking Ruby's hand. She gave him a firm grip but avoided eye contact.

"Hi. Thanks for letting me come." Her words sounded flat and scripted.

"Don't make it a habit. Gas is expensive," Bram said. "Load up. You got one last leg to this journey."

They put the bags and the dogs in the back of the truck. Ruby idled behind, making sure that Ivas slid in first so that she wouldn't have to sit in the middle next to Bram.

"It's a bit of a drive from town," Bram said. "We go in for supplies every couple of weeks. If you ever need to get away, you're out of luck. I know you kids can get bored, so you'll have to make your own fun on the farm. Traverse will show you all the games they've come up with. You from the same town as Ivas?"

"Yeah."

As they drove, Ruby kept looking over her shoulder at the dogs, as if worried they would fall out.

"You ever been this far inland?"

"Not really."

"The mountains are sure pretty, and we got a lot of wilderness. Explore all you want, but be careful. It's not too terribly hard to get lost or run into wild animals out here. Keep your dog with you when you go on walks."

"Okay."

"And quit talking so much. Ivas can't get a word in edgewise."

Ruby rewarded Bram with a soft but sincere giggle, finally relaxing a bit in her seat. Her attention was focused on the passing countryside as they worked their way uphill, bumping along the dirt road.

"Are there bears?" Ruby suddenly asked.

"Yeah, but they're pretty solitary and don't come near the farm. If you're worried, tie a bell to your ankle."

"Really? Is that like…a backwoods superstition?"

"No, it's so the bears'll hear you coming."

Ruby laughed again.

"If they hear you coming, they'll go the other way," Bram said.

"Are there wolves?"

"Coyotes," Ivas answered that one.

"Most animals you're going to see are deer and rabbits," Bram said.

When the farm came into view, Ivas unnecessarily pointed it out to Ruby. She grew quiet again. The house was large, having been passed down through the family to host several generations, so there were many bedrooms and large common spaces. The barn was further back, with the fenced pasture where sheep were grazing.

"Just over that hill, there is a lake," Bram said, pointing. "If you're staying the whole summer, we'll have to do some fishing and swimming."

"Do you have a boat?" Ruby asked. "I know how to sail."

"No sailing needed here. You'll have to paddle," Bram said.

They pulled up to a patch of dirt that had been designated as parking for the family vehicles. Ivas noticed that Cherry's truck wasn't there.

Aster was beside himself, barking at the sheep and the new landscape in general. Ivas took his and Blanc's leashes while Bram got the bags. Ruby stayed close to Ivas.

"Here, we'll put them in the dog pen for now," Ivas said. Blanc already knew the way, but Aster kept pulling at the leash, choking himself as he tried to smell everything they passed.

"I don't know how I managed to give you the most temperamental dog in the bunch," Ivas said apologetically.

"He's a handful," Ruby said, shaking her head.

At the pen, Aster's brothers and sisters all came out of their respective homes to greet them. The pen was large, with a doghouse for each dog and a cover for shade at one end. They watched the more excited dog with confusion. None of them rushed the gate to try to get out, but waited patiently as Ivas opened the gate.

Ruby's mouth dropped. "How did you get them to do that?"

"Lots of work." He said it casually, but it felt good to be admired for his hard work.

"But...they're the same age as Aster, and there's three of them!"

"I'll teach you how to do the same with Aster," Ivas promised.

Blanc went inside obediently, but Aster put up a fight. Ivas and Ruby had to manhandle the dog into the pen and shut it before he could run back out.

"Aster might be a hopeless case," Ruby sighed.

"No such thing," Ivas promised. "Come on, let's meet the family and have some food."

A member of the family was already standing there when they turned around.

"Ivas! Hey, man!" Bram's son Eli was tall, lean, and sported long, dirt-brown hair. He was a young man not yet old enough to drink, still working his way through college. He towered over Ivas as he stepped forward and hugged the shepherd.

"Ruby, this is Eli," Ivas said, giving Eli only a short pat in return.

"What's up, Rubes?" Eli held out his fist and Ruby bumped it.

"Not much."

"So cool to have you here, man, it's going to be a lot of fun. Don't let my dad work you the whole time. I'll show you all the best sneak-away places, okay?"

Ruby nodded and looked at her feet.

"We're going to be teaching her how to handle herding dogs," Ivas explained. He pointed at the pen. "Aster there is hers."

"Far out. Ivas is a wizard with herding, even better than my dad. Speaking of which, Mom said to bring you guys inside. It's time to eat. I gotta find Trav." Eli gave them a salute and jogged off, his sandals slapping against the grass. Ivas started walking the opposite way toward the house, with Ruby following closely.

There was a mudroom entrance through the porch, but Ivas took them to the front door straight into the kitchen. The smell of food perked them both up. Connie looked up from setting the table.

"There they are!" she squealed, wiggling forward to take Ivas's hands. "And look at this beautiful dear," she cooed at Ruby, giving her a hug. Ruby couldn't help blushing a little. She had never hugged an adult shorter than her before. Connie only came up to the top of Ruby's chest.

Connie was the opposite of her husband in almost every way. While Bram was stout and firm, she was tiny and plump with a mess of curly hair.

"We are so happy to have you staying here! My name is Connie, and you come to me for anything, okay?"

Ruby smiled and nodded shyly.

"Aw, look at you, so quiet. We'll break you of that," she teased. "You must be so tired from your trip. Go wash up and come eat— Oh! But you don't know the house. Here, let me give you a tour— Or, no, wait, I've got the stove on..."

"I'll show her around," Ivas cut in. "We'll wash and be right back. It smells great."

Connie gave Ivas a grateful smile and went back to the food. Ivas guided Ruby through the home—a large house covered in photos and childhood paintings, lopsided hand-made pots holding fresh flowers, chairs covered in blankets, books, and magazines. Shoes and clothes were stashed everywhere, and every available surface was covered in some sort of project, from art to a broken appliance to piles of things waiting to be cleaned. There were plenty of bath-rooms, so the two split up.

Ivas doused his face in cold water, shaking off the day's travels, and scrubbed his hands and arms with soap. He felt refreshed and found Ruby looking a little better too, though tired.

Back in the kitchen, the rest of the family was gathering, all talking in a cozy cacophony of conversation. Eli was back, and Bram was helping set out food.

Everyone took their seats, Ruby sitting next to Ivas. One chair remained empty and Connie sighed.

"Eli, were you not able to find Traverse?" Connie asked.

"Look, she knows when food is. She'll show up or eat later," Eli shrugged.

"I wanted Ruby to have a family meal and meet every-one!" Connie shook her head and turned to Ruby. "Tra-verse is our daughter. She just turned eighteen and is wild as a..."

"An eighteen-year-old," Bram finished.

The table laughed.

"What's so funny?"

Ivas looked up as Traverse entered the kitchen. She wore shorts, a spaghetti strap shirt, and no shoes, showing off her ebony skin. Her black hair was fluffy, piled into an afro on her head.

Connie gave her daughter a pointed look. "Go wash and come eat. We have a guest."

"Oh, yeah. Hey, Ivas." Traverse waved.

"And *this* is Ruby," Connie said pointedly.

"How old are you?"

"Sixteen."

"Cool."

"Go wash. We're eating now."

"I'm going, I'm going." Traverse skipped off and Connie waved at everyone to dig in. Ruby noticed that Eli only ate the vegetables and bread. When Bram tried to take two rolls, Connie took one away, hissing something about the doctor to him.

Ruby took a little of everything and dug in, feeling like it was Christmas. Since it had just been her and Hannah for a while now, their meals had become small and easy, so the hearty array of homemade food was a welcomed treat.

Traverse returned and plopped down at the table. "So, Ruby, you in trouble? Running from the law?"

"What?" Ruby tried to swallow her mashed potatoes.

"Why else would you come out to the backwoods?"

"Not really your business," Bram said.

"My dad died," Ruby said. The table quieted and all eyes turned to her. She had considered keeping it a secret, being mysterious, but she didn't like the idea of the Carns thinking she was a juvenile delinquent on the run. "He disappeared awhile back and…things have been hard, so we thought I should get away from, like, all the stuff that reminds me of him."

"He *disappeared*?" Traverse's mouth dropped. Ruby felt kind of proud, putting the older girl in awe.

"Shit, dude. I'm so sorry," Eli said.

"Thanks. I'm okay, just…you know. Oh, and thank you, for letting me stay."

"Of course!" Connie said. "I love having a full house. You're just in time for Eli's birthday, too. It'll be a party with everyone here."

"Mom!" Eli whined.

The conversation turned to lighter subjects and they finished their meal. Ruby ate heartily and heaved a deep sigh, sinking back in her chair.

"You want to rest a bit or see the farm?" Ivas asked.

"Farm," Ruby said, hopping up.

"Oh, me too," Traverse said, following.

"Coming, Bram?" Ivas asked.

"No, I need to digest for a bit," Bram said, heading for the back patio. Eli stayed to help Connie clear the table.

Ivas took Ruby outside and showed her the different pastures. There was a large pond with ducks behind the house, as well as a vegetable garden. They then went to the sheep pasture where the animals were grazing.

"These here are Scottish Blackface sheep," Ivas said. "You're just in time to help with sheering, too."

"Cool," Ruby said sincerely. "I've never sheered a sheep before."

"It's a pain in the ass," Traverse laughed. "Our guy will be here tomorrow, Ivas."

"I've got good timing then." Ivas turned to Ruby and motioned with his hand. "This circular pin over here is what we've been using to train the dogs. They're still less than a year old, so we've only been training for a few months."

"Oh my gosh, did he tell you what he tried to name the dogs?" Traverse asked Ruby. "*Numbers*! He started calling them One, Two, and Three."

"Ivas, I thought the name 'Blanc' was bad." Ruby shook her head disapprovingly.

"I gave them proper names," Traverse said proudly. "Come on, let's go see them."

They headed up to the dog pen, where they were greeted by a storm of barks. Aster was jumping up on the fence as if he could climb out.

"Since their mom's name is Blanc, I named them all different words for white. That's Lefko—Greek. Then Abyad —Arabic. And Shiro is—"

"Japanese," Ruby interrupted proudly. Traverse nodded in approval. "I named mine Aster." Ruby pointed to the obvious dog.

"Wow, he's…"

"Got potential," Ivas said. "Even if he can't herd, we can get some obedience instilled in him."

"Where's their dad?" Ruby asked.

"Bram lent him out to another breeder with a bitch," Traverse said. "We'll get him back soon."

Ruby snickered at the word bitch.

"Trav, would you mind grabbing a leash and treats? I thought we could try walking Aster for a bit," Ivas said. Traverse gave him a sarcastic salute and jogged off, her bare feet patting the grass.

"Ivas," Ruby said quietly, "why is Traverse…black? Is that racist to ask?"

"She and Eli are both adopted," Ivas explained with a patient smile. "Connie can't have kids, so they fostered for a couple of decades. Eli and Traverse were the ones that stuck around."

"Oh, okay, that's cool," Ruby relaxed. She scratched at her collarbone, pulling at the collar of her shirt. Ivas caught a glimpse of something there, a refraction of the light, but before he could put a proper thought to it, Traverse returned with the leash.

Ivas showed Ruby how to harness Aster around his chest

so that it would turn him around when he tried to pull away. The three of them walked the dog around the perimeter of the treeline, Ivas holding the leash firmly. Every time Aster slowed down and stayed by Ivas's side, he got a treat, but it was hard for the young dog not to be distracted by the woods. Ruby watched in amazement as Ivas used a sure, strong hand to make him heel.

"This is amazing," she said. "I've been fighting him for months, you've already got him walking with you!"

"I have a lot of experience," Ivas explained. "You take the lead and give it a try."

Ruby did so, pleased to not have her shoulder pulled from its socket for once, though Aster still struggled. The dog whined and paused at a trailhead.

"Aster," Ruby called, offering a treat. Aster whimpered and doubled back, circling around Ruby, tail tucked between his legs.

"That's weird." Ruby looked into the trees, trying to see what had frightened the dog.

"Probably smells a coyote," Traverse said, peering into the woods. "They've been getting more bold lately."

Ivas swallowed.

I killed one...

"Bram is talking about getting another Great Pyrenees to guard the stock. We had one a long time ago, but she got too old. Want to see the barn?"

Ruby agreed and Traverse took the lead. Ivas let the girls get ahead, staring into the woods for the tale-tale sign of glowing eyes, but nothing moved. He let a shiver run down his neck and through his back before continuing the walk.

They finished the tour of the farm and looped back around to the dog pen. Ruby tossed treats into a corner to make Aster go in, and while the puppies were distracted, Ivas called Blanc forward.

"Time to round up the sheep," he said with a smile.

Traverse and Ruby sat themselves on the fence and watched as Ivas entered the pasture.

All the sheep heads perked up and Blanc laid down in the grass, awaiting orders.

Ivas hesitated, staring out at the field. He looked down at Blanc, then at the sheep, who, after a moment of inaction, went back to their grazing.

What is it...

What's the word...

Ivas scratched his head as if he could physically jostle the memory of the phrase he had forgotten. He could hear the girls talking behind him.

"It's so crazy that they can say a word and the dog knows what to do," Traverse said.

"It is pretty cool," Ruby agreed. "Do you do any herding?"

"A little bit. I've only lived here about four years, so farm life is still pretty new to me. Ivas tell you we're adopted?"

"Yeah."

What's the word...

Ivas's breath quickened and he closed a fist into his shirt. Blanc looked up at him, confused, still waiting.

Ivas's mouth went dry and he couldn't swallow. Gray spots blinked across his vision.

"Ivas, you okay?" Traverse's voice sounded far away.

He realized that he was on his knees and the grass was coming closer. Then he saw white and felt a warm body beneath him.

Blanc.

He heard the girls' voices, but his ears were ringing too loud to understand them. He laid still instead, focusing on breathing. Eventually, the spots faded and the ringing stopped.

"...Ivas, honey, talk to me."

That was Connie's voice. Ivas looked up into her worried face. It felt like he had only been out for a second, but it was long enough for the girls to go get help.

"What happened? Are you having chest pain?" Connie asked, touching his forehead.

"I'm alright, I'm alright," Ivas said, waving his hand to clear the hovering faces of the three women away.

"You're not alright. You scared the hell out of us," Traverse said.

"Don't swear," Connie muttered, studying Ivas's face.

"It was just a fainting spell. I must have gotten too hot or tired." Ivas sat up and got to his feet. The girls watched him warily, Connie kept her hands near his arm.

"Come inside, let me get you some tea," Connie insisted.

"Let's just go to my cabin so I can lie down," Ivas begged. Connie relented and changed course, helping to guide Ivas to his room, even though he walked without trouble.

"I'm *not* leaving you alone," Connie said sharply as she opened the door. Ivas slipped inside, turning on the light. Blanc followed right at his feet.

"I'll stay with him," Ruby quickly volunteered. She went inside as well, going to the stove while Ivas sat on the bed. "Ivas, do you have tea?"

"Top cabinet."

"I'll be back in just a few minutes," Connie said. "I'll have Bram put the sheep away."

"Thank you."

Traverse hesitated, not knowing who to stay with. Ruby put the kettle on, and Ivas waved her away. Putting her hands up in surrender, Traverse followed Connie, shutting the door.

When they were gone, Ivas doubled over to put his head in his hands.

"Ivas…" Ruby spoke softly, turning away from the kettle to go to him. She sat on her knees, watching him nervously.

"It's gone." A tear dripped from his nose. "I don't know how to herd. That goddamn—"

"What do you mean? Are you having amnesia?"

Ivas dropped his hands, revealing his red face shining with bright tears. "You had to pay a price to get your message to me. I paid it for you and…" He looked down at his hands. They trembled like autumn leaves. "That monster… It took… I don't know how to talk to Blanc. I can't remember the words. I don't know how to bring the sheep in…"

"The Messenger took that from you?" Ruby's whispered question came out horrified. "Ivas, that was my price. You shouldn't have—"

"No," Ivas snapped, making Ruby jump. "*You* shouldn't have gone out there in the first place. You were being eaten alive. I wasn't going to let the Messenger take anything else from you." Ivas sighed, deep and heavy. "I just… Herding is what I do; it's all I know. Now it's all gone. I don't remember anything my grandpa taught me."

Ruby let herself fall back on her backside, crossing her legs. "I'm sorry for calling you."

"No, don't ever be sorry for calling for me. Always call for me." Ivas sat up, popping his back. He took the sleeve of his shirt and wiped his face dry. "I don't know what I'm going to do. I'm literally here to teach the dogs how to herd."

"You still remember how to train the dogs. You were doing magic on Aster," Ruby said.

"Herding is different. There's a whole different language to use, knowing how to move the sheep, and the timing…"

The kettle started to whistle. Ruby jumped up and snatched it off the stove before it could get too loud.

"I can't believe it's all gone," Ivas whispered.

Blanc moved at that point, startling Ivas. He had forgotten she was there. She came to his side and rested her head on his knee. Her eyes twitched upward to look at him worriedly.

"What am I going to do?"

"I'll help you," Ruby said. She came back holding a mug with a tea bag floating inside. The hot water left a train of steam. "We'll figure something out. That house is filled with books. There must be something."

Ivas took the mug. It was hot, but he desperately needed something to clutch. Blanc licked his wrist. In the corner, he saw his shepherd's staff leaning in the corner with its unique crook, and he didn't know what it was for.

CHAPTER 6

THE HORNED GIRL SHEDS HER ANTLERS

Cherry walked through the woods, a whistle around her neck and eyes on the ground. She heard the shouts of people around her, all echoing the same name over and over.

"Siobhan!"

Siobhan...

Cherry panned her eyes back and forth, looking for any clue—a footprint, a scrap of fabric, even a granola bar wrapper. The foliage was thick and could easily hide anything. She tried to focus beyond the wall of leaves.

She heard a dog bay several yards out and looked up hopefully, but then it quieted, undoubtedly having spotted a squirrel.

The shouts of Siobhan's name became fewer, and then it got too quiet. Cherry dug deep into her diaphragm and bellowed a shout that sent birds screaming and flying. She even paused and closed her eyes to listen for an answer, a whisper for help, anything.

A whistle broke through the forest, making her jump. A cold sweat bloomed over her neck. Cherry turned and jogged toward the sound. She reached the whistle-blower first, a man in an orange vest with a grey beard. He noticed her and held up what he had found.

A tennis shoe. Some mud was on the soles, but it was fresh and clean otherwise. Cherry couldn't remember if they had a description of Siobhan's shoes.

"Hers?"

"Maybe," the man said, studying the ground further, as if the second might be around. Another searcher arrived and nodded.

"It's hers. Family said she was wearing blue and white sneakers."

The bearded man stuck a little orange flag in the ground where he had found the shoe.

"Group leader will be here in a minute. They got a bit ahead," the new person said.

"This is my fourth search," the bearded man said, staring at the shoe. "Been a volunteer for about ten years now."

"How many of them did you find?" Cherry asked.

"Only one came back," he said ruefully. "There was a hunter several years back. It was broad daylight. He was hunting with a friend and they had walkie-talkies. Did everything right to stay safe. But then they lost sight of each other and he just disappeared. Never found a trace of him, not even the walkie-talkie."

Cherry shuddered. The creep down her spine settled as a heavy weight in her stomach.

"Then there was a toddler. This was back when I was a young man. The kid wandered away from the family's camp. They only looked away for a minute but never saw him again."

"Who was the one that came back?"

"A teenager. They were out walking, playing around, and didn't come home that night. We all went out the next morning. It was real foggy, and we didn't have much hope of finding her. I was walking with one of the dog trainers. The bloodhound was sniffing at the ground, fully concentrating. We reached some water that was too deep to cross and were about to turn around and go back, but the trainer stopped. She had been doing this a long time and just had a gut feeling. We turned back around and there in the fog, right in front of us, was the kid. She was standing maybe five feet in front of us, 'bout ankle-deep in the water. The dog didn't even smell her, and I swear she hadn't been there a second ago."

"God," Cherry whispered. "Was she all right?"

"Seemed fine, physically, but she was confused, like she was in a trance. Didn't seem to know where she was. Funny thing was, we weren't even a mile from town. She had been gone all night. We figured she'd be miles away, deep in the woods. But she was right there in a creek that local kids played in all the time."

"Do you think we'll find Siobhan?" Cherry asked.

The man studied the shoe. The group leader arrived and took it from him, noting the location on his map. He bagged the shoe and put it in his pack.

"Impossible to tell," the man said finally.

The search resumed. They bowed their heads and walked on.

~

"Your hair is so pretty," Traverse said, gathering up Ruby's long red locks.

"So's yours. There's so much volume. Mine just lays flat and boring."

"Nah, you just got to know what to do with it." The two girls were in their pajamas, seated on the bed in the guest bedroom. Traverse combed and twined Ruby's hair between her fingers. It felt good to have it played with. Ruby smiled and, when Traverse pulled too hard, held back a grunt. Traverse frowned when she ran her nails over Ruby's scalp. It felt as if something was there, and yet…

Traverse shook her head and ignored it. She divided Ruby's hair into sections and weaved them together into one long braid. "Leave this in overnight and you'll have a nice wave in the morning."

"Thanks." Ruby pulled her hair over her shoulder and giggled.

Connie poked her head in. "Got everything you need, Ruby?"

"I think so."

"Well, don't hesitate to ask."

"Or just take it," Traverse said. "We've got so much junk, Connie wouldn't even notice."

"Oh, like I wouldn't notice you 'borrowing' my turquoise necklace?" Connie challenged.

"You're just mad because it looks better on me."

"Everything looks good on my beautiful girl," Connie cooed, taking Traverse's face in her hands and giving her a kiss. Ruby felt a pang of homesickness watching Traverse fight the affection. She had already spoken to her mom on the phone for a couple of hours, but she suddenly felt like packing her suitcase and making a run back for the sea just so she could get a kiss goodnight.

"Sleep time, girls. Got a long day tomorrow," Connie said. "That means your own bed, Trav."

Traverse rolled her eyes but hopped up off the bed. She allowed herself to be distracted by a book Ruby had packed along.

"I've never met an adopted family before," Ruby said, interrupting Traverse's pursual of the novel. "Is it weird?"

"In a way, I guess," Traverse shrugged. "Wasn't sure I'd fit in with a white family on a farm of all places, but now I don't really want to be anywhere else."

"That's really sweet."

"Better than foster care. See you in the morning."

"Goodnight."

When the door was shut and she was alone, Ruby released a sigh and fell back into the bed, letting herself bounce.

Her head itched.

When she reached up to scratch, her fingers bumped her horns. She closed her eyes and tried to sleep through the strange smells and the lack of ocean sounds. She dosed off, then woke to a dull ache in her head. She grabbed her antlers and pulled, which provided some relief. Outside, bugs were screaming, and her room felt too hot. She kicked the blankets away and dosed off again.

Ruby woke to her head throbbing. She blinked at the window, which had turned a pale blue, indicating the early morning. Giving up on sleep, Ruby rose and dawned her shoes and jacket.

At the back door, she remembered how Traverse had walked around barefoot, and kicked her shoes off again, stepping outside into the cold, wet grass. The feel of icy dew on her bare feet shocked her system in a good way. Ruby stepped out, feeling heavy with the early morning but enjoying the sweet taste of new air and the sleepy baas of the sheep from the barn.

Ruby walked through the backyard, past the vegetable garden and the pond. The ducks were not awake yet. She went to the woods and stepped between the trees, feeling a strange itch that required a certain scratch.

Scratch, scratch, scratch...

Her antlers bumped against a low branch and felt good,

relieving her, temporarily, of the throbbing. Seeking more, she leaned against a thick trunk and rubbed her antlers against it, catching the tips in the bark so that they held and *pulled...*

With a crack, a piece of her antler came off and the weight eased. Ruby found another tree, one with nice thick grooves in the bark that she could sink her horns into. She rubbed and pushed, easing that itching feeling in her head, and after a few more scratches, the entire horn came off.

Then the other.

Ruby sighed with relief and stared down at her detached horns. She touched her hair and felt the remnants of stumps, which would no doubt heal over time. The itch and heaviness were gone. She touched the scratches in the tree her horns had caused, running her fingers into the gashes. She suddenly realized that, upon waking this morning, she hadn't looked out the window to see if her father's boat had come in.

Ruby turned and picked up a small piece of antler. She cupped it in her hand and squeezed tight.

Something moved between the trees. Ruby caught it in the corner of her eye and turned her head, but it seemed that only the shadows were moving.

The wind shifted, pulling her hair over her face. It sounded like something large taking a deep, long sniff. As she left the woods, a branch snagged her shirt and she pulled away. Some leaves rustled loudly behind her, and Ruby turned her head to see a squirrel staring her down.

As she walked back to the house, the ducks quacked and greeted her a good morning from the pond. The grass glistened in the yellow sunshine and swaths of cobwebs appeared on the ground, like fallen handkerchiefs.

From the barn, the sheep calls heightened and Ruby could just make out the silhouette of Bram releasing the

Scottish Blackface into the field. When she stepped inside, she heard the clatter of pans in the kitchen and quietly snuck back to her room.

When Ruby laid down, dirty, grass-covered feet hanging off the edge of the bed, the throbbing and the itching were gone. Antler still clutched in her hand, she took a deep breath and finally fell asleep.

CHAPTER 7

THE SHEPHERD FINDS A SNAIL

Ruby was jolted awake by a knock at the door. The sun was blazing now, fully shining into her room. Ruby's mind panicked at the idea of being late for school before remembering that it was summer break. The door creaked open and Connie poked her head in with a smile.

"I know you teenagers like your sleep, but it's breakfast time."

"What time is it?"

"Breakfast time."

"I mean the—"

Connie chortled at her joke. "Seven o'clock. You've got plenty of time to eat and dress before the shearer gets here."

Ruby followed Connie down the hall and found that Eli was the only one at the table. "Where's everyone?" she asked.

"They already ate. We're pretty early risers."

"Not me. I'm on summer vacation," Eli said, enjoying a bowl of cereal.

"What do you like, Ruby?"

"Cereal's fine."

"Then I'm heading outside. My garden needs to be weeded." Connie waved and headed for the back door.

Eli passed a bowl and spoon to Ruby, who poured herself the cereal and milk. She frowned at the taste.

"What is this?" she asked, double-checking the box.

"Oh, you're probably tasting the sheep's milk," Eli said.

"For real?" Ruby took a spoonful of just milk and sipped it. "Wow, that's really good."

"We milk the ewes ourselves," Eli said proudly.

"How long have you been here, Eli?" Ruby asked. "Ivas said you were adopted."

"Yeah, I came here when I was about eight, I think? Loved the farm life when I was a kid. I think a lot of the other fosters hated it 'cause they couldn't sneak out to parties and sh- stuff, but I liked the quiet. Plan on sticking around, too, once I'm done with college. I'm getting my degree in agriculture."

"That's cool," Ruby said noncommittally.

"Gonna study abroad first, though. Don't want to settle down *too* soon, you know? Got to get out and see the world while I'm young."

That sounded more interesting. "Where are you going to study?"

"There's a cool program in Japan I'm looking at, hoping to spend the next semester there."

"Wow, that does sound cool. I want to go abroad, too."

"You should, dudette. Travel is the best teacher you'll ever have." Eli raised his cereal bowl, offering a toast. Ruby raised hers as well and they clinked the bowls together before draining the last of the sheep's milk.

"Welp, time to get to work."

Ruby stood and followed Eli outside, where the morning glories hadn't yet folded in the sun and the smell of dew was still fresh. A new truck was parked with the other vehicles and a strange man was talking to Bram. He was younger and callused, wearing a ball cap and dirty denim.

"That's Ethan. He's a traveling sheep shearer," Eli explained. "It would take any of us forty minutes to shear just one sheep. Takes Ethan five."

Ethan gave them an acknowledging wave. Bram turned and waved as well. "Get everyone rounded up."

Traverse and Connie were fetched from the garden. The only person missing was Ivas.

"Connie said to leave him be today," Eli said. "Said he had a fall yesterday?"

"Yeah, he's feeling kind of sick," Ruby said sadly.

They walked along the fence line to the barn where a woman Ruby hadn't seen before was waiting.

"You haven't met Cherry yet," Eli noted as they approached. "Ruby, this is Cherry. She works on the farm doing…everything."

Cherry turned and gave Ruby a smile before taking off her glove and giving her a handshake. Cherry was tall and large with a full belly and tanned skin. Her long hair was twisted into a bun, but a few strands had escaped, giving her a windswept look.

"'Everything's right," Cherry said, giving Eli a slap on the shoulder. She was taller than him.

"Any luck yesterday?" Eli's tone turned a little somber. Cherry sighed and shook her head.

"What happened yesterday?" Ruby asked.

"I was volunteering with a search party," Cherry explained. "A woman was out hiking in the woods and went missing. We walked all day but didn't find anything."

"That's awful." Ruby frowned.

"Happens more often than we'd like," Cherry said. She looked at Ruby warningly. "Don't go off wandering by your-self. It's really easy to get lost."

Traverse joined them along the fence. Ruby was surprised to see that Blanc was with her. "It's easy to what?"

"Get lost," Eli said.

"Yeesh. Rude."

"No! I mean—"

Traverse laughed. Eli rolled his eyes.

"Did you see Ivas?" Ruby asked Traverse.

"Yeah, Connie had me bring him some food. Wants him to lay in this morning. Lucky duck."

"You don't even have a hard job," Cherry said. "Now, are we ready to get started?"

"Aww, damn. Dad's probably steaming," Eli said. The four of them headed to the barn where the sheep were waiting.

Everyone had a job on sheep shearing day. Ruby watched from the fence as Bram and Blanc brought the sheep into the barn. From there, Ethan wrestled them one at a time into a paddock, where he flipped them onto their rear ends and began the shearing process. Ethan's face was hard and focused as he took the coats off in one piece. She laughed, watching the sheep just lay there, too confused to try and get back on their feet. There was even a netted hammock that the sheep were laid back on so that Eli could clean and trim their hooves.

"Spa day!" Connie joked.

From there, they went into a shoot where Connie and Traverse gave them their shots and checked for worms. After that, they were free to reenter the pasture, looking lighter and bright-eyed.

The wool was placed into boxes. Ruby took a clump, rolling the raw wool between her fingers, somehow soft and coarse at the same time.

"Save those scraps for me, Ruby," Connie called. "I'll put them in with my tomato plants."

So, Ruby took it upon herself to gather the wool scraps

into her shirt. Everyone had their job. With her shirt lifted from her midsection, she felt eyes on her and turned, surprised to see Ivas standing to the side, staring. His sudden appearance shocked her and she jumped.

Can he see them?

She tried to keep her shirt lowered while not dropping any wool. She walked up to Ivas. "Hey, Ivas. You feeling okay?"

He blinked. "Yeah, better. Got some sleep. Thought I'd help but looks like you're just about finished."

By the time the last sheep was sheared, it was well past lunch and everyone was starving. Connie served sandwiches —Eli made his own vegetable version—and lemonade on the porch and Ethan joined them, telling Traverse and Eli about where he had been so far and where he still needed to go. Ruby felt herself drawn in by the stories, fascinated by the idea of someone traveling for a living.

"Hey, Ruby." Ivas caught her attention quietly. "Come here for a second. Want you to look at a sheep with me."

Ruby lowered her plate. The others didn't notice them depart since they were busy with their meals and Ethan's stories. Ruby followed Ivas off the porch and around the house back toward the barn.

"What's up?" she asked, confused.

Ivas seized her arm and yanked her shirt up.

Ruby yelped, her face heating up. She slapped at Ivas, riling up Blanc, who danced around them, wondering what game was being played.

"Stop!"

Ivas pulled her shirt up higher, tilting his head to see better. Ruby stopped struggling and sighed, annoyed.

"Ruby, what the hell—?"

She yanked her arm away and shoved her shirt back down. "I'm fine."

"What *are* they?"

Ruby shrugged. "I dunno. They got on me when I was… you know, in the ocean. They don't hurt me." She turned around and pulled her shirt up some more, revealing her bare back.

Except that it wasn't bare. Covering her skin were a handful of snails, leaving shining trails all over her flesh, which glimmered with rainbow light under the afternoon sun. Ivas leaned closer. They weren't actual bugs, that much was clear. They were the wrong color, wrong…everything. One in particular caught his attention. It was clear like glass, its body swirled up inside its transparent shell. He touched it with the tip of his finger and it did not react.

"They crawled on you while you were out on the ocean?"

"Yeah. I think they were trying to get away from those monsters." Ruby lowered her shirt again.

"Well… Jesus, why didn't you say anything, Ruby? Let me pull them off."

She stepped away, shaking her head. "They're scared."

Ivas raised his eyebrows. Ruby took a deep breath and sank down, sitting on a chopping stump. Blanc licked at her face.

"They're not hurting me. Some have already left on their own, but the others are still scared. They don't know where to go."

"How do you know they're not hurting you?" Ivas bent down, balancing on his haunches.

Ruby swayed, thinking. "It's, um, it's hard to explain. So, they kind of have feelings, but don't? It's not the same as how you and I have feelings… Ugh." Ruby slapped her knees. "Look, our feelings come from chemicals in our brains and shit, right? So, these guys don't have that. They feel the way you feel deep inside, like how you feel from your soul. But they don't have skin and bodies to keep their feelings inside, so I can *feel* their emotions. Like little jots of electricity on my body."

Ivas frowned.

"Imagine if someone poked you with a stick, and every time they poked you, you could feel how they were feeling. So, for a second, you felt sad, and you knew it was because they were feeling sad. Does that make sense?"

"A little, but it doesn't explain what they are or what they want."

"They don't *want* anything," Ruby said. She lifted her shirt again, revealing her stomach. Resting above her navel was a snail shining purple and blue, like an oil spill. Blanc leaned forward and sniffed at it, ears laid back. "They're just here, waiting until they get to where they need to be."

"Where's that?"

"It's different for all of them." Ruby lowered her shirt again, pushing Blanc away as the dog tried to lick her stomach. "Some dropped off me right away when I got back to shore. A couple of others left at the train station. Every time they leave, I can feel how content they are, like you just solved a big puzzle. When I tried to pull one off, it was scared and hurt."

"It must have something to do with The Dead God," Ivas muttered. Saying the name reminded him of what the monster ate. It made his skin crawl. "Are you sure it's safe? Do you feel any different? Sick? Tired?"

"I've actually been feeling better since we came here," Ruby said, touching her head. "My horns fell off."

Ivas looked at her skull, staring past the glamour and realizing it wasn't there anymore. "That's good. That's a relief."

"Why?"

"What do you mean?"

"I mean, why are you always so concerned about my

horns? Why is it so bad that I have them?" Ruby didn't sound mad as she asked, but genuinely curious. She plucked a snail that had crawled onto her neck into her hand and studied it. "What are you, little guy?"

Ivas took her hand. Ruby looked him in the eye.

"It's not about the horns, Ruby. Those are a part of you. They are your power, your will, your strength. What I don't want is for you to put yourself in danger going after supernatural things that could hurt you. You're just sixteen. That's not fair."

Ruby frowned at that. "Not fair?"

"Not fair that you should have to fight something like that. You should have a normal life."

Ruby wasn't sure about that, but she didn't say anything. She broke eye contact and looked down at their hands instead. "This one likes you."

Ivas looked down as well and saw that the snail—the color of milky water—had slithered onto his finger, resting in the place where a wedding band might have gone. Ivas lifted it closer to his face, watching it slowly journey over his knuckle. Ruby reached for it, but Ivas stopped her. "Let it stay. I'll feel better if I know they're not dangerous."

He lowered his hand and stared at her again. "Ruby, please tell me about these things. I know what you've been through—we went through it together. You're not alone, and you don't need to keep secrets from me. Please?"

Ruby blinked, surprised by how hurt Ivas sounded as he begged her. She hadn't meant to keep it a secret, she just... was used to it.

"I will. I'm sorry."

"Promise?"

Ruby laughed. "Yeah, I promise."

"Okay." Ivas sighed and stood up, pulling Ruby up with him. "Let's go finish lunch."

CHAPTER 8

THE REAPER MAKES A CALL

The afternoon was hot and everyone was ready for some fun after the long day of sheep work. Traverse latched onto Ruby once she returned from the barn with Ivas and took her to the lake on the far side of the farm.

"I don't have a swimming suit!" Ruby protested as the older girl pulled her along.

"It doesn't matter," Traverse said. "Strip down to your comfort level. This is going to be the best thing ever, you'll see."

Ruby didn't believe her. "I spent my life on a *beach*. I don't want to jump into a slimy lake."

When the water came into view, Ruby couldn't deny that it did look inviting. The gentle water shimmered in the sun, and there was a shoreline where feet had trampled the grass away over the years. A few ducks quacked and retreated at their approach.

Traverse took off her shirt, then her pants, leaving on her bra and underwear. Ruby stared and chastised herself. She liked looking at other girls in the locker room at school, fascinated by everyone's unique bodies. But she had been caught and tormented for it and tried to curb her desire to stare.

She shyly took off her own shirt and pants as well, double-checking over her shoulder to ensure no boys were looking. Ahead of her, Traverse charged into the water, splashing and squealing. The ducks quacked loudly, as if protesting her fun.

Ruby took a more cautious approach, dipping her toes in. The water was warm from the summer day and soft sand was on the bottom. "There's nothing dangerous in here, is there?" Ruby asked, wading in up to her calves.

"You literally swam in water with sharks in it and you're worried about our lake?" Traverse teased.

Ruby made a face at some algae that floated by, but Traverse was right, the water felt great against her sweaty, hot skin, and she dived in up to her shoulders, paddling out next to Traverse, who gave her a friendly splash.

"Feels good, right?"

"Yeah, this is awesome," Ruby said. "It's nice that there's no tide or big waves."

"Just watch out for the giant catfish," Traverse warned. "They like to…eat toes!"

Ruby felt something brush against her leg and squealed despite knowing very well that it was Traverse's foot. She splashed the older girl in retaliation, and they broke down into a fit of giggles.

A sensation of relief and contentment struck her, and Ruby felt the pull and disappearance as a snail let go. She smiled at the feeling, truly glad to be in this place, somewhere safe where she, and the snails, could find their way.

They swam until it was too dark to see and finally returned to the house, hungry and exhausted.

～

*T*he next morning, Traverse listened to music as she walked to the pond, holding a bucket of duck feed. Morning chores were well underway for everyone. Ivas fed and walked the dogs with Ruby, continuing to work on Aster's training. Connie was burying sheep wool in her vegetable garden, and Bram and Eli were taking care of the chickens.

Traverse preferred plugging her ears with music and working alone. She wore a tank top and oversized coveralls rolled up to her calves so she could walk barefoot across the grass. Even with headphones on, she could hear the ducks quacking in welcome as she approached. She smiled at them as they came splashing out of the pond and dropped the cornmeal mix onto the ground. They gorged themselves happily.

Traverse looked up and scanned the area, enjoying the beauty of the early morning—blue skies and sheep-shaped clouds—and checking for anything out of the ordinary, as had become her habit as a farmer. Odd shapes, flashing eyes, broken fences, all things that could cause trouble.

What she saw was a shadow. Momentary, but enough to make her stomach flip. It was human-shaped, yet not human at all. It stood at the edge of the tree line like a deer at dusk, perfectly still and invisible if it wasn't for Traverse's trained eyes.

But the longer she stared, the more she didn't see anything at all, just normal shadows cast down from the leaves, dancing in the wind.

She closed her eyes, shook her head, and looked again. Everything was fine. The ducks finished their meal and headed back to the water, quacking contently to each other. Traverse went the opposite way, heading back to the house, not liking how her stomach still hurt with fear.

~

ack at the house, Connie was at work in the kitchen. The scent of sugar filled the air as she pulled a cake from the oven. Bram was on decorating duty, taping streamers to the ceiling. When Traverse walked in, Connie threw a bag of balloons at her.

"Inflate those."

"By myself?" Traverse protested. The bag was small, but there were fifty balloons inside.

"Just do as many as you can. Bram has Eli cleaning out the barn and I want to have this done before he gets back."

"He knows it's his birthday. It's not a surprise."

"It's still fun. Less talking, more blowing."

Traverse groaned. She sat down and got to work inflating the colorful array of balloons. Ten in and she began to feel lightheaded. Twenty later and she was ready to pass out. Bram walked past her, inadvertently kicking a path through the balloons as he went.

"I think I'm done."

"No, no, do some more. I know you've got the hot air in you." Connie didn't look up from her icing work.

"There's no more room on the floor!"

"We'll hang them up."

Bram groaned at this declaration, having just put the step stool away.

The door opened. Connie dropped her pipping tool to jump out, but it was only Ivas and Ruby.

"Thank god," Traverse said, holding out the bag. "You're taking over balloon duty."

"Whose birthday?" Ruby asked, sitting down. She placed a red balloon to her lips and filled it up.

"Eli, remember?" Ivas ducked under some streamers.

"Hey, Connie," Ruby tied off her balloon and bopped it

into the pile, "would it be okay if I borrowed some of your craft supplies? I just need something to make a necklace with."

"Of course!" Connie said. She added a blossom of icing to the cake, completing the circle of flowers. "I've got twine, chains, bead string, whatever you need. Just go through the craft room and help yourself."

"Ooh, craft room clearance," Traverse winked. "You're in the big leagues now."

"Trav! Tape up the balloons!" Connie ordered.

"Ugh!" Traverse made a big show of complaining. "Why should I throw a party for the man that abandoned us?"

"He went to college."

"Left us destitute and without an heir."

"I'm going to destitute you in a minute," Connie warned.

"What does that even mean?"

"You don't want to know."

Ruby flicked a balloon into Traverse's face. She caught it, threatened to throw it back, then taped it up on the ceiling instead. Connie finished her cake, writing Eli's name in big cursive letters before adding the candles.

"Okay, now everyone, hide!" Connie said. The table was set and the balloons had become an invasive species thanks to Ruby's contribution.

"He knows what we're doing," Traverse said.

"It's still fun. Now, hide!"

Everyone picked a spot, ducking behind the stove, under the table, or for Bram, who couldn't bend down too long, behind a load-bearing post. Everything went quiet, and Ruby heard a loud popping sound. She looked over and saw that Connie was cracking her knuckles.

"How long do we have to wait?" Ivas asked, pressed up beside the fridge.

Connie sighed. "Bram, go call for him."

Leaving his hiding spot, Bram went to the front door, stuck his head out, and scanned the area. Before he could call out, they all heard the mud room door slam closed.

"Oh! Oh! Surprise!" Connie yelled as Eli stepped into the kitchen. Startled by the change of entry, everyone else stumbled forward, giving haphazard "happy birthdays."

"Mom, I told you not to make a fuss," Eli said, bending down so his mother could kiss his cheek.

"I'm always going to fuss over my boy. Now, happy birthday to you…"

Everyone joined in the song and Eli blew out his candles. They all ate cake while watching him open presents. A vegetarian cookbook for poor college students, some new clothes, and a tiny pocketknife covered in dirt from Traverse.

"Whoa, nice one!" Eli said admirably, studying the little silver handle. He tried to fold it open, but it was rusted shut.

"What am I missing?" Ruby asked.

"So, the first time I was here for Eli's birthday, I didn't have anything to give him, so I just went looking around the farm for whatever I could find. I dug up an old coin and gave it to him, and now it's our tradition to give each other whatever we can dig up on the property."

"Last year, I found a horseshoe," Eli said proudly.

"I had to go deep in the forest for this guy," Traverse said. "I almost had to give you another rock."

"Awesome find. I bet if I clean it up, we can get it open."

"You two are adults with money now," Connie said disapprovingly. "You could give each other *real* presents."

"This is way more fun."

"When's your birthday, Ruby?" Traverse asked.

"Spring. We already missed it," Ruby said, disappointed.

Next, Eli got to pick a game to play and whatever he wanted for dinner. He chose poker, since it was the only game he could think of that would accommodate the number of players. This was apparently a common game because Bram brought out a large pickle jar of pennies to use for bets.

There were no breaks from farm life, however. After a few games in which Bram obtained all the pennies, it was back to work. Connie and Eli went to the kitchen to get started on Eli's requested meat-free dinner. Everyone else headed outside to wrap up the day.

"So, how's farm life so far?" Traverse asked. The two girls stood on the wooden fence, watching Ivas and Blanc gather the sheep into the barn.

"I love it," Ruby grinned. "Can we go swimming again tomorrow?"

"Actually, I have something else to show you. We'll go after I finish morning chores."

"What is it?"

"A surprise," Traverse teased.

~

*I*n the morning, Ruby woke later than the rest of the household. The home was quiet as she searched the kitchen for breakfast. She helped herself to another bowl of cereal and sheep milk, then went in search of the craft room.

Ruby took advantage of Connie's many craft supplies to make a necklace from the piece of horn that had fallen from her head. Using leather strips, she tied the antler up and dressed it with wooden beads. She knotted the ends and slipped it over her head. It felt good to have a piece close to her.

Power, will, strength...

"Very pretty!" A voice from the door startled her. Connie

stepped in, pulling off her gardening gloves. She looked down at Ruby's project. "Did you find that outside?"

Ruby nodded.

"Traverse liked to collect animal parts, too. She would find antlers, snake skins, even skulls sometimes."

"What did I do?" Traverse's voice echoed to them from the mud room, followed by the slamming door.

"I was telling Ruby about all the cool things you would find when— Will you put shoes on?"

Traverse walked into the room, feet covered in mud and grass. "Oh, sorry."

"My god, child, go clean your feet. You're going to step on a hornet one day and you'd better not come crying to me when you do."

Traverse rolled her eyes and went to the bathroom. Ruby could hear the pipes clanking in the walls as she ran the bath. "Hey, Ruby!" Traverse shouted over the running water. "Let's go hiking when I'm done. I'll show you all the cool trails."

"Yeah!" Ruby agreed eagerly.

"Are you done with Ivas for the day?" Connie checked.

"I haven't seen him."

"Go work with him and Aster for a bit, then you guys can hike. Just be back before it gets dark. I'll have Eli help me with dinner."

Ruby heaved a sigh but did as she was told. Shoes on, she headed outside to the dog pen. Aster was there, but the pen was short one pup.

"Where's Shiro?" Ruby asked, opening the gate. Aster jumped up on her, covering her shirt in muddy paw prints. Ruby quickly pushed him off gand got the leash on his collar. The other dogs watched them patiently.

"Why can't you follow their example?" Ruby asked. She scanned the area and spotted Ivas in the training corral with

Shiro. Blanc was lying in the grass outside the fence, watching her daughter.

Ivas just stood there, shoulders slumped and eyes vacant. Ruby carefully approached. He didn't notice until she said his name.

"It's gone. All gone," he whispered. Ruby twisted the leash in her hands. "I can't train the puppies. I can't even talk to Blanc."

"You can still do obedience, though, right?"

"Yeah, just nothing to do with sheep herding." He finally looked at her. His lips were pale and eyes heavy.

"Have you gotten any sleep?"

"Only a little," he confessed.

"Can you help me with Aster?"

"I… No, I really need to work with the pups. Even if it's just some obedience training. Just walk him around the property and use the tricks I taught you yesterday."

"He's pulling again," Ruby said with a sigh. "He doesn't listen to me."

"You have to keep working with him. It takes time and repetition." Ivas ran a hand through his hair tiredly. "Just keep at it."

Ruby felt lost looking at Ivas. He seemed completely broken and scared, but she didn't know what to say.

Ruby surrendered herself to the task of training Aster, but any progress they made seemed to have been lost, as if Aster had already gotten bored of the novelty of being obedient. Ruby tried everything Ivas had shown her, but Aster just seemed to fight harder.

Several exhausting hours later, Ruby looked up at the training corral, but Ivas was gone. Ruby gave up and put Aster away again.

"Come on, man, can't you work with me here? You did so good for Ivas! What am I doing wrong?"

Aster only gave her a tongue-filled grin in response.

"You're lucky you're cute."

Ruby stumbled into the house, where the smell of lunch made her stomach rumble.

"I heard that," Connie said from the kitchen. "Come in and eat."

"Don't we need to wait for everyone?" Ruby asked, stepping into the dining room.

"Usually the household comes and goes for food since everyone gets pretty busy." Connie put a plate of simple pasta together and Ruby eagerly accepted. Traverse joined her shortly after.

"Ready for our special hike?" she asked around a mouthful of food. Ruby nodded eagerly and scarfed down the rest of her meal.

The door slammed as they raced outside, heading for the trees. The sun was in its decent, making the shadows long and cooling the day. Ruby laughed happily as they raced through the evening air. The trailhead Traverse took her to was well worn by years of feet, patted down to dirt and tree roots.

"What I'm about to show you is top secret," Traverse teased, winking at Ruby from over her shoulder. "No adults allowed."

"But you're eighteen."

"Yeah, but I mean, like, *adult* adults."

"What is it?"

"You'll see."

Ruby enjoyed the walk. Her face warmed in the patches of sunlight that fell through the leaves like golden magic. The air smelled sweet and moist, filled with honeysuckle. Eventually, the trail opened up next to a creek, and they followed this to a large tree that cradled a hut in its branches.

"Check it out," Traverse said proudly. "This is our secret treehouse. Eli and I built it together after Connie and Bram officially adopted me."

"Wow," Ruby gasped. "That is so cool! You built it by yourselves?"

"Well, I mean, Bram helped *a little*." Traverse chuckled. "Anyway, you can come here any time you need to get away, okay?" They jogged up to the tree where planks were nailed into the trunk, acting as a ladder. The treehouse itself was fairly small—they weren't able to stand up in it, and there was room for maybe four people to sit down on the floor comfortably, but it was dry, with a real glass window and various old pillows on the floor. Old paperbacks, sketchbooks, CDs, and comics were littered in the corners.

"This is the coolest thing ever," Ruby said, settling herself down and picking up one of the books—an old horror novel with a screaming woman in a loose dress on the cover.

"Yeah, any time we got something that our parents didn't allow—like horror books—we hid them here. Sometimes, my friends and I would have sleepovers, and we would sneak out here and do witchcraft until we fell asleep."

Ruby looked up in surprise. "Witchcraft?"

Traverse smiled. "Yeah, dude. We'd light candles—super dangerous, by the way—then we'd draw chalk symbols and try to cast spells and things. Oh, wait..." Traverse went to a corner containing a couple of board games and held one up. "One time, one of my friends brought this Ouji board. That was really fun."

Ruby's eyes widened. "Whoa, did it work?"

"Nah, we just pushed it around spelling things like 'butt' and 'farts.' My friend Cassandra tried to scare us by pretending there was a ghost, but it was just make-believe." Traverse set the board on the floor, unfolding it to reveal the alphabet, surrounded by suns and moons. "No idea where the planchette is. I think we lost it."

Ruby stared at the board, then touched her necklace. "What about this?"

Traverse shrugged. "We can try it if you want."

Ruby slipped the antler off her neck and placed it in the middle of the board. It was small enough and slid across the surface easily.

"Who are we talking to?" Traverse asked, placing her fingers on the horn. "I'm always a fan of Elvis myself."

Ruby chuckled. "It's whatever. I'm just messing around."

"Hello?" Traverse called. "Is there anyone here who would like to talk to us?"

They watched the board for a moment. Ruby licked her lips.

The horn moved.

Ruby yelped and yanked her hands away as if she had been shocked. Traverse jumped, then laughed. "Did you just scare yourself?"

"No! It was you!" Ruby laughed as well and threw a pillow at Traverse's head. The older girl flopped over in defeat.

"Not me, kiddo. Must have been a ghost."

"Hey, you never know," Ruby said mysteriously. "I've seen things."

"Oh yeah? Lots of spirits over at the beach, huh?" Traverse stood up, ducking her head, and headed for the door. Ruby followed, slipping her necklace back on.

"But yeah, you're welcome here any time. We only have one rule, and it's mostly for Eli, but no porn."

Ruby made a face. "Gross."

"I'm guessing you don't have siblings. Boys are *so* gross."

The two girls giggled as they walked back down the trail, taking their time to skip rocks and watch minnows in the creek. The golden light turned red and then blue as they became lost in conversation. Lightning bugs blinked at them from the tall grass. Traverse finally noticed the waning day and motioned for Ruby to hurry back to the house.

The squeal of a coyote made their hair stand up.

"Are coyotes dangerous?" Ruby asked.

"Not really. They're mostly scaredy cats."

"It sounds like a ghost."

"I know," Traverse agreed solemnly.

Then, the coyotes were screaming all at once, howling and yipping as if they were in pain. Ruby grabbed Traverse's hand and the older girl pulled her into a run, following the trail with a familiarness that came from years of experience. They didn't stop until they broke through the trees and saw the lights of the house. Only then were they brave enough to look at each other and laugh.

CHAPTER 9

THE SHEPHERD MAKES A CALL

Ivas stared down at the books he had gathered from the house. He had found anything that had a sheep on the cover or mentioned herding, spread them on the floor of his cabin, and explored the pages.

He started by memorizing the words. "Come by," "Away to me," "Lie down." He read what each command meant, hoping that at some point he would have a moment of inspiration and it would all come rushing back, but it was as if he had no idea what sheepherding was, except that it was his job.

He tried to summon the memory of his grandfather, all the long days spent learning to be a shepherd, but they had become faded in his mind. Anything the man had told him, all the hours sitting on the fence and watching him work, had become uselessly muddled.

The worst part was Blanc. Training her had been the happiest he had been since his parents died. He and Blanc had connected from the moment his grandpa pulled her out of the kennel and presented her to him as his very own sheepdog.

"Come by… Away…" He said the words, but they meant nothing to him. Would Blanc even know what he wanted from her? Why did sheep even need to be herded?

He closed his eyes and rubbed them until he saw spots. He tossed the book aside and stood up, deciding to take on a different challenge instead.

It took Ivas a while to find Old Popper's number. The paper was crumbled up in one of his other pockets.

He headed to the house, walking through the dark. Dinner had been eaten, and Bram had taken care of putting the sheep away. Ivas knew he could only feign illness for so long.

Inside the house, things had quieted down. Everyone had settled into their comfy chairs or bedrooms to read or listen to music. He passed the living room where Bram and Connie were chatting over the radio.

He took the phone out onto the back porch for privacy and dialed the rotary phone, turning each number at a time until it was complete.

It rang enough times that Ivas thought it wouldn't be answered, and then, as he was about to give up, the receiver clicked.

"'ello?"

"Mr. Poppermill?"

"Speaking."

"It's Ivas… S'barge. How are you, sir?"

"No complaints."

Ivas smiled at that. "Is Archibald still staying with you?"

"Not sure I could get him to leave if I wanted to," Poppermill said. "Luckily for him, I like having the company. Though he's got my books all out of order. You wanting to talk to him?"

"Actually, I was wanting to ask you a question, another story question."

"Shoot."

"Do you know any stories about snails or slugs?"

"You always ask about the most specific things," Poppermill said.

"Sorry."

"No need to be sorry, just wondering how you get these ideas in your head."

Ivas heard a second voice in the background.

"Something about snails," Poppermill answered, talking away from the phone. "I don't really know any specific stories about snails, do you?"

Ivas heard the voice start to ramble and Poppermill stopped him. "Here, here, just take the phone. Tell Ivas."

"Hello, Ivas!" Archibald's voice took over the soundwaves. "How are you? I can't thank you enough for introducing me to Mr. Poppermill. I'm trying to talk him into coming to the university with me to talk about his collection."

"That sounds nice. Do you know—"

"Ivas thinks it's a good idea, Mr. Poppermill!"

"Good, I always take my life advice from the shepherd's boy," Poppermill responded sarcastically from the background.

"Arch," Ivas spoke up, "I was wondering—"

"But it would be such a boon to the academic community!"

"Archibald!" Ivas shouted. "Snails. I need to know if you have any stories about snails."

"Snails? Hmm, insects are often used in literature as a metaphor for ghosts and the afterlife. There's butterflies, scarabs, spiders… Depends on which culture you ask. Now, those all represent ghosts—people who have already passed on. Snails are unique in that they represent new souls."

"What does that mean?"

"Means they haven't lived a life. They're new, they haven't been born yet. Certain cultures say it's bad luck to kill or salt a snail because it means that someone, or something, won't have the chance to be born. Seeing a snail when you're pregnant is supposed to be good luck because it means the baby will be born healthy."

"Okay, okay." Ivas was relieved to hear that they weren't an entity for evil. He lifted his arm and regarded his snail, which had chosen to rest in the dip inside of his elbow. It was easy to forget that it was there. It didn't bother him physically, but when he remembered its presence, he was able to immediately find it on his body. "So, they're not bad then?"

"Not at all! In fact, they're the most neutral creations out there, can't harm or help. Some don't even really consider them souls. More like...the potential for a soul. This is a point often argued in philosophy. Now, that wasn't my favorite class, but I did enjoy our debates on the ideas of the soul, where life begins, that sort of thing. Some argue it's when we take our first breath, or first heartbeat. Others felt it was when we were able to form conscious opinions..."

Ivas realized that Archibald was ranting now, but that was okay. The snails wouldn't harm Ruby, and that was all that mattered. After a couple of failed attempts to tell Archibald goodbye, Ivas simply hung up the phone.

~

"...*M*e, personally. Yeah, I said that the first indication of the soul is the ability to laugh. What, I ask you, is a clearer indicator of a life being lived? Hello? Ivas? Oh, must have lost the connection." Archibald hung up the antique phone and turned to see that Poppermill had made them some tea.

"J'ya tell him about the things that hunt souls?" Poppermill asked.

Archibald's eyes brightened and he hurriedly swallowed his biscuit to answer. "Oh! You mean like soul eaters?"

"Mmmhmm. I've read lots of stories about things like that. There are things you gotta do when you die to make sure they don't come and gobble up your soul."

Archibald nodded. "Every culture I've read has some version of that. Do you think I should have told Ivas? Is it important?"

Poppermill shrugged and sipped his tea. "Probably not."

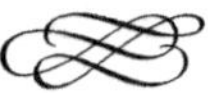

CHAPTER 10

THE HORNED GIRL TALKS TO GHOSTS

*R*uby made sure everyone was busy with their chores before slipping away into the forest. A couple of days had passed and she was becoming more comfortable with the Carns, growing used to the scream of cicadas and the yelping of coyotes at night.

There wasn't much for her to do on the farm. The day before, she had gone out with Traverse and sat on the fence, watching as the older girl used a scythe to cut the long grass in one of the fields. Ruby had been mesmerized by the movement and sound as Traverse swiftly swung the tool left and right, cutting the alfalfa evenly in one stroke. Each step she took was another swath of grass down. She let Ruby try it next, but the grass just fell over, dodging the blade when she used it.

"You have to be closer to the ground, and swing it fast," Traverse instructed.

The next day, Ruby followed Eli around the farm, helping to feed all the animals. They took the alfalfa Traverse had cut and gave it to the sheep, then visited the ducks and chickens. The buckets were heavy, but it was worth it to see the little birds run up to them excitedly, clucking and quacking and flapping their wings. While the chickens ate, they gathered their eggs into a basket and took them back to the house.

Connie had also been harvesting. The kitchen table was filled with tomatoes, zucchini, potatoes, corn, cabbage, onions, carrots, and other vegetables from her garden.

"Too much again," she said, shaking her head.

"Send it to the neighbors." Eli shrugged.

"What if we sold it?" Ruby suggested. "Mom and I would always stop at produce stands when we went on drives to the city."

"Not a bad idea. It's been a while since we had a stand. We'll all go into town next week and take it to the farmers' market."

The next morning, Ruby decided to return to the treehouse.

She knew it wasn't the right thing to do. It wasn't wrong, but it wasn't healthy either. She was supposed to be using this trip to get over things, but her horn came from magic, and it had *moved* when she and Traverse tried it on the Ouija board. She was sure of it.

The game was still laid out on the floor when she climbed up into the tree. She placed her antler necklace in the middle and gently rested her fingers on top. They trembled and she tried to take a deep breath before calling out to the open air.

"Dad?"

She felt that wasn't enough. There were probably lots of "Dads" out there, so she called his name.

"If you're there, say something." She stared hard at the broken antler, both terrified and eager for it to move. "I got your letter. I stopped the Dead God. Are you safe now?"

The horn shivered under her trembling fingers.

Then, it moved.

First to the H, then E, then on to L and O. Ruby's heart sank, knowing that whatever she was talking to wasn't her father.

"Hello," she said glumly. "Who are you?"

N-O—N-A-M-E

"Sure."

The antler didn't move.

"What do you want?" Ruby pressed.

F-O-O-D

Ruby frowned. She felt fear, but it wasn't hers. "What kind of food?"

E-S-C-A-R-G-O-T

If Ruby had hackles, they would have risen. She swiped the horn down to the word "Goodbye" forcefully.

She lifted her shirt and looked at the snails that rested on her stomach. "Don't worry, guys. I'll keep you safe. I promise." She grabbed the Ouija board and tossed it back into the corner, chastising herself. She should have known better. Her father wasn't a ghost. He had passed on, was at peace, and she needed to find peace as well.

The disappointment still lingered on her face as she climbed down from the treehouse and left the woods, hands in pockets and eyes on her feet. She had almost reached the house when Ivas's voice stopped her.

"I was looking for you," he said. Blanc trotted up and licked her hand. Ruby pulled it away. Ivas wasn't looking much better from the last time they had spoken. He was pale and bags had formed under his eyes. "Let's go work with Aster a bit."

Ruby didn't answer, just followed Ivas back to the dog pens. The other dogs looked up calmly while Aster jumped up on the fencing, making it clang. Ruby rolled her eyes.

Ivas opened the door and let Aster out. The excited animal jumped up on them, and it took a few loud commands from Ivas to get him to sit. He handed the leash to Ruby to tie around the dog's chest. She tried to get it into place, but Aster immediately left the sitting position to jump up on her instead.

"Sit!" she ordered. Aster did not obey. Ruby slapped his hide sharply, making the puppy yelp and tuck his tail. "Sit, Goddammit!"

"Ruby!" Ivas stepped forward and snatched the leash from her. Blanc's ears folded back warningly. "You don't strike an animal! What's the matter with you?"

"Nothing," she growled.

"If this is how you treat him, then he's not going back with you."

"Whatever. He's a shit dog anyway."

Ivas stared, a mixture of confusion and anger on his face, not knowing what to say. Ruby turned and stomped away. He heard a soft gasp from her, a tearful sound.

He stood awhile, watching Ruby head down the hill and into the farmhouse. He looked down at Aster, who looked back worriedly, licking at Ivas's hand and shuffling his paws as if to say, "I'm sorry."

"You're okay, bud," Ivas reassured him, providing ear rubs until Aster's tail started wagging again. He went ahead and gave Aster his walk, then went in search of Connie.

He found her in the backyard swing, skin sweaty and hands dirty from a day of weeding. He sat next to her.

"So, you know about teenagers, right?"

"I've had a few pass through this house."

"Ruby's acting weird. I think something happened." Ivas explained the incident at the dog pen.

Connie shrugged. "That's just kind of regular teenage behavior. We've had all kinds when we were taking in fosters. They were all lost, unwanted, full of confusion and anger, and they acted accordingly. Some days things were good, but most were hard, full of yelling and fighting. Ruby's the same. She's been hurt, and when you're that age, you don't know what to do about the hurt."

"Would you talk to her? I have no idea what to say."

"Sure. Did she go to her room?"

"She went in the house, so I guess so."

"I'm sure you were the same at that age," Connie teased.

"I'm pretty sure I was a perfect angel," Ivas joked. "Were Eli and Traverse the same way?"

"Still are," Connie said with a shrug. "Eli's parents were in jail for the entirety of his childhood. Traverse's dad ran off and her mom died in childbirth. You don't just grow out of that." Connie scooted herself to the edge of the swing and hopped down.

"Did you ever get tired of it?" Ivas asked, "Must have been really hard trying to take care of so many troubled teens."

"Honestly, some days were a nightmare," Connie admitted, casting her eyes down, as if ashamed. "Some we couldn't help at all. Things their parents did before they were born made it impossible. There was one boy..." She sighed and shook her head.

"What happened?"

"Let's just say he was particularly troubled. He ran away, the first and only of ours that did. Never did find out what happened to him." Connie raised her head and met Ivas's eyes. "I was relieved when he did, Ivas. I've never felt that way about any of the kids, no matter how bad they got. But this boy... He had something truly wrong with him. He hurt the animals and the other kids. Lied and stole. Almost burned the barn down once."

Ivas shuddered.

"So, I think we can handle whatever Ruby is going through," Connie said confidently. "Go find Bram for me. It's his turn for supper tonight."

Connie dusted off her hands and washed them in the kitchen before heading to the guest room. The door was open, but Ruby wasn't there. Connie did a quick search of the house, and when she didn't find Ruby, she stepped onto the front porch.

She spotted the redhead on top of the hill next to the dog pen, playing with Aster. There was no leash; Aster was free, running in circles and rolling in the grass, his white fur turning green. Ruby chased after him and gave him ferocious belly rubs before feeding him a treat.

Connie smiled and went back into the house.

~

"I'm sorry," Ruby said again, feeding Aster yet another treat, knowing it was definitely too many and not caring. "You're a good dog."

Aster wagged his tail, happy to hear it.

"Sit," she said.

Aster did so.

"Great job!" Ruby praised. More belly rubs and treats followed. "Let's try a walk."

Ruby regarded the leash but decided against it. Instead, she made sure Aster saw that she was carrying a treat and started to walk along the tree line. Aster eagerly followed, eyes locked on the snack. After a few feet with Aster staying by her side, he was rewarded, and a new treat was produced. They continued their walk this way. Every time Aster became distracted by something, Ruby quickly brought his attention back to the food and kept him at her thigh.

"Good boy, Aster, good boy," she whispered, feeling almost tearful at the success. "I don't like leashes either."

She watched the sky turn red as they walked back to the pen, the clouds slashed against the sky in oranges and pinks, the sun like a bloody wound. The shadows stretched long and deepened in the woods.

Aster stopped walking and stared.

Ruby paused and held the treat to his nose, but he didn't pay it any heed. The green-stained fur on his back began to rise and spike up, his triangle ears laid back.

Ruby looked into the woods and saw multiple pairs of eyes staring back at her. She couldn't tell what possessed them, their bodies blending into the shadows, but their eyes reflected back the setting sun, glowing gold and red.

Aster growled lowly in his throat.

Another set of eyes appeared, these much higher than the others, floating forward as their owner came closer. Ruby could just make out a strange outline of a body.

A long, skinny hand stretched out from the trees—the only part of the creature that left the woods—it looked to be made of sticks and mud.

The creature made a sound like creaking wood and screaming cicadas. Aster snarled at the sound and Ruby took a fearful step back.

From the cacophony of noise the creature emitted, Ruby was actually able to make out some words and realized the thing was trying to speak.

She heard the word "...*snails*..." and her eyes locked on its grasping hand.

"No," she choked on the word.

A clear, guttural growl rumbled from its throat. The eyes came closer.

Ruby looked down at Aster, then at the dog pen where his siblings were also staring at the trees, wide-eyed and fur-spiked.

Ruby ran to the pen and threw the latch up. Immediately, the dogs came out and formed a line along the trees, not entering the woods but daring anything to step beyond them. Saliva and foam dripped from their mouths as they showed their teeth and snarled madly.

The lower eyes blinked out, retreating from the threat of the Burger Blanc Suisses. The creature made a noise like a bear—a sound of warning—before stepping back and disappearing into the dark wilderness.

When it was gone, the dogs slowly relaxed, fur lying down and tongues panting tiredly. Ruby let out the breath she had accidentally been holding and quickly ushered the dogs back into the pen before running as fast as she could to the farmhouse and locking the door behind her.

It wasn't just *her* fear. She could practically feel the little snails trembling against her skin. She tried to whisper reassurances to them, but the words died in her throat as she went to her bedroom and saw the forest outside the window. She closed the blinds, then shoved the bed to the opposite wall. She practically ran to the dining room when dinner was announced.

CHAPTER 11

THE REAPER TELLS A GHOST STORY

"Hey, Trav, are there any stories about the woods around here?" Ruby asked. The two of them sat on Traverse's bed, listening to music from the radio and flipping through various magazines. The bed was laid out with snacks and sweets.

"What do you mean?" Traverse laughed and showed Ruby a recipe from her magazine that involved setting vegetables in gelatin. Ruby made a face.

"Like, legends? Or ghost stories?"

Traverse's eyebrows shot up and she smiled wickedly. "Actually, there is something like that." She closed her magazine and sat up. Ruby put a pretzel in her mouth, eyes wide. "This was before I came to the farm, but Eli told me about this foster boy that Bram and Connie took in—he was really messed up. They caught him with one of the chickens once, holding it by the legs and ready to sacrifice it to the devil. Another time, Eli claims the boy snuck into his room and watched him sleep."

Ruby went tense, chasing her pretzel with some chocolate.

"He was really bad, even tried to burn the barn down once. One day, he disappeared. Connie said he ran away. Not uncommon for fosters, you know? But Eli said that's not what happened, said he was eaten by a monster that lives in the forest."

"What monster?"

"It doesn't really have a name. I think it's similar to the Leshy or Wendigo, but all the foster kids before me called it Creeping Bones. It's sort of become an inherited legend around here—Eli would tell the story to new fosters to scare them. Its body is built from the bones of those who get lost in the woods. If you go out there alone, it'll hunt you and tear out your bones, add them to its body. If it's hungry, it'll eat the rest."

Ruby swallowed. "And that's what happened to that boy?"

Traverse shrugged. "If he went into the forest alone? Maybe. He was never found. Never heard from again."

"Are you bullshitting me?" Ruby challenged, narrowing her eyes.

"He really did disappear," Traverse said sincerely, almost sadly. "It really tore up Connie and Bram. Creeping Bones has always been a ghost story we tell new fosters so that they don't go into the woods by themselves—because you *can* get lost out there, and they will *never* find you. It's happened to hikers before. A few years ago, this girl had been hiking the mountain outside the farm and just disappeared. Bram and Connie helped with the search party."

"Damn." Ruby sank back, her body getting sore from keeping a stiff posture.

"Yeah, the wilderness is really dangerous out here. Eli said Creeping Bones will put a spell on you so that when you try to get back home, you end up walking in a big circle and not even realize it. Then, when it's dark and you're too tired to run, that's when it comes for you."

Ruby rubbed her palms against her bare arms, brushing against one of the snail shells resting on her shoulder. "What else does it do?"

"It has eyes that shine like a coyote's, and it controls the forest animals through fear and promises of sharing human meat. If predators come onto the farm, it means Creeping Bones is hungry. Sometimes, it'll try to lure children into the trees with a cute bunny or fox."

"So, it can't come onto the farm?"

"It can't enter any human settlement or path. It's a spirit of the wild woods—that's its domain."

"Where—"

"RAH!"

The girls screamed as the door suddenly burst open, and Eli stormed in, arms raised and face pulled into the most frightening expression he could manage. He doubled over into laughter at the sight of their terror.

"Cheesus, Eli!" Traverse shrieked. She grabbed a pillow and attacked without mercy. Ruby joined in, slamming a second pillow into his head.

"You jerk! You scared us!"

"That's the point," Eli said, dancing away from their attacks. "I heard you guys talking about Creeping Bones." He pointed a teasing finger at Traverse. "She thinks it's real."

"Shut up!" Traverse rolled her eyes.

"If the grass gets up too high around the trees and fields, she cuts it down with the scythe," Eli continued, "cause the land has to be worked with human tools to keep Creeping Bones away."

"That's just what Bram said to make me do chores," Traverse said.

"But you still do it religiously." Eli fell onto the bed and picked up one of the magazines. Ruby landed a hard shot to his face with the pillow.

"Like you don't leave your light on at night." Traverse smirked.

"I fall asleep reading."

"Sure you do."

"So," Ruby spoke up, "how does one, hypothetically, get rid of Creeping Bones?"

Eli shrugged. "You don't. It's a forest spirit. It kind of *is* the forest—if you look beyond the silly ghost story side of it. The way to avoid 'Creeping Bones'—" he used air quotes there, "—is to be smart: don't go out alone, know how to survive the wilderness."

Traverse plopped down next to her brother and opened one of the chocolates. "I was telling her about Joseph."

Eli's expression darkened. "He was a messed-up kid. I know it's bad to say, but no one was sad when he disappeared."

"That bad?" Ruby said.

"Dad had to lock the dogs up in the barn because Joseph —we called him Siph—would sneak out at night and torture them. I remember hearing them yelping and crying one night. I ran out with Dad and we found Siph in the dog pen with one of Dad's leather belts, whipping the poor dog. He was having *fun,* smiling about it. If Creeping Bones is real, then he did us all a favor."

The room grew quiet. The cry of an owl made them all jump and then laugh nervously, slowly melting away the tension. Eli pointed out a page in one of the home décor magazines and told Traverse to cut it out for Connie. Ruby picked up a cookbook and looked for a dessert they could bake together later. The ghost story was slowly pushed to the back of their minds, but that night, the three of them slept in Traverse's room with the lights on.

CHAPTER 12

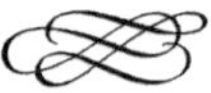

THE SHEPHERD LEARNS TO COUNT

Bram and Ivas stared at the barn door, both painfully aware of their own breathing. The wood was scarred with claw marks, the handle shredded by teeth, lying broken in the grass. Something had literally dug its way through, and in the barn, a sheep was dead. Whatever had broken in had managed to corner it and tear out its neck.

"You didn't hear anything last night?" Bram asked.

"Heard the sheep talking at one point, but they weren't panicked."

"You figure they would have been screaming bloody murder." Bram sighed and rubbed the back of his neck. "We'll look into reinforcing it today. Use a metal barricade."

"I just killed a coyote last week, now this. What's got them so active?"

"I don't know, but it's not out of hunger. Look, they didn't eat any of it, just killed it."

"We need to bring in Magnus," Ivas said.

Bram nodded. "I'll make the call. Until then, I think you and Blanc better stick to the fields and keep an eye on them."

Ivas nodded. It was the first time Bram had actively ordered him to watch the sheep, and his stomach twisted with fear. He went to the back of the barn and slowly lifted the latch for the door. The sheep eagerly pressed against it. He fully opened the door to the impatient ewes and rams waiting on the other side. Like a blanket being whipped out, they flowed into the field for a day of grazing.

Blanc looked up at Ivas, and even she seemed worried.

Ivas swallowed. He had memorized the commands over the past few nights, but putting them into action was an entirely different matter. Would Blanc know what to do?

Looking over his shoulder, Ivas made sure there were no witnesses. He clutched his staff tightly in both hands.

"Okay…" He looked down at Blanc, who stared up at him, eyes friendly and tongue hanging out. "Come by."

Blanc took off. She ran down the field along the sheep and started to turn in a clockwise motion when she reached the back. The sheep bleated worriedly and jogged away.

That meant she was too close. "St- Ah, get back!"

Blanc slowed down.

"Okay, okay…" Ivas studied the sheep, trying to determine where they would go once he gave the order. "Walk on."

Blanc slowly moved forward, and the sheep responded by pushing the herd to get away from her.

"Lie down."

She did so.

"Walk up— I mean, walk on!"

She hesitated.

"Walk on!"

At this, she moved again.

"Come by."

Blanc finished making a circle around the sheep, pushing them to the other side of the field. When she reached Ivas, he told her, "That'll do," and she came to a stop at his feet.

Ivas rubbed his face with his sleeve. He felt exhausted and nervous. The sheep hadn't really moved anywhere, and he wasn't sure if they were supposed to, wasn't sure if he had done anything *right*.

He looked down at Blanc and knew she felt the same. She and him had spoken the same language, had worked so smoothly and flawlessly together, and now it was lost. The years it took to build that connection were gone. Ivas sank down into the grass and pulled her into his chest. Blank licked his cheek.

"I'm sorry. I don't know how to do this."

Blanc leaned into his embrace, dropping all her weight on him. Ivas felt like crying but pushed the feeling away.

"We just have to keep trying, okay? Can you be patient for me?"

Blanc tilted her head, looking at him upside down. Ivas kissed her snout.

"Okay, let's try again." Ivas stood up, and Blanc eagerly jumped to her feet. "Away."

~

A few more practice runs around the field left them both tired, Blanc's tongue hanging out and coated in white foam. Ivas gave the "that'll do" command, and Blanc came to his side.

A noise made Blanc turn her head to the house, and Ivas followed her gaze, spotting the three kids coming out for the day, each holding a coffee cup.

Ivas frowned thoughtfully and pulled up his sleeve to find the snail he had taken from Ruby. It was nestled in the crook of his elbow, hidden in its shell. He had actually forgotten it was there.

The potential for a soul...

The three kids had abandoned their mugs on the porch and ran to his side, peering cautiously into the barn at the dead sheep. Bram must have said something.

"I'll get a shovel," Eli said dutifully.

"What did this?" Ruby asked.

"A coyote, I suppose. The door is covered in claws and teeth marks, and the handle is snapped off. Don't know what else it could be."

Ruby and Traverse looked at each other with worried expressions.

"I'm going into town," Bram announced, coming up behind them. "If anyone wants to come, get ready. Tell your brother."

Traverse looked to the edge of the trees where Eli was working on a hole. Digging one big enough for the sheep would take a few hours.

"I want to come," Ruby said.

"Me too." Traverse nodded.

"Ivas? Want anything?"

"A soda pop."

"A'ight, you girls go get dressed." Bram walked away and the girls started for the house. Ruby hesitated and turned back to Ivas. The morning dew was dampening the hem of her pajama pants.

"Hey, Ivas? I'm sorry about yesterday."

Ivas looked at her and tilted his head. "Are you okay?"

"Yeah, I was just… I'll tell you about it later. I went back and apologized to Aster, worked with him a bit. He did really well."

Ivas nodded. "I'm glad to hear it."

"I don't really think he's a bad dog."

"Good."

Ruby turned away but hesitated again. "Um, Ivas? Don't go into the woods today, okay?"

"Why not?"

"I'll tell you later." This time she finished her journey to the house.

Ivas furrowed his brow and looked down at Blanc. "What the hell does that mean?"

Blanc panted, having no answer. Ivas set himself up on the wooden fence, finding a good perch that gave him a clear view of the field. He watched as Bram, Connie, Ruby, and Traverse got into the truck and drove away. Eli loaded the dead sheep into a wheelbarrow and rolled it away to its grave.

Ivas watched the sheep graze in the field. There was another part of shepherding that he had learned, one that was a bit more easy than actual herding. Sitting on the wooden fence, he looked over the sheep and started to count.

"Yan, Tayn, Tethera…"

It was apparently very important to keep an accurate count of the sheep, and there was a special way to count them just for shepherds. The unique numbers only went up to twenty. When he reached the end, he made a notch in his staff with a pocketknife and started again.

"Yan, Tayn, Tethera…"

Don't go in the woods today…

Ivas swallowed but stayed concentrated on his work. "Dik, yanadik…"

Another notch. He glanced toward the woods and immediately lost his place, the sheep he had left off on lost in the sea of wool.

He put his staff aside with a frustrated huff and jumped off the fence.

"Blanc, stay," Ivas ordered. Blanc's ears perked up and she stared at him as he walked away, seeming uneasy that she was being left alone. "Need you to watch the sheep," Ivas added over his shoulder. Blanc settled herself down in the grass and turned her attention back to the ewes and rams.

Ivas made his way to the tree line, opposite from where Eli was still working on burying the animal. He walked along the forest's edge, peering into the shadows where rays of sunshine fell through the gaps.

A sheep is dead...

Don't go into the woods...

Ivas took a breath and stepped closer into the tall grass, trying to make sense of what was happening.

Then something came forth from the thick brush and grabbed his shirt.

Ivas screamed as he was yanked into the woods, pulled along the ground through dead leaves leftover from the fall. He fought what had a hold of him and found that it was a hand like the branch of a tree—its skin was bark and its nails were mismatched animal claws. The arm was covered by a layer of moss—like fur.

Bare grapevines entwined his body, and the hand left his chest, shredding his shirt instead. Ivas screamed and called for help until the creature's other hand covered his mouth, forcing him to be silent.

Ivas's gaze focused, and he took in the head of the thing holding him. It was made of darkness and trees, animal fur and bones, all spliced together like a collage made by someone who needed a body but didn't have the materials it needed for a proper one. Its eyes were like a coyote's, shining in the darkness, and on top of its head was a tangle of horns made of sticks, all tangled together and held by ivy.

The unnatural eyes landed on Ivas's arm, and with its free hand, the creature plucked the little snail from the safe fold of Ivas's elbow. Ivas struggled and made muffled cries behind his gag, but the monster ignored him. It lifted the snail, studying it closely, then tilted its head back and opened its mouth, revealing rows of various mismatched teeth—like it had collected them from different animals. Some were bleached white, others rotten. A long, black tongue rolled out of its mouth, on which the creature placed the snail. Thick, dark saliva dripped to the ground. It pulled the snail into its mouth, and Ivas flinched when he heard the sickening crunch of it biting into the shell.

It swallowed loudly, then looked down at Ivas, who felt the sting of tears as its claws dug into his face. It made a strange sound, like a branch cracking in two, but was cut off by a distant but nearing bark. The creature looked up, released Ivas, and folded itself into the forest. Its limbs became trees, the moss took hold of nearby rocks, and the earth swallowed the bones.

Ivas gasped and scrambled to his feet, moving toward the barking. He tried to call out, but his voice was hoarse and broke when he tried to use it. He stumbled through the thick wilderness, feeling like a blind man. He heard a human voice, and finally managed to call out.

Eli appeared, tearing through the plant life in a panic. Relief filled his expression when he spotted Ivas.

"I heard you scream. Blanc was going crazy. What happened?"

"A-animal," Ivas gasped. Eli took his arm and led him out of the woods.

"What kind? You didn't see a bear, did you?"

Ivas didn't answer.

"Shit."

Eli helped Ivas through the farm and back to the house. Even though he wasn't actually injured, Ivas found it diffi-cult to walk and keep his balance. His heart was beating too fast, mind racing. Eli set him on the couch and said something about tea before rushing to the kitchen.

Blanc rested her head on the couch next to Ivas's as he lay down. She licked at his face, and Ivas could feel the sting of injury from the monster's claws.

He looked down at his bare chest, his shirt torn away, hanging off him in tatters. He looked at his elbow and felt a pang of hurt in his stomach, remembering the snail that had housed itself there. He couldn't stop the tears from really flowing then, and when Eli returned, he put the cup of tea down and went to Ivas's side, asking where he was hurt.

The hurt was everywhere.

CHAPTER 13

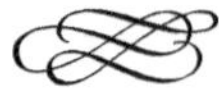

THE GUARDIAN COMES

Magnus was a Great Pyrenees, large even for his type, with a thick coat of white fur and eyes like an old preacher. Ruby would have been terrified of the giant if it weren't for his apathetic expression.

Bram explained to Ruby that Pyrenees were the preferred dog for guarding livestock—they were kind to their flocks but fiercely protective. They had arrived at a neighboring farm that had several Great Pyrenees and were willing to lend them out. Magnus had hopped up in the truck without any fuss and laid down. To Ruby, he seemed too lazy to do any real guarding.

"When Magnus is around, don't mess with the animals," Bram warned Ruby as they drove away. "He's familiar with us, but he doesn't know you, and he will snap. He's a working dog and needs to be treated as such."

Ruby looked through the back window into the truck bed where Magnus was lying on his side, his large pink tongue hanging out. Traverse winked.

"So, why don't you guys have a Great Pyrenees?" Ruby asked.

"Usually, our dog, Nettle Grey, is enough to scare off any predators," Connie said.

"That's Aster's dad," Traverse added.

"But he's loaned out for breeding right now."

The next stops were to a hardware store, where Bram purchased a new metal handle for the barn door, and then the market, where Connie picked up groceries. It was late into the afternoon when errands were finally done and they headed back to the farm.

Eli was waiting for them on the porch as they pulled up. He stood and went straight to the driver's side door.

"Help your mom with the—"

"Something happened to Ivas," Eli said quietly, but not quietly enough that the others didn't hear. Ruby, Connie, and Traverse all turned their heads.

"What happened?" Ruby asked.

"Not sure. I think an animal attacked him."

Bram swore and jogged to the house with Eli at his side. The girls looked at each other. Connie motioned for them to grab the bags of groceries.

"Let's put these away, then we'll check on Ivas," she said. Ruby and Traverse loaded as many bags into their arms as they could manage and raced into the house before throwing the bags onto the table and running to the living room.

Bram was bent over, studying Ivas's face. The two spoke quietly to each other. Ruby pushed herself in and noticed his shredded shirt.

"Ivas—!"

Ivas's eyes snapped to her, and Ruby shrank away. He looked angry.

"You're damn lucky," Bram said. "He got his teeth on your face but no marks on your chest. You guess it was the same bear that broke into the barn?"

Ivas didn't answer, but Bram seemed to have the answer for himself already. "Looks like we're going bear hunting."

"Dad—" Eli said imploringly.

"Don't start with me," Bram snapped. "We've got a man-killer, and I'm not letting it roam around with the family on the farm."

Eli deflated, looking down at his shoes.

"I'm going to go check on the guns right now and call Cherry. You don't have to hunt it," Bram told his son kindly before leaving the room. They could hear his voice as he spoke to Connie in the kitchen. Eli heaved a sigh and followed his father. Traverse sat next to Ivas on the couch.

"How big was it?"

Ivas looked at Ruby with haunted eyes, ignoring Traverse's question. Ruby averted her gaze.

"You didn't tell me," he said accusingly.

Ruby blanched. "I *tried*."

"No," Ivas stood up, letting his shirt slide off his shoulders so he could hold it out and shake it in front of Ruby's face. She winced. "You knew and you didn't tell me."

"Ruby knew about the bear?" Traverse asked.

"I told you not to go into the woods," Ruby murmured.

"And then ran off without an explanation."

"I didn't have *time*—"

Ivas grabbed Ruby's forearm, squeezing. It didn't hurt, but Ruby yelped in fear. Traverse jumped up and shoved her palm against Ivas's shoulder.

"Knock it off," she growled.

Ivas let go of Ruby. "I thought…after everything, that we trusted each other. You said no more secrets."

"What is going on?" Traverse demanded.

"You want to tell her?" Ivas asked. "Cause I sure as hell don't know."

Ruby sighed and met their eyes. "It's Creeping Bones."

Her audience furrowed their brows.

"What is that?" Ivas asked.

"It's a ghost story," Traverse said. "I told her about it last night. It's not real, Ruby."

"Maybe not, but there is something in the woods. I saw it yesterday, before you told me the story. That's why I asked."

"Sometimes the woods can play tricks on you," Traverse said. "The shadows can make the normal seem abnormal. I've also seen weird things in the woods, but it's not real. It's just a bear. It's probably sick or has mange, making it look like a monster."

The floor creaked and they turned to see Connie enter. She held a steaming bowl, which she offered to Ivas. "Drink this. It's a warm broth that'll help with the shock."

Ivas accepted and sipped at the warm drink. The taste of garlic, bay, and onion filled his mouth.

"Sit down so I can disinfect your face," Connie ordered. Ivas obeyed, taking a seat while Connie stepped away to grab medicine.

"Traverse," Ruby said, "we should take your scythe and clear out the brush around the woods, right?"

"Yeah, I can do that." Traverse shrugged. "If it'll make you feel better."

"Take Blanc with you," Ivas said. At the mention of her name, Blanc sat up from where she had been lying next to the fireplace and walked up to them, tail wagging helpfully.

"Will do. Come on, Blanc." Traverse whistled lightly and the Berger Blanc Suisse followed her out of the room.

Connie returned with witch hazel and a cotton swab. She sat next to Ivas and began applying the medicine to the bloodied marks on his face. He hissed at the sting. Ruby slipped away.

"It ate the snail," Ivas said loudly.

Ruby froze in the doorway, then quickly scampered away as Connie questioned Ivas about his odd statement.

It ate the snail...

Fear flowed from the little creatures on her back. Ruby quickly went outside, stumbling onto the porch. She looked out on the farm, happy to see precautions being made. Magnus was in the fields, lying in the grass with his gentle eyes on the grazing sheep. Bram and Eli were at the barn, installing the new handle. A rifle leaned against the wall next to them.

Ruby heard the familiar swish of the scythe and followed the noise to the trees where Traverse was swinging methodically at the bushes and vines growing there. Blanc was at her side.

Ruby sighed deeply and squeezed the porch railing, stretching her arms, deeply aware of how the forest circled the entire farm except for the single dirt road that led them in and out. The trees seemed so tall and black, like the bars of a cage.

~

Traverse swung the scythe methodically, lost in the whoosh of the blade through the grass. It had gotten tall, and little saplings had sprouted, but that was to be expected this time of year. Pausing her work, she looked up into the forest with a frown.

It was Creeping Bones, that was what Ruby had said. Traverse would have shrugged it off as a childish attempt at attention-seeking, but Ivas seemed to take her words seriously, had given his own cryptic message. What were the two of them hiding? Why did Ivas really bring Ruby here?

"Come on, Blanc," Traverse said, shouldering her tool. The dog perked up and jumped to her feet as Traverse slipped between the trees. There was a creek in the woods, shallow and usually dry, except during the spring rains. It made a U-shape, looping close to the farm but not crossing the boundary before continuing its journey through the forest.

The foster kids used this creek as a guide for wilderness adventures, a way to keep from getting lost. That was why they told stories of Creeping Bones. Traverse didn't know where the legend began, but the point of it was to keep kids safe.

"Don't go into the woods alone," Traverse said out loud. Blanc glanced at her. "Creeping Bones will rearrange the trees and turn you in circles so you can't find your way home. Stay to the creek because when it gets dark, that's when it gets you."

The creek had high dirt walls tangled with tree roots and shelves of rock. It was beautiful and wonderfully fun. Even as a young woman out of her childhood, Traverse liked climbing up on the rocks and crawling under logs. There were some puddles of water here and there, clogged with leaves and rippling with the dances of pond skaters. The goal was to walk as far as you could until the water became too deep to pass or the brush too thick.

"There was once this kid," Traverse told Blanc, "that liked to go off into the woods by himself. He wouldn't follow the rules. So, one day, Bram took him on a walk. They went a couple of miles out, and then Bram hung his hat on a tree branch and told the kid to lead them back to the farm. The kid tried, but after an hour, they ended up back at the tree with Bram's hat. They had made a big circle."

Traverse paused and used her scythe to cut away a thick bramble of thorns from their path. "That's how Bram is. He doesn't tell you not to touch the electric fence, he takes a pork steak and throws it on so you can see what will happen."

Once the way was clear, they continued on.

"I guess my point is, would Bram make up a story about a monster? Connie wouldn't—she hates scaring kids."

Blanc had no input on the matter, interested in sniffing a stick instead.

"And if they didn't make up the story, where did it come from?"

The blade wielder...

Traverse followed the sound, noting a squirrel watching her from a tree.

She keeps the barrier...

The wind rattled tree branches together. Traverse almost didn't spot the deer standing still as stone above her, looking down into the creek bed. A frog paused on a stone, and from under a rock, a snake slithered forth.

Reaper of the wood...

A group of birds in the trees. A dragonfly on a leaf. They were all staring at her. Blanc growled briefly.

"Come on," Traverse said, turning and hiking swiftly back. Her rush made her clumsy, causing her to slip on a stone and break the skin of her knee open. All around her, on either side of the creek, birds, chipmunks, and even a raccoon stood frozen and staring, eyes following her as she ran. Blanc barked at the wild animals, but none fled.

Testing something, Traverse approached the most skittish of animals—a bird sitting on a tree root. It did not move as she approached it, though she could see its chest heaving, moving faster and faster as she came closer. All of its feathers trembled, but it did not fly away. Traverse was so close she could see herself reflected in its black, unblinking eye.

She held the blade of the scythe to its throat.

Its breath was fast, too fast. Its heart gave out and the little bird fell to the stones of the dried creek, dead.

~

*E*li followed Bram and Cherry along an overgrown hunting trail. He did not carry a gun, but the other two had rifles resting on their arms, pointed at an angle to the ground. The long summer day gave them plenty of daylight, even after waiting for Cherry to arrive.

"You don't have to come, Eli," Bram had told him.

But Eli felt that he did. What if Bram and Cherry just started shooting any animal with teeth? Someone had to be the voice of reason. Someone had to say, "Stop, don't kill it," when everyone else's minds were on slaughter.

Growing up, Eli always felt that Bram was too cavalier about killing things—shooting at rabbits that entered Connie's garden, feeding the family deer and squirrels, shooting coyotes that came too close.

Eli knew better, knew the consequences, knew how important every life was.

Someone had to be there to say "stop."

So, he followed, feeling tense and uneasy, which was an unusual feeling in the woods that were his home. There wasn't anything dangerous here; there couldn't be. Dozens of children had passed through this farm, played between these trees. How could something dangerous appear now?

Things seemed normal in the forest. Birds sang, thick rays of sunshine sliced the air, and squirrels made a ruckus in the leaves. Bram searched the ground for scat and tracks while Cherry scanned the area.

They walked for a while, but everything seemed normal. There were no bear tracks where Ivas had been attacked, and no other evidence of a large animal either. Bram seemed frustrated. Eli was relieved. Maybe there was no bear at all.

Then again, *something* had attacked Ivas. *Something* had broken into the barn.

As the sun started to set, Bram announced that they would call it. "I'll sit out tonight and keep watch with Magnus."

"Want me to stay as well?" Cherry asked.

"Nah, go home and get some sleep. Maybe we'll get lucky and this thing will have moved on."

"Maybe. I guess as long as Magnus is here, it's alright," Cherry said, though her voice was doubtful.

Eli let himself fall back out of earshot of their conversation. Bram was smart. He was experienced and knew the farm and woods better than anybody. But Eli had learned a lot too, learned new things in college that Bram didn't know, and he wanted a moment to himself to look and listen.

He looked at the plants, listened to the birds. Animals were shy, they didn't like coming close to people-places in the country. Eli had been surprised when he went to school by how many more animals he saw in town than at the farm, and it was because they had less room to live and there was food near people-places. This wasn't the case in the country. The Carns were smart about keeping temptations like food out of the equation, and there was plenty of wilderness to go around. Animals didn't come to the farm unless something was wrong—either sickness or starvation.

So, Eli was looking for something different than his father—signs of distress.

He was so focused that he didn't notice Bram and Cherry disappear around the corner. He did notice how things suddenly went quiet, and the shadow that paused over his head.

Then something was around his mouth, his arms, lifting

him up, silencing him, and pulling him close in a tight embrace he couldn't escape.

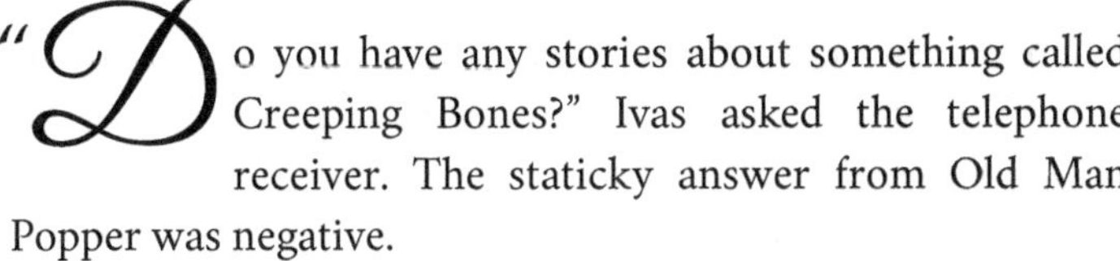

"**D**o you have any stories about something called Creeping Bones?" Ivas asked the telephone receiver. The staticky answer from Old Man Popper was negative.

"Never heard of it."

"It's a monster that lives in the forest. It makes itself out of human bones and eats souls," Ivas explained.

"Eh." Ivas could hear the shrug in Poppermill's voice. "Got lots of stories about forest monsters that eat people in general."

"How do the stories end? Is there a way to kill them?"

"Not generally. Stories like that, the moral is to not go in the woods at all, or at least be respectful."

Ivas heard another voice behind Poppermill's. "Is that Archie?"

"Aye, he's packing up. Better say hello."

There was a clatter as the phone was passed.

"Hello, Ivas!" Archibald's chipper voice appeared. "Got a call from the university, so my t-time is up. But good news! Mr. Poppermill has agreed to come with me! He's going to bring some of his collection, and we're going to look into archiving it. Isn't it wonderful? I feel like the Brothers Grimm, or maybe just the one. I never had a b-brother, but perhaps that is lucky as they tend to bully each other and I'm more of a pacifist. Of course, maybe having a sibling would have toughened me up—"

"*Archie,*" Ivas raised his voice pleadingly, "I'm sorry to interrupt. That is good news, but I have an important question about killing forest monsters in stories."

"Forest monsters? Quite a few of those in every culture. The Native Americans had the Wendigo, of course. Then there's the Sasquatch, Hiisi, Peikko…"

"Is there a way to kill them?"

"Um," Archibald seemed perplexed by the question. "That's not how the stories work, Ivas. You don't kill them; you fear them, learn from them. Also, you can't kill things that aren't real."

Ivas gritted his teeth.

"I was told a story once—not read. This was told to me in the traditional oral manner, which is a whole other subject I won't get into—"

Ivas sighed with relief.

"There's a small mountainous desert village that tells the story of a goat herder and his family who lived in the wilderness. They lived mostly isolated on a mountaintop, visiting the village rarely.

"One year, a strange, harsh winter struck the mountain. A huge blizzard rolled through, blocking off the mountain passes to the village, leaving the family trapped. When the pass finally cleared, only the husband came down. Everyone assumed that his family had died from sickness and starvation, but he had a different story to tell. He said that a monster had killed his family. He claimed to have seen it, but when a hunting party went up with him to kill the beast, no evidence was found, and the shepherd seemed a bit… unhinged. He heard things no one else did and felt that something was watching him.

"The villagers felt that he must have lost his mind from grief and invented the monster. Sometimes it's easier that way, you know? You can't take revenge on an illness, so he invented a foe for himself. Some even suspected that he had killed his own family. After all, the winter had been hard and the desert region wasn't used to snow. He must have gotten very hungry.

"Nonetheless, the shepherd returned to the mountaintop, determined to catch and kill the monster, but he didn't go alone. The story varies on this point. Some say it was a brother, a neighbor, a deputy who wanted to prove the man's guilt. Either way, another went into the mountains with the shepherd, and he was the one who returned to tell what happened next.

"Apparently, there *was* something on that mountain. They could hear it stalking them at night, found its monstrous tracks, and heard it breathing and growling in the darkness, but they couldn't kill it. The witness said that he saw the shepherd fire point blank into its chest, and the monster still killed him, tore his head right off his neck."

Ivas shuddered.

"I don't remember how it ends, I'm afraid. I believe the w-witness managed to trap it, but I can't remember how."

"You sure? Think about it," Ivas said.

"I'm s-sorry. It's been a long time since I heard this one. I'll s-see if I can find it again."

Ivas sighed. "That's okay. You're leaving soon anyway, right?"

"Indeed! I'm terribly excited. Hmm, you know, maybe there wasn't a trap. Only the witness returned to tell the tale, and he could have easily lied. Maybe there really wasn't a supernatural creature. Maybe it was the goat herder all along."

"Why would he lie?"

"Sometimes, Ivas, it's easier to tell the story of a monster than admit that man was the m-monster all along."

CHAPTER 14

THE GUARDIAN'S SECRET

*E*li was missing.

He hadn't come back with Bram and Cherry, who, upon returning to the farm, had waited five minutes, then went back into the woods, calling his name. Eli did not respond, and an hour later, he still hadn't returned. Connie and Ivas joined them. Traverse returned as well, having not seen Eli at the creek.

"The animals are acting weird, though," she said quietly to Ivas.

"Weird how?"

Traverse hesitated, not sure how to answer. Bram interrupted, calling to them to help search.

"Take your scythe," Ivas told her. "I'll take Blanc."

The adults all split up and entered the woods. Calls of Eli's name filled the air.

Ruby stood on the porch, feeling sick to her stomach. She didn't need Ivas to tell her that it wasn't safe to go into the forest, not with her skin covered in the invisible snails.

It ate the snail...

Ruby pressed a palm to her mouth and took a deep

breath. She kept telling herself that this wasn't Creeping Bones, that Eli just got sidetracked and would be back any moment. But as the shadows grew long with the setting sun and the others still hadn't come back, the dread made it more and more apparent that Eli wasn't just lost.

Finally, after standing for hours watching the darkness creep in, Ruby clenched her fists and stepped off the porch. She went to the field where the sheep had already gathered near the barn door, ready to go inside for their evening meal. Magnus sat near them, lying in the grass.

Ruby opened the gate and called to the large dog. He stared at her.

"Magnus! Come here, boy!"

He panted, not even wagging his tail.

"Fine!" she snapped and slammed the gate closed again. Feeling that she didn't have time, she ran to the dog pen and called for Aster instead. The pup ran out of the pen eagerly, jumping on her.

"Good boy. Come on." Ruby locked the gate and headed for the woods. Aster followed at her side.

At the start of the trees, Ruby hesitated. Aster didn't, stepping past the bramble to eagerly sniff the ground. Ruby followed him. They didn't have to walk far, only just out of sight of the farm before the animals appeared. Squirrels looked down from the branches, rabbits peered out from under the brush, and she caught the flash of coyote eyes off in the shadows. Even as Aster barked and sniffed at the frozen creatures, none of them moved. Their eyes remained on her, unblinking, even as their bodies trembled in terror.

There was movement in the brush and from the thick curtain of summer leaves, Eli appeared.

He was not alone.

His body was wrapped in grape vines and thorns, and his

eyes were closed as if he were asleep. The vines moved his body forward like a puppet.

Aster yelped and whined, stepping back behind Ruby in fear. Ruby herself had to fight the urge to run.

Standing over Eli was the grotesque form of Creeping Bones, its body built of bark and rotting animal limbs. It made a noise from its mouth like crickets, then placed its hand—a warped appendage made of mud and tree roots—on top of Eli's head. Small vines grew from Creeping Bone's hand, sliding over Eli's jaw, teeth, and tongue. The small vines worked his mouth, forcing it to form words. Eli straightened and opened his mouth.

"I am stronger now. If you want the boy back, you will give the snails to me." It was Eli's voice, but not his words. Ruby felt bile rise in her throat. Behind her, Aster was growling and crying.

"Please, just let him go. You've already taken a snail."

"If you do not give them, I will take them," the Eli-puppet said.

"I won't let you."

"You have no power here. You have shed your horns."

Ruby felt her nails dig into her palms, cold sweat blossoming under her arms. Then she felt pressure around her ankles and looked down to see that thorny vines had stealthily begun wrapping themselves around her. Ruby cried out and tried to yank her foot away. The thorns instantly tore through her pants and cut her skin, making her yelp.

Aster was now screaming. Branches came down and tangled themselves in Ruby's hair. She tried to fight them off, to pull free and run, but the woods were working against her. Sharp rocks jutted upward under her feet, tripping her.

Creeping Bones came forward, casting Eli aside to focus on Ruby. The girl scrambled back, kicking and screaming along with Aster. Creeping Bone's horrible hand came down for her.

Then it froze.

A blur of white threw itself forward into Creeping Bones, too fast for her to make out what it was. She felt its softness, like fur, brush against her arm as it rushed by.

With Creeping Bones pushed away, Ruby focused on freeing herself. She pulled her legs from the thorns and untangled herself from the tree branches. Her eyes watered as strands of hair were yanked out. She finally got her footing and looked up.

Creeping Bones had fled, and she saw something the size of a man wearing a white coat sink to their knees and lift Eli's unconscious body.

"Magnus?" Her brain staled with confusion, uncertain of what she was seeing. The fur was Magnus's, but the shape was wrong. The creature did not answer her or look back but turned and started moving swiftly to the farm.

Ruby scrambled to follow, to get a look at her rescuer, but almost tripped over Aster, who was behind a tree, tail tucked and shivering. She picked him up with some effort and quickly followed after Magnus, who was just a flash of white amongst the green.

Ruby tried to run and catch up, but Aster was too heavy for her to move that fast. When she broke out of the forest, she found Eli lying in the grass with Magnus—this time clearly a dog—sitting beside him.

"Wh-what was— Are you a—?" Ruby didn't know how to phrase her question, and Magnus didn't seem interested in answering it anyway because he turned away and headed back for the sheep field.

"Wait!" Ruby called after him and set Aster down, but Magnus didn't heed her. Ruby went to Eli instead and checked on him. At the touch of her hand, he stirred and blinked.

"Eli, are you okay?"

Eli groaned in response and winced, making a face as if he had a bad taste in his mouth. "Where's..." He looked around. "Did I pass out?"

"I think so. Can you walk?"

Eli carefully tested himself, sitting up, waiting for the dizziness to pass, and then standing with Ruby's help. She looked down and saw that Aster was gone. A quick, panicked scan of the area revealed that he was back at the dog pen, lying beside the door, eyes sad and nervous. His siblings poked their noses through the fence to give him reassuring licks.

Ruby helped Eli back to the house. As the sun finished its decent, the others began to return, one by one, and the house was filled with cries of relief, then with questions that Eli couldn't answer.

"I don't remember," Eli murmured when asked what had happened to him.

"I just found him passed out in the grass," Ruby said, meeting Ivas's eyes knowingly. "I was walking Aster and he smelled him."

"Alright." Bram stood up and spoke firmly, instantly making Traverse and Eli stiffen, a voice Ruby recognized from her own father. "Whatever the hell is going on, I'm ending it. No one goes into the woods, understand? Not by yourselves, not at all. In fact, teams of two if you're going outside at all. Cherry and I are going to lay out traps, and she's agreed to stay over for a couple of nights."

"Do you still think it's a bear?" Traverse asked.

"No, this is people. Rustlers or poachers is my bet."

"Oh God." Connie pressed a hand to her chest. Bram

touched her shoulder. "Cherry, Ivas, and I will take turns keeping watch the next few nights."

Ruby knew it wouldn't help, but she was surprised no one had mentioned it yet. "Should we call the police?"

Eli scowled and Connie stiffened, eyes darting to the floor.

"We take care of our own problems," Bram said firmly. "We'll chase off whoever this is—if they haven't already been scared away."

Connie heaved a big sigh and slapped her knees. "I'm going to make dinner."

"It's Traverse's turn, though."

"I need something to do," Connie said, waving her hand in the air. Traverse got up and followed her anyway. Eli said he was going to bed. Bram put an arm around his shoulders to help him to his bedroom.

Cherry sighed. "Just as I was thinking of quitting," she muttered, standing up and pulling out a pack of cigarettes. She stepped out into the backyard.

Ruby and Ivas met eyes.

"It was Creeping Bones," she whispered.

"It took Eli?"

Ruby nodded. "In exchange for the snails." She looked up imploringly. "Ivas, what do we do?"

"We need to send you home," Ivas said decisively. "If the snails aren't here, it won't be able to come after them. No point in attacking anymore."

Ruby nodded in agreement. "Yeah, yeah, that's true. Could we leave tomorrow?"

"I think that would be best. And it would help if you tried casting the snails off when we do. You're putting yourself in too much danger and I don't want to risk this thing trying to follow."

Ruby sighed but relented. "I'll try. I don't want to be near that thing anymore. What about you? Will you come back? Is there a way to get rid of it? What if it still attacks the farm?"

"I will take care of it," Ivas said, "somehow. Getting rid of the snails is the first step though. Just stay in the house tonight. Tomorrow, I'll tell Bram that you're scared of the poachers and want to go home."

"Okay."

Ivas heaved a deep sigh, so heavy Ruby felt her own shoulders sink. "I need to put the sheep away."

"I'll come with you."

Outside, the twilight was soft on the horizon. Watching Ivas, Ruby could see the clear difference in his skill. Things that seemed so flawless before were now a struggle as he sent Blanc into the field to gather the stray sheep. It took much longer as well. Her heart ached for him.

"Have the books helped?" she asked quietly.

"A little. They can't replace a lifetime of experience. Give me a minute, okay? I have to count them."

Ivas counted as the sheep filed into the barn. "Yan, Tayn, Tethera…"

Whenever he got to giggot, Ivas stuck out a finger and started again. It was like watching a child learning math for the first time.

When the last sheep entered, Ivas sighed and closed the door. "I've never felt so tired."

"'Cause of counting sheep?" Ruby asked, trying to joke. Ivas didn't seem to notice. He bent down and rubbed Blanc's ears, letting her lick his cheek.

"She's been so patient with me. It's not easy on her either."

Ruby bent down, petted Blanc, then plucked some long grass blades from the dirt. At that angle, she noticed the Great Pyrenees sitting in a corner of the field. He had been watching the whole time.

"Magnus isn't what he seems," Ruby said. She sat back and began braiding three pieces of grass together. Ivas looked at the dog sitting calmly, long pink tongue hanging from his mouth.

"What do you mean?"

"When I found Eli and the… Creeping Bones, Magnus saved us both. But he wasn't a dog. He was standing up and wearing his fur like a coat."

Ivas went to the guard dog and rubbed his hand over Magnus's back, catching the thick fur between his fingers. Magnus seemed indifferent to the pats.

"Is that true, bud? You can tell us. We've seen stranger things than you."

Magnus licked his own nose and yawned. Ivas leaned back on his heels thoughtfully. Even though he was familiar with stories of selkies and werewolves, none seemed to fit Ruby's description of Magnus.

"You're sure it was him?"

"Definitely."

"Hmm. I guess if he doesn't want to show us, that's his business." Ivas shrugged his shoulders and stood up. "Come on, let's get some dinner."

CHAPTER 15

A GHOST COMES

*E*li didn't eat at dinner, only nibbled on some bread while Connie looked at him worriedly.

His mouth hurt, his throat was sore, and it was hard to swallow. His stomach lurched when he did, so he gave up and went to his room early. He heard his father and Cherry preparing for their watch, the click of guns being loaded, the hushed talk of paranoid voices.

This time he didn't blame them. He had his curtains drawn, the blanket pulled up to his nose, and the light on. Connie checked on him, but he wasn't a scared foster child anymore. He was a grown man, and he waved her off.

When she was gone the fear truly sank it.

Too quiet and dark.

His mouth ached horribly. He tried to remember what had happened, but when the memory started to rise, he quickly pushed it back down, physically shaking his head like he was shaking off a nightmare.

He didn't want to know.

He gave up on sleep and sat up, wrapping a blanket around his shoulders. He looked through his books, but none kept his attention. There was a television in the craft room. As kids, he and the other fosters would sneak in after lights out to watch the late-night news and whatever static-filled movie was playing. They were always caught.

In the end, he couldn't bring himself to leave the bed.

The hours slowly waned on, creeping into the morning. Sleepiness was finally clouding his mind, and Eli felt that he would, thankfully, succumb soon.

Then something tapped at the window.

Adrenaline surged as Eli shot his head up, eyes glued to the covered window. His body was so tense that even breathing hurt.

The curtain parted and a face peered in at him through the dark glass. Eli felt nausea rise and was glad he hadn't eaten anything.

"Eli..." the apparition said.

Eli groaned and sank down into the bed. Tears filled his eyes and ran down his cheeks. The boy in the window stepped through the glass and into the bedroom. Eli tried to scream but only croaked.

The boy smiled at him, a big, horrible smile that was sincere in a malicious way. Eli shook his head violently, hurting his neck.

"No, no, no, no, no— Siph. No, Siph..." he blubbered.

"Yes," Siph said, stepping to the foot of the bed. "I'm here, Eli. I've always been here. I'm still in the woods."

"No!" This time he managed a small yelp. "You're dead! Go away!"

Siph cast his eyes down, almost ruefully. "I am dead, and you let it happen." Siph turned around and pointed at the back of his head. There was a perfect circle there. The skin was burned and the hair was matted with black blood. "This is what they did. I didn't see it coming. Didn't know it had even happened."

Eli shook his head more. Dizziness overcame him, blackness swirled at the edge of his vision, threatening to pull him under.

"You're still so weak," Siph taunted. He was on Eli's bed now, knees resting on either side of his hips. He looked at the bedside table and reached out a hand. Eli turned and watched him stroke the pocketknife there, the one from his birthday.

"Do you remember?" Siph whispered. He turned back to Eli and placed his hands on Eli's cheeks. Ice cold and real.

Eli couldn't pull his head away, only cry silently as Siph held his head in place, staring at him with matte eyes, eyes that didn't shine in the lamplight.

"Creeping Bones said it would let me out if I got it what it wanted. I live here now, Eli. We'll sleep together in this room every night until you give it what it wants."

Eli gritted his teeth, unable to shake his head no.

"It wants the girl with red hair. Until you give her to it, you're all mine."

Siph leaned forward, pressing his icy lips to Eli's forehead. This time, Eli was finally able to scream. He thrashed and howled, tearing the blanket in the process.

The bedroom door flew open.

"Eli!" Traverse screamed her brother's name, grabbing his arms to stop him from slamming them into the walls. Eli came back to himself, looking around to search for the ghost, but Siph was gone.

He looked at Traverse and started to bawl, face oozing, unable to speak as Traverse asked what had happened. Connie was in shortly after. They both held him, rocking him back and forth between them.

"I think he had a nightmare," Traverse said to Connie as Eli sobbed into her shoulder.

Connie looked at the wall above the bed where the

plaster was cracked from Eli's fist, then down at the cotton sheet that had been torn nearly in two.

"Let's take him to the couch," she said tiredly. They guided Eli into the living room. Connie made a warm tea that would soothe him to sleep, something with chamomile and lavender. Eli only sipped it despondently.

He kept looking at Connie with a strange expression, like he was trying to remember something and didn't trust the memory.

"Did you have a nightmare?" Traverse asked.

Nod.

"About the monster?"

Eli frowned.

"Kind of?"

He sighed. When he spoke, his voice was hoarse, but the tea seemed to have helped. "I dreamed of Siph."

Both of the women visibly stiffened.

"Kids, it's been a very hard day," Connie said lamely. "Try and get some sleep, okay? Things will look better in the sunshine." She kissed them both on the cheek. Eli flinched away from her lips but relaxed as she hugged him.

Traverse settled on the couch next to her brother, asking if he wanted to listen to some music. Eli agreed as Connie stepped away into her bedroom.

Connie and Bram shared a room at the top of the hall with a private bathroom. She went there now and stepped onto her special stool—one that Bram had built for her to reach the sink—and stared into the mirror.

Siph...

Siph, their poor son, dead. Still a child.

She popped her knuckles as she looked over the counter. Brush teeth, take pills, comb hair. She had a checklist for bed, but just stood and popped her finger joints.

Over her shoulder, Connie thought she saw movement.

When she turned, she thought she saw Siph's face peeking in at her through the crack of the door.

The room was, of course, empty when she opened it.

"We couldn't run forever," she whispered to the room, resignation in her voice.

She climbed the miniature steps into bed and pulled the covers up, leaving the light on.

~

Outside, Bram and Cherry jumped at the strange sounds of the forest—the crack of twigs, sudden glints of light, even whispers, like a human voice.

Bram sore he heard something say…

"It's me, Abe."

~

In Ivas's room, Blanc sat at the door, growling. Ivas sat with her, holding his staff—the one he had strangled the coyote with—and stared at the door as well. Outside, he could hear the death noises of an animal.

~

Ruby lay in bed. She had heard Eli scream but stayed still, feeling so much like a stranger that it was like she wasn't really there. She touched her head, but it was bare.

In the end, no one slept that night.

~

When the sunlight came, everyone was already up. Eli and Traverse groggily stirred from the couch as Connie went into the kitchen to make coffee. Bram and Cherry had come inside just before dawn. Bram went straight to the shower. Cherry sought out a recliner to sleep on.

Outside, Ivas felt like all of his senses hurt at once. The sun was too bright, the smell of the sheep too potent, the morning too cold. He hobbled to the barn to free the animals while Blanc checked the interior for stragglers. Magnus took his post in the field.

When Bram came out of the shower, he found Connie in the bedroom waiting for him.

"Didn't sleep?" he asked.

Connie looked at him, her expression dark. "Eli woke up screaming last night. He said he had a nightmare about Joseph."

"It was a stressful day, and he's always been sensitive."

"It's the curse, Bram," Connie said. "I know it."

"There's no curse."

"Did you two see anything last night? Animals? People?"

"No."

"I knew that what we did would come back to haunt us someday. I just didn't want it to affect the children."

"It's not haunting us," Bram insisted. He went to his wife and took her shoulders. "I mean… It haunts us in a mental way, yeah? We took that on ourselves, we knew the cost, but this isn't that. There's no curse, just some bad luck."

Connie sighed. "I'm so worried. Ivas got hurt, Eli disappeared. Something bad is happening, and I don't think it's just bad luck."

Bram heaved a deep sigh and hugged Connie tightly. She

hugged him back, wrapping her arms around his damp, naked chest.

"I'm not going to let anything happen to our family."

"But what do we do?"

"I'll think of something." Bram released her and stepped away to find a change of clothes. "We can always get away from the farm for a few days if we need to."

Connie looked down at her stairs, not answering. Bram pulled a clean shirt on and kissed her head. "It's going to be alright. Stay in the house with the kids today. I bet Ruby would enjoy some board games."

Connie chuckled a bit at that. "I don't know if I want to scar the poor girl with how Trav and Eli play Ludo."

Bram relaxed at her laugh. He squeezed her shoulder and left the room, commenting on needing coffee.

Connie's smile disappeared when he left, replaced with deep, dangerous thoughts.

There were ways to break curses.

～

"She wants to leave?" Bram frowned at Ivas, who had joined everyone in the kitchen for food.

"With everything that's been happening, she's just scared and homesick," Ivas shrugged. "I told her I'd take her home today."

Bram sighed. "Yeah, you can use the truck then. Hate to have her leave with a sour taste in her mouth."

"Yeah, I wanted to take her to the lake again," Traverse said, disappointed.

"It's probably for the best," Eli murmured. "Doesn't feel safe around here."

The room became somber.

"You're right," Bram muttered, seeming angry at the admission.

"I'll try to get back by tonight," Ivas promised.

"Take the night if you have to."

"Where is Ruby anyway?" Connie asked. She had bacon cooking in a skillet. "Is she still asleep?"

Traverse volunteered to check and returned, reporting that the guest room was empty. Knowing the unpredictability of his ward, Ivas stepped back outside to look. He spotted Ruby leaning on the fence, looking out at the sheep. Aster was chasing dragonflies around her feet, and on the other side of the fence, Magnus lay in the grass.

As Ivas walked closer, he heard Ruby speaking.

"I know what I saw. It's okay. You can tell me." She was speaking to Magnus, who completely ignored her. "Come on, I already know, alright? Are you a werewolf? A shapeshifter?"

Again, no answer.

"I thought werewolves changed at the full moon," Ivas said, announcing his presence and stepping up next to Ruby. The girl sighed.

"He must hate me. He won't even look at me." She pouted, resting her chin on the post.

"He doesn't hate you. He has a job to do. Guard dogs like Magnus can be very single-minded. Don't take it personally."

Ruby stepped away from the fence, the cuffs of her pants getting soaked in the morning dew. "Are we still leaving today?"

"Yes, I think it's for the best. If the snails are gone, Creeping Bones won't have any reason to bother the farm."

Ruby nodded. "I'll miss everyone, though. Do you think we can come back?"

"I don't know. We'll have to see. Let's go eat breakfast and get packed, okay?"

Back inside, Ruby inhaled a plate of bacon while exchanging contact information with Traverse. Eli was in a heavy sleep in his bedroom, so she let him be. Connie made her a sandwich to go, and Bram passed the truck keys to Ivas.

"Hey, wait." Traverse pulled Ruby into her bedroom and picked something up from her dresser. "I have a present for you."

"Really?" Ruby set down her bag.

"Yeah, I was going to clean it up and give it to you at the end of the summer, but since you're leaving now…" Traverse held out her hands and opened them like a pop-up book. In her palm was a pin with an image of a compass.

"Ta-da! Your first found-item present."

"Whoa, you found this?" Ruby took the pin, only a little bigger than a coin, and rotated it in her fingers, chipping some dirt away with her thumbnail. It was a good quality, made of pewter, with the arrows of the compass sticking out from its round body. The needle on the back was still intact.

"Yeah, in the creek yesterday. It's awesome, right? Sometimes, you get some good stuff washed up there."

The N for north was a little faded, but otherwise the colors were there. Ruby poked it into her shirt. "I shall wear it always. I'll find a present on the beach to send to you."

"Please do." Traverse pulled her into a hug, and Ruby returned it tightly.

Apologies and goodbyes were passed around until Ivas ushered Ruby out the door. Aster was leashed and put in the back of the truck, and they were ready to go.

Ivas breathed a sigh of relief as the vehicle started up and they headed down the dirt driveway. Getting Ruby away from the farm put his mind at ease.

As they reached the edge of the farm, where the woods crept along the road, something suddenly ran out in front of them. Ivas jumped and slammed the brakes but knew it was too late. His arms jerked the steering wheel, causing the truck to turn sharply and hit the ditch.

Ivas whipped his head around wildly, knowing he couldn't have seen what he thought he saw, but when he looked through the window, his eyes focused on a coyote—one covered in dirt with a swollen neck and missing eyes. His stomach dropped. The creature stared at him with empty sockets, seeing him despite its rotted soft tissue.

A flurry of panicked barking snapped him out of the trance.

"Shit, shit, Aster!" Ruby shoved her door open to clamber out of the car.

"Ruby, no!" Ivas cried out and tried to grab her, keep her in the safety of the cab, but she ignored him and scrambled outside. In the corner of his eye, Ivas saw the coyote turn his head toward the sound.

Ivas quickly opened his own door and jumped out, waving his hands and yelling. "Over here! Hey, right here!"

The coyote turned its attention to Ivas. It began to growl, more of a gurgling sound, and foam slipped from its mouth. Ivas heard claws clattering against metal, Ruby scream, then a flash of white as Aster shot past him and attacked the coyote.

Yelps and screams filled the air, fur flew, then blood appeared. Ruby started to jump around the bed of the truck, but Ivas shoved her back and grabbed a tire iron. He charged the two canines and brought the metal rod down on the coyote's head.

It did nothing.

The coyote pinned Aster to the dirt, its strong jaw locking around the pup's throat. Ivas struck with the iron again—fur broke off and flesh parted, revealing skull underneath, but the coyote did not yield. Ivas felt bile rise in his throat. He struck the creature once more, this time cracking the bone. Ivas turned away and fell to his knees, fighting back vomit as the coyote's brain became visible. Ruby was babbling and swearing behind him, her voice full of tears.

A different kind of voice spoke over hers. It had words Ivas recognized, but the sounds that made them were of the forest—the buzz of a wasp, the grass in the breeze.

"Give, or I'll kill the pet." The 'k' sounded like the snap of a twig.

Ivas looked up. In the shadows of the trees, just past where the truck had crashed, Creeping Bones stood. Ruby screamed into her hands. "No, no, no…"

"Give me the snails." The 's' sound floated from the rustling leaves.

"Don't hurt my dog," Ruby sobbed. The coyote jerked its head and Aster yelped in pain. Ivas watched uselessly. The tire iron had pieces of the dead thing on it.

Ruby clambered away from truck, trembling and crying. Ivas watched as she pulled a snail off her neck, her hand shaking. She looked at Ivas pleadingly.

He tried to think of an answer, something he could do, but he knew the coyote could kill Aster before he could do anything. He looked back up the drive, as if something might present itself. They were out of view of the house, but on the crest of the hill, he saw something coming.

It took him a moment to process what he was seeing. It was Traverse, and in her hands, posed over her head like the angle of death, was the scythe.

Eyes going wide, Ivas threw himself out of the way. Traverse ran with a speed almost inhuman and when she reached the coyote, she swung her blade, swift and sure, across its mangled neck, severing it cleanly from the body.

Aster was immediately on his feet, running to Ruby. He had to shake himself to dislodge the decapitated head of the coyote from his neck. Ruby wailed and wrapped the dog up in her arms, getting blood and white fur on her clothes.

From the woods was a sound like a scream—full of cicadas and rabbits and howling creatures. Ivas covered his ears and Traverse looked up fearfully, brandishing her weapon.

"Back to the house!" Ivas shouted. The girls ran, Ruby carrying Aster in her arms. The screaming faded, and the only sound became their panting and the crunch of dirt under their shoes. It was too quiet, and Ivas ran faster, feeling that something was hiding in that silence. Ruby started to fall behind with the weight of the dog. Ivas took Aster from her and pushed her ahead.

The three of them all tripped over each other getting into the house. Ivas stumbled under the weight of Aster, and Traverse knocked a cup off the counter with her scythe. The noise brought out Cherry, who stared at them blankly.

"I just wanted to take a nap," she said shaking her head.

"Cherry, holy shit," Traverse stepped forward, bumping the refrigerator. "I was walking out to get the grass on the west side, right? And I saw Bram's truck in the ditch! And when I got closer, there was a freaking coyote attacking the dog!" Traverse held out the scythe to the wide-eyed woman. "I cut off its head, Cherry! It's head!"

"You saved Aster!" Ruby said, taking the dog back from Ivas. "It was going to kill him!"

Seeing red against Aster's stark white, Cherry went from bewildered to concerned. She went to the dog and checked his neck.

"Is it bad?" Ruby asked.

"Doesn't look too bad," Cherry said. "I see the bite marks, but he's okay. I think he might be hamming it up a bit."

Aster licked at Cherry's hands, giving his tail a slight wag.

He did seem to be enjoying the extra attention. Ruby sighed and squeezed him tight. "Thank God."

"Ivas, you're shaking." Traverse looked at him worriedly. Ivas quickly sat down and rested his head in his hand.

"Can I get some water, please?"

Cherry obliged, filling a cup. "You crashed Bram's truck?"

"The coyote ran out in front of us," Ruby said.

"Oh, I see, and Aster attacked it." Cherry passed the water over and Ivas sipped it.

"What did Aster attack?" Connie's voice made them all jump. The smaller woman was holding a basket of tomatoes and staring at them with worry. Traverse eagerly relayed the story again, emphasizing the part where she had taken off the coyote's head.

Connie dropped her basket and covered her mouth with her hands, tears springing up in her eyes. Tomatoes rolled across the floor.

"Connie, it's okay. No one is hurt."

Connie didn't answer. She shook her head, her expression wild. Cherry went to her and put an arm around her shoulders to calm her down. "What is it? What's wrong?"

She just kept shaking her head, lowering it to hide her tears.

"Okay, okay, let's go sit you down. Ruby, go clean up Aster. Traverse, grab those tomatoes. Ivas, I'll help you get the truck out in a little bit." Cherry led Connie away while the other two went to their assigned tasks.

Ivas stayed at his seat and sighed deeply, clutching his cup far too tight.

～

*R*uby cooed and kissed Aster's nose as she cleaned the blood off his fur. She sat on the bathroom floor with a wet cloth in hand. As Cherry had said, there was little damage. She patted the bite marks with some iodine. Aster lay in her lap, tongue hanging out and happy to let her do as she pleased.

The door opened and Traverse slipped inside. "How's the patient?"

"All good," Ruby said, stroking his ears. "Good thing he's got all his shots, so we don't have to worry about that."

Traverse slid down the wall to the floor opposite Ruby, studying her.

"What's up?" Ruby asked.

"I saw something in the woods."

Ruby didn't look up, her voice conveying no surprise. "Yeah?"

"Yeah, and I heard that scream… Ivas wasn't attacked by a bear, was he?"

Ruby swallowed.

"And Eli…"

She nodded.

"Cheesus, Ruby." Traverse squeezed her own forearms. "Did Ivas see it, too?"

"He knows about it."

"Why? Why is it…?"

Ruby reached under her shirt and pulled something out from her chest. Aster sniffed at her closed fist, searching for a treat. Ruby opened her fingers. "Do you see it?"

Traverse frowned, looking down at Ruby's bare palm. "No?"

"You have to really look, Trav. Remember what you saw in the woods."

The animals were watching…

Are there any ghost stories?

I saw...

Then, as if it had been hidden by a trick of the light, she saw the glimmer of a shell and two little antennae. Traverse jerked up in surprise. "Oh."

"It's not a snail," Ruby said.

Traverse then saw another sitting on Ruby's cheek, and another hiding behind her ear. "No, it's not."

"Creeping Bones wants them. I've been trying to keep them safe." Ruby sighed sadly. "That's why Ivas was trying to take me back home."

"That's why all this stuff has been happening. It's… Creeping Bones has been coming after you."

"It's my fault," Ruby said, hugging Aster closer. "The snails can't leave and… Eli almost got…"

"It's not your fault," Traverse said, reaching out to pat her knee. "You've been trying to protect them."

"Creeping Bones managed to steal one when it attacked Ivas."

"I'll take them." Traverse took her hand off Ruby's knee and gently picked up the snail.

"But… No, I—"

"It's okay." Traverse took the one from her cheek. "You've had them this whole time. I can help. I'm older."

"It'll come for you instead."

"That's okay, we can—"

"It's *not*," Ruby said warningly. "It's really not okay."

Traverse quietly took another snail, then another. Ruby patted Aster off her lap and took off her shirt. One by one, Traverse plucked the gastropods from her back, stomach, and shoulders. Soon, all of them were settled on Traverse, leaving iridescent trails along her dark skin as they slid under her clothes to hide away.

"Wow, it's like they're barely there," she whispered.

"Can you feel them feeling?"

"It's like having emotions that aren't mine."

Ruby smiled. It felt good to share with someone who understood. "Thank you, Trav." Then she was on her knees, hugging Traverse around the neck. The older girl hugged her back.

"You know I got you, girl."

CHAPTER 16

THE NIGHTMARE RETURNS

Eli remembered being a young boy when he came to live with Connie and Bram, around eight years old. His life before them was blurry, and he preferred it that way. He loved the farm and the other kids. The house was a whirlwind of activity and distractions. There was always a chore to do, homework to be done, people to play with. There wasn't time to be sad or wonder where his mother and father had gone. Bram and Connie became "Mom" and "Dad." The farm was his home, and he was lucky. So many kids were moved to other houses, to God knows what. Eli was lucky.

But there was a part of living on the farm that was blurry too, and that was when Siph came to live with them.

Eli had been at the farm for a few years by that time and had become comfortable with the lifestyle. He was a seasoned foster, there to guide the newcomers. Two little ones were already living in the guest room, so when Siph came along, Eli graciously agreed to share his room.

Siph was very quiet at first but quickly opened up. He wasn't an easy foster, which often happened with the teenagers. They were usually angry, got into trouble, got into fights. Connie and Bram were well-practiced, though. They knew how to calm them down and make them comfortable enough to handle the next day, and the one after that. It was hard work—and didn't always pay off.

Siph took a lot of work, but it wasn't enough in the end.

Eli frowned, trying to remember. Siph had been crafty and lied so easily, it scared Eli. He would steal food and blame it on one of the little ones. He pulled pranks that would hurt people—like a nail on the stairs—and when he got caught, he would cry and apologize. Once the adults' backs were turned, the tears would immediately stop and Siph would run off to find another problem to cause.

Sometimes, the problems were so much worse, like when he hurt the dogs or dropped a match in the barn. Eli remembered feeling bewildered by Siph's behavior.

"We can't understand what kind of pain he's been through," Connie had tried to explain to Eli one night.

"But he's not in pain now," Eli had protested. "This is a good place. He doesn't have to act that way."

Connie sighed sadly. "It's hard to explain. Some people feel like they do have to act that way, even more so when they're somewhere good."

"But *why?*"

Connie hadn't been able to explain, and even now, as an adult, Eli struggled to understand.

"Hey."

Bram's voice brought Eli back to the present as he entered his room. What time was it?

"You've been sleeping awhile. Come out and eat."

"Y-yeah." Eli sat up and shrugged the blankets off. He felt stale, like bread left out of a bag.

"Your mom said you had a bad nightmare last night."

Eli shuddered. Everyone kept calling it a nightmare.

"About Siph?" Bram prodded.

"Yeah."

Bram cleared his throat in that way that said he needed to talk but wasn't keen on the conversation. He sat down on the bed next to Eli, looking at some comic books on the floor. "You have nightmares like that before?"

"I— Uh, no, I don't think so. I haven't even thought about him in years. Ruby was asking about him, I think. Maybe that put him in my head."

"You know, Siph wasn't...a very good kid."

"Yeah."

"Do you remember?"

Eli turned the question around in his mind. It seemed to him a part of it was missing, like there was something specific Bram wanted to know but didn't want to ask outright.

"He tried to burn down the barn and hurt the dogs."

"Do you remember the time he tried to hurt you?"

Eli frowned. "He, uh, sat on me while I was sleeping."

"Hmm." Bram took a deep breath. "And what was he holding, Eli?"

"What?" Eli looked at his father's face. Bram met his gaze.

"Your mother and I agreed that if you couldn't remember, then that was for the best. But I don't want you remembering in some nightmare. It's best to remember in the light of day and know you're safe."

"He— But, there was..." Eli sharply inhaled. In his mind, he saw Siph looking down at him, sitting on his chest so he could barely breathe. Blood in the sheets. Siph smiling. And in his hand...

In his hand...

Do you remember?

Eli's eyes slowly dragged themselves to the corner of his sockets and saw the pocketknife sitting on his bedside table.

"Oh shit." Eli groaned and buried his head in his hands. "I remember. He fucking... He had a knife. He cut me with it."

He had done it slowly. He sat on Eli's chest so that he couldn't move or shout, and with a pocketknife—that *same* pocketknife—he had cut a bit of Eli's neck. He had said something about an artery being there.

It bled a lot.

The pain had been enough to squeeze out a scream and Bram had come, saved him, stopped the bleeding.

"Siph isn't here anymore, Eli. He can't hurt you."

Eli shuddered and leaned against Bram's shoulder. The other man put an arm around him. Eli pushed himself in closer. Soon, Bram had both arms around his son, rocking him as he sniffled.

"I'm sorry. I'd rather you'd never remembered that."

"Me too."

A moment of quiet passed.

"Did he do anything else that I repressed?"

"He would try to physically fight me a lot. Once, he attacked your mother. He even..." Bram trailed off.

"What?"

"I'd rather not talk about it."

"Dad, did Siph really run away?" Eli remembered the hole in the back of Siph's head.

This is what they did...

Bram patted his knee. "Come on, let's go eat." He stood up and left Eli's room quickly, not waiting for him to follow.

~

"Ivas got the damn truck stuck in a ditch," Bram grumbled. It might have been teasing, but it was hard to tell with Bram. Everyone was gathered, and a meal of breakfast for dinner was laid out.

Eli smiled weakly.

"Cherry and I worked at it all afternoon, but there's too much mud," Ivas said.

"We'll get the tow tomorrow. Don't worry," Bram said, patting his shoulder. He leaned over to his wife, whispering a joke to her. Connie only gave him a weak smile. Bram quietly tried to check on her while the rest of the table talked on.

Traverse and Ruby sat side by side, smiling and talking quietly together. After dinner, they went out onto the porch and sat cross-legged, bare-footed, playing cat's cradle and making string figures with pieces of yarn. Traverse showed Ruby the steps to create specific shapes, how to loop the circle between their fingers to make different patterns. Ruby copied, cheering when she successfully made the yarn into a spider web, a cat with whiskers, then a Jacob's ladder.

"We played this all the time when we were kids," Traverse said. "Remember, Eli?" she called through the screen door. The older boy was washing dishes.

"Huh?" Eli looked up from his work, distracted.

"Connie always taught the fosters how to do it. When we were being annoying, she would give us a piece of string and tell us to go make a star."

"Kept your hands busy," Connie chuckled. She was wiping down the table.

Ruby giggled. "It's surprisingly enjoyable."

"Eli, I think that dish is clean," Ivas said. He was on drying duty, and Eli had been scrubbing the same plate for several minutes.

"Oh." Eli gave his head a shake as if to clear it. "Sorry."

"I'll get those." Bram stepped up, gently pushing Eli away from the sink. "Go outside with the girls, get some air."

Eli joined them on the porch but turned down his own piece of yarn, staring off toward the horizon as the sun sank down. Ivas and Cherry stepped outside, Ivas heading to the barn.

"Are you going to stay up again tonight?" Traverse asked Cherry.

"Nah, heading home. You guys take it easy." Cherry waved and went to her car. Ruby watched nervously, but Cherry drove off the farm without issue.

Without a word, Eli rose and went inside his bedroom, though bedtime was still several hours away.

"Eli? Are you feeling alright?" Connie tried to ask. Her only answer was the click of his door shutting.

Bram took Connie's shoulder comfortingly. "He's alright. Let the boy rest."

Connie sighed shakily, wringing her hands. She called the girls inside, despite their protests that it was a warm night.

"There's still danger out there. Something is wrong in the woods and we need to stay inside. Ivas, you should stay, too."

Eventually, Connie convinced everyone to gather together in the dining room for drinks and a card game, even agreeing to let Blanc inside to lie under the table. She drew the line when Ruby asked if Aster could come inside too.

Cards were dealt and everyone settled in, comforted by their four walls and electric light.

～

*E*li listened to the soft chatter of his family from the bedroom, his bedsheets clutched in his hands. The curtains were drawn over the window, and his lamp was on, but it didn't stop the presence of the small figure shrouded in a misty blue as it manifested in his bedroom.

"Hello, Eli." Siph smiled at the grown man cowering under his covers.

Eli whimpered.

Siph approached the foot of the bed. "Did Bram tell you what I did? Do you remember now?" The boy took Eli's big toe between his fingers and yanked it. It felt real, and Eli yelped, but he couldn't move.

"I was trying to cut your throat. Do you remember asking me why? I don't remember what I said. I probably just laughed at you because I didn't have an answer. Not that you would understand. Have you ever had an itch you couldn't reach? But in your heart? Your soul? Cutting your throat would have scratched that itch for me. Maybe. Maybe not."

Siph crawled into the bed, legs and arms on either side of Eli's body. "Did they tell you what I did to the little ones?" His grin was huge. His skin began to rot away as he spoke, revealing the skull underneath. Some of his adult teeth were still buried beneath the baby teeth, giving him a double grin. "Could Abe not *bear* to tell you my sins?"

He leaned in close enough to kiss Eli's lips. "I touched them, in all their forbidden places. Touched them, made them cry, and told them it was their fault, that if they told anybody, they would be in trouble. The fucking brats ratted me out, though, after I started hurting them. Guess that was the last straw for Abe."

To emphasize the last straw, Siph began to turn his head, slowly cranking it until the spine snapped and the wound in the back of his head was visible. Eli was crying now, his body shaking.

"The kids tried to call to you once. You were next door, and they tried to call your name for help, until I slapped them into shutting up." Siph giggled at that. His head continued its rotation, going back to its original place. His skin and eyes were back. "They were *so* scared."

Eli closed his eyes, teeth gritting as he tried to fight back.

"Give Creeping Bones the redhead, Eli. Give her over

and I'll go away forever. I'll finally be free of the woods, and you'll be free of me. It's what we both want, right? So just do it, Eli. Do it, do it, you fucking coward. Do it. Do it!"

The door opened and Eli realized he was screaming.

~

*E*veryone heard Eli's screams this time. Connie jumped so hard she knocked over her cup. The cards fell as everyone jumped to their feet with a chorus of chairs scraping.

Connie and Bram got into the room first. Everyone else stayed at the head of the hallway, watching as they guided Eli out of his room. He still had a hold of his bed sheet, sobbing into it. Connie and Bram took him away to their room to calm down. They could still hear his cries, muffled by the closed door.

Ivas heaved a shuddering breath and turned away, murmuring something about finding a stronger drink. Traverse put her arms around Ruby's shoulders and led them to her bedroom. They sat on the bed together, backs against the wall and knees pulled up. Traverse pulled out her portable music player and handed Ruby an earbud to share the music.

"This is really good," Ruby said, soaking in the powerful voices. It was kind of like rock and roll but stronger, harder. "Back home, everyone just listens to folk music."

"I only really listen to black girl bands. Gotta get my culture somewhere."

"Oh my god," Ruby said. "You're probably the only black person for miles."

Traverse nodded with an exasperated eye roll.

"Is it weird?"

She shrugged. "Sometimes. They've had a couple of other black fosters in the past, but they moved on."

"Why didn't you?"

Traverse tilted her head, thinking about it. "I like the farm. I liked being useful. Bram actually taught me how to do things even though I was a girl. Having stuff to work on —not just boring stuff like school, but real stuff, things with your hands, things that mattered. I could get a toolbox and work on the tractor and it would be *fixed*, you know what I mean?"

Ruby nodded, smiling. "My dad was teaching me how to sail…before he disappeared. I loved it, the feeling of steering a big craft in the giant ocean. It felt real. Training Aster has kind of been like that, too."

"You still have your mom, right?"

"Yeah, I just needed to get away from everything that reminded me of him."

"Has it worked?"

Ruby realized that it had, a little. Not just because of Creeping Bones. Waking up without the ocean beyond her window—staring at the horizon for a boat that was never coming. She had even gone a whole day without thinking about him.

"Does Eli get nightmares all the time?"

"Never," Traverse said with a frown. "I'm worried about him. He's so optimistic, annoyingly so. I don't know what could be freaking him out so much."

A memory flashed in Ruby's mind, of Eli's mouth and jaw being worked like a puppet. She shuddered.

"Was it Creeping Bones? Is that why we couldn't find him the other day?"

Ruby nodded a little guiltily.

"We'll find a way to get rid of it," Traverse said. "There's got to be something."

"It would be better if you got away," Ruby said. "The snails need a safe way to leave. Maybe you could sneak off the farm if we keep Creeping Bones busy."

"Hmm, that's not a bad idea. How, though?"

"I'll talk to Ivas. We'll come up with something."

"Let's talk to him now. The sooner, the better."

The music was paused and they left the bedroom. Ivas was in the living room with the deck of cards, playing a game of solitaire. He had a glass of amber liquid next to the game. Blanc looked up and beat her tail against the floor.

"I don't usually drink, and now I remember why." He picked up the glass and sipped, wincing at the taste. "Stuff's nasty."

"You okay?"

"Yeah. Just doesn't do my nerves any good hearing Eli scream like that. They still in their room?"

"Yeah. Actually, Ivas, can we—"

The sound of a door opening down the hall cut Ruby off. They all turned their heads to see Bram step down the hall, joining them in the living room.

"Eli drifted off again," he said.

"Is he okay?" Traverse asked.

"Had a nightmare again. Can't get hurt from a nightmare." Bram sat down and took Ivas's drink, finishing it off.

"Did you guys need something?" Ivas asked.

They shook their heads and returned to the bedroom, whispering quietly late into the night.

CHAPTER 17

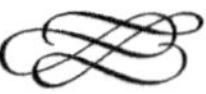

THE GUARDIAN SPEAKS

In the morning, Cherry, Ivas, and Bram worked together to get the truck out of the ditch. It rattled and coughed when they started it, so Bram took it to the garage for repairs. Traverse started to follow but was distracted when she saw the growth coming from the forest.

Everyone noted the strange burst of weeds and saplings growing around the edge of the woods, even though the yard had been fully maintained yesterday. Wildflowers dotted the hill in bright colors, tall grass swayed, and even young trees were visible.

Traverse grabbed her scythe and went to work pushing the wilderness back.

"Stay in the house," Ivas warned Ruby. "This thing is getting desperate. How is it able to do this? It controlled a dead animal, and now the forest is spreading."

"Maybe because of the snail it ate," Ruby said. She was fresh out of the shower and barely in her clothes. She carefully put her compass pin in place on her shirt. "That's why it wants them so bad—they make it more powerful."

Ivas sighed deeply. "As soon as the truck is fixed, we're leaving."

"Actually, Ivas." Ruby dipped her voice into a low whisper. "Traverse has the snails now. *She* needs to get out of here, and we need to distract Creeping Bones so she can."

Ivas whipped his head around to her. "What? She knows? When?"

"After the car crash. She wanted to take them to keep me safe. If Creeping Bones thinks I have them, then I can go into the woods. It'll come after me and Traverse can escape."

"No, absolutely not."

"Why not?"

"Because that thing will kill you!" Ivas hissed. He shuddered, remembering his own attack. "You don't do anything. You stay inside. When the truck is fixed, the three of us will leave together. Understand?"

Ruby raised her shoulders defensively. "Creeping Bones already stopped us once."

Ivas shook his head. "Go inside."

"I want to work with Aster. He got really scared yesterday."

"Fine, but stay in my sight."

Ruby ran to the dog pen, where the canines greeted her eagerly. She almost didn't notice Eli standing nearby.

She jumped in fear, noticing the figure standing in the corner of her eye. "Jeez, man, you scared me."

Eli looked sick, pale, eyes dark and heavy. He had been staring at the woods, but now studied her.

"Are you okay? It sounded really bad last night."

Eli shook his head. Ruby wasn't sure if he was answering her question or dismissing her. She opened the gate and picked up Aster. "Need some puppy love?"

Eli looked at Aster and gave him a slight smile. He rubbed an ear, and Aster licked his cheek.

"Thanks."

"Maybe you should go take a nap?"

"Yeah." He yawned heavily and turned away. Ruby watched him worriedly.

~

*E*li fell onto his bed. He hadn't slept the night before, only dozed off now and then in the early morning hours, and those naps were haunted by bad dreams.

The sunshine in his window was comforting, and the blanket was warm. Eli wrapped himself up, eager to escape from his terror-filled thoughts and finally sleep.

Then Siph came.

Seeing the ghost in the daytime startled Eli so badly that his head hit the wall. Stars burst over his eyes, blinding him. When his vision cleared, he saw Siph on his knees at the foot of the bed, staring at him with a dark expression.

"Creeping Bones found me after I started to rot," Siph said as if continuing a bedtime story that Eli had interrupted. "It let the animals eat me, then took my bones for itself, used them for its own body. I live in its rib cage, curled up tight inside. It eats at me, slowly, a little bit every day."

Eli watched as Siph's body started to rot. The skin pulled away from his fingernails until they fell onto the bed. His eyeball crinkled up like a piece of paper. The skin peeled away, revealing the horrible row of second teeth.

"You can't imagine how much it hurts," Siph said. "It's going to take you too, Eli. If you don't give Creeping Bones what it wants, it'll take your bones and lock you away, too."

Eli leaned over the bed and threw up on the floor, dry heaving painfully as his empty belly tried to end the nausea.

When he looked up again, Siph was still there, standing in the corner of his room, watching. "I'm not leaving this time, Eli. We're together now, you and me, and when Creeping Bones takes you, we'll be together forever."

Eli threw the blankets off and ran.

~

Connie sat in her garden, staring at the woods. Her poor son was having nightmares and the wilderness was creeping into the farm. Something was very wrong. She clenched her hands, popping the knuckles one by one, pressing a little too hard if they wouldn't give.

She thought of Siph. Of sacrifices and consequences.

How did one stop a curse? When she and Bram made their decision, she accepted that someday she would have to pay for it, but nothing had happened to her or Bram. Instead, it was happening to her family.

She popped her thumb, the crack loud and a little painful.

"Truck's good to go. You finish the weeds today?"

She usually heard her husband's heavy footsteps approach, but this time she was startled, her mind nowhere near her ears.

"Oh, I got a little distracted," she said, looking down at her dirt-covered gloves.

"What are you thinking about?" Bram grunted with effort to kneel down next to her.

"Curses."

Bram glowered. "I don't want to hear no more about curses. That's your mother talking."

Connie flinched. They didn't talk about her mother—ever. The woman who gave birth to a dwarf and was convinced that *she* was cursed. She had done...bad things to try and break that curse.

"I'm not my mother. I'm not going to hurt anyone," Connie whispered. "I was thinking salt...or a chicken."

"As much as I love fried chicken, I don't think sacrificing one will help with nightmares. Eli is just remembering things that he had repressed. He'll get past it."

"It seems like there's more than just the nightmares. Something is wrong on the farm."

"Then we leave the farm if we have to."

Pop. Pop.

Bram took her hand and squeezed it tight. "This isn't a curse, Connie, it's guilt. The moment you heard Siph's name, you've been spiraling."

Connie sighed and leaned into Bram, like her body was deflating. "I thought I had finally accepted it, that I was evil. That I would someday pay for what we did. The fact that I haven't is worse."

Bram put an arm around her and kissed her head. "You are not evil, my dear. There's not a mean bone in your body."

Connie shook her head. "We did an evil thing."

"Yes, we did. And I wouldn't take it back."

Connie sighed. "Me neither."

~

The sun was setting. It was time to put the sheep away, and Ivas couldn't keep an eye on both Ruby and Blanc. A handful of sheep had scattered out over the field, and he was helping her bring them in.

"Look back!" he called over the field, struggling to help her pull in the stragglers. He didn't know how to balance the commands properly. Every time Blanc turned around to get the separated sheep, it only scared them further afield.

Ruby had stayed outside all day, working with Aster on his training. Traverse had slowly orbited them as she cut down the brush that bordered the woods. Her dark skin shined with sweat by the end and her hands were blistered, but she had taken back the land they had lost. She tiredly dragged herself to the house to shower.

Ivas shouted at Ruby to go with her but couldn't tell if she had heard him. He turned back to his work, calling orders to Blanc. She circled the loose sheep, laid down, circled the other way, slowly pushing them toward the herd and the barn.

~

*R*uby heard Ivas but was busy praising Aster. They had worked all day and he was finally showing progress. Ruby wondered guiltily if the coyote had scared some obedience into him. Aster sat and laid down, even stayed up to a point, and kept by her side as they took walks around the house.

She kissed his nose and rubbed his ears so hard his back leg came up to bat at the air. Noticing the long shadows, she guided the dog back to the pen, and he went in without a fuss.

When the lock fell, arms came down around her. Ruby barely got out a yelp before a hand clamped down over her mouth. The other arm went around her waist, and she was lifted off her feet.

Ruby kicked and flailed. The dogs started barking and jumping. Her capturer pulled her away and carried her toward the woods.

"What did you do?" Eli's voice hissed next to her ear. Ruby's eyes went wide, hardly believing that the mild-mannered vegetarian was kidnapping her. She rammed her elbow into his arm and tried to kick his shins. He took her closer to the trees.

"There's a ghost in my room. He says Creeping Bones wants *you*. What did you do?"

Ruby put her hands around Eli's fingers and managed to pull his hand away. "Let go!"

"I haven't slept in three fucking days!"

Ruby started screaming.

Eli tossed her.

She hit the ground, landing on the thick floor of dead leaves. The moment she left the border of the farm, the trees seemed to close up behind her like a wall. She scrambled to flee the woods, but thorny vines caught her legs and rocks jutted up to cut her hands.

From the leaves and roots, Creeping Bones rose. It manifested only the top half of its body, staying low near Ruby, who began to tremble. It used the forest to speak to her—the chitter of a squirrel, the creak of branches.

"*I will make this painful for you.*" It reached for her with a gnarled, clawed hand, wrapping the appendages around her throat and pulling her toward its face. "*I will bite each of them off and take a piece of you with it.*"

It began to search her, and Ruby screamed. She felt hands land on her arms, trying to pull her backward.

"Stop!" Eli was yelling, "Let her go!"

"Leave, or your ghost will always stay."

Eli faltered, his grip loosening.

Ruby reached for the antler piece around her neck, searching for strength, wishing for her claws back. Creeping Bones opened its mouth wide, revealing mismatched, stolen teeth—all pointed canines—and a black, dead tongue.

Eli yanked her back, breaking the vines, even as Ruby cried from the thorns piercing her. They fell backward, tangled in each other. Eli groaned in pain as a rock jutted from the ground, punching him in the back.

They both heard a deep, ferocious bark and turned to see a wall of white that was Magnus rushing into the trees. Teeth appeared around his snarl, and the whites of his eyes overtook the warm black.

Magnus and Creeping Bones locked together in a cyclone of blood, fur, and fangs. As white fur flew, Ruby saw human arms and legs appear. Magnus was grabbing at Creeping Bones, trying to tear it apart.

"Ruby! Eli!" They both heard Ivas's frantic voice behind them, accompanied by Blanc's high-pitched barks. They scrambled to their feet, no longer impeded by the wilderness, and retreated out of the forest. The shepherd grabbed them by their shirts and dragged them away, making them trip in his panic.

The three of them went down, and they took the moment to look up to the spot where Magnus and Creeping Bones fought.

"Magnus!" Ruby cried.

The dog, who now possessed the arms and legs of a man, stumbled from the woods, throwing himself out of its clutches. He collapsed into a heap, gasping, trying to crawl further away. His body heaved with the effort.

Ruby clamored to her feet, and Eli followed. They went to Magnus's side, and when they arrived, they saw that his human limbs were gone. A normal dog lay before them, panting and whimpering.

"H-he's got lacerations everywhere," Eli said, parting the thick fur to see the injuries better. In doing so, he spread blood everywhere. Magnus growled at him, and Eli pulled his hands away. Blanc circled them all worriedly, making small whines.

The young man had gone pale, overcome by a feeling of numbness as he sat back, too frightened to think properly. Ivas came to their side and gently touched Magnus's head.

"Easy, boy, you're alright. It's not bad, is it?" He spoke gently and stroked his ears. Magnus sighed.

"Is-is he...?" Ruby tried to speak, but tears choked her voice.

"He's alright," Ivas said quietly. "I've got a special med kit for dogs. Let's take him to my room. Eli?"

Eli blinked at Ivas. His body hadn't stopped shaking.

"Go inside, Eli. Get us some water, yeah?"

Eli nodded but didn't seem to hear him. His eyes were vacant, his expression blank. He slowly stood up and began walking away, toward the house.

"Come on, buddy," Ivas said encouragingly to Magnus. "You got this. Hop up."

With some effort, Magnus pushed himself to his paws. He walked with a slight stumble. Blanc licked at his face helpfully. Ivas shooed her away. "That's it, good job. Come on."

Ruby followed, agonized by their slow pace. She kept checking over her shoulder, expecting Creeping Bones to come chasing them.

They finally made it to Ivas's tiny cabin and eagerly went inside. Magnus laid himself down on the floor and Ivas went to his wardrobe. Not knowing what to do, Ruby lowered herself down on the bed.

It was a twin mattress on a metal frame that squeaked when she sat down. Ivas had his own bathroom, and even a stove, next to which was a table and chair for one. Sitting on that table was a tiny television not much bigger than a shoe box. On the windowsill were soap carvings of various animals.

From the wardrobe, Ivas fetched a small canvas bag. He sat down next to Magnus and opened it, revealing a collection of medical items. Ruby watched silently as he put a fabric muzzle over Magnus's nose first, then began wiping down each injury with a disinfectant wipe. Magnus tried to snap at him when the disinfectant started to sting, but he remained calm otherwise. Ivas spoke to him reassuringly.

Soon, his white fur was restored. "Nothing looks too serious," Ivas said. "The bleeding stopped anyway. Might try to take him to the vet later."

Ruby's tense body finally relaxed at the news, her shoulders sagging.

"I saw what you were telling me," Ivas said. "I saw him change." He rubbed Magnus's ears as he removed the muzzle. "How'd you do that, huh? How'd you do that?"

Ruby went down to her knees in front of Magnus and took off her necklace. "You can tell us; it's okay," she said, presenting the antler piece. "I can change too."

Magnus sniffed at the bone she offered for a long moment, then looked at her, then Ivas. From beneath his body two human arms and legs appeared, as if they had been folded up under him the whole time. His dog legs went limp, like empty jacket sleeves.

From his head a human jaw appeared with a mouth, but no eyes or nose. His dog head remained in place, like a mask. Ruby saw, with some discontentment, that his dog eyes, nose, and ears still moved. It looked like a puppet. It made her stomach twist.

Blanc's fur stood up suspiciously, watching Magnus for any wrong move.

Magnus opened his human mouth and spoke with it. "Forest gave gift."

His voice was halting and strange to hear, as if he didn't quite know how to use it. Ruby couldn't help the fear she felt from the *wrongness* of his semi-transformation. She backed away until she touched the wall. Blanc came to her side. Ivas looked nervous, too, but he didn't move.

"The forest?" he asked. "Something in the forest gave you the ability to change like this?"

Magnus looked at him with his dog eyes. Ruby shuddered.

"Pup disappeared. Lost."

Ivas frowned.

"I smell for girl pup. I have strong smells. I find the pup. Help the two-legs."

"One of your puppies went missing?" Ivas asked.

"Two-leg pup."

"A human kid?" Ruby guessed. Magnus sounded broken. It was worse than trying to understand someone who didn't speak the language. His pitch changed randomly, and his tone was alien.

"Trees took the two-leg girl pup," Magnus continued. "Trail changed, forest tricked, but I have strong smells. I find pup."

Magnus hesitated here, looking down, as if thinking about his next words. "Tree wolf wouldn't give pup back."

"Tree wolf?" Ruby asked for clarification.

Magnus growled in frustration. "Bones. Trees. Two-leg-eater."

"Are you talking about Creeping Bones?" Ivas asked.

"Creeping Bones took a child that got lost in the woods," Ruby translated.

"Death came. Pup was howling. I ask forest for more. Need to talk as two-legs. Need to grab as two-legs."

Magnus held out his hands to them. "Forest gave gift."

Ruby clutched her antler, hand trembling.

"I grab, I call, break! Run." Magnus took a breath. "Save pup. Happy two-legs."

Ivas and Ruby looked at each other. "The forest changed him—just like the fog changed you," Ivas said quietly. "Are you hurt anywhere, Magnus?"

"No hurt."

"You sure?"

Magnus frowned, seeming confused by the question. Instead of answering, he folded his human limbs beneath his torso and they disappeared. A bow of his head banished the human jaw as well.

A thoughtful silence filled the cabin as they stared at Magnus, who curled up and closed his eyes. Blanc lowered her head onto her own bed, brows twitching as she darted her eyes between Ruby and Ivas.

"So, what happened?" Ivas asked quietly. "Why did you go into the woods?"

Ruby's eyes widened, remembering something. "It was Eli. Something is wrong with him. He said there's a ghost in his room."

"Then we'd better go find him."

CHAPTER 18

THE FARMER PERFORMS AN EXORCISM

Connie stared at the trees. She had noticed Eli as she left the house—distracted and heavy-eyed. He had said something about needing water but barely seemed to notice her. Connie sighed sadly and continued on her task.

The sun was down, and there was a light in Ivas's cabin. Bram was on dinner duty, and Traverse had not risen from her nap, tired after a long day of reaping the unnatural growth from the forest.

In her hands, Connie carried a small bag filled with salt, crushed eggshell, and ground sage from her garden. It was an old remedy for protection. Her mother used to deny that it was witchcraft. Witches were bad, but this was *natural*, like lemon and honey for a cold.

Something was happening to her home, something dangerous, and though the salt and shell mixture seemed a little weak, Connie felt she had to do something. Perhaps sprinkling it along the barrier of their farm could keep whatever evil was haunting them at bay.

But would it be enough? Would salt keep away a ghost, or would she need to pay for this sin in blood?

It wasn't hard to find a scab on her hand—an injury from the garden—and pick it until it bled. A line of red curved over her finger and into her palm. She took a handful of the protective mixture, letting the blood weave into the white, wincing as the salt hit the open wound.

She approached the trees and let her blood and tears fall.

~

They found Eli by the water hose. He was holding it but hadn't turned the spout. He just stood there, staring, as if he had forgotten what he was doing.

When Ivas said the boy's name, he jumped in surprise, dropping the hose.

"Oh shit, I forgot— I… Is Magnus okay?"

"He is." Ivas had left Magnus and Blanc in his cabin. Eli looked at Ruby, then down at his shoes, clutched his arm, and dug his fingernails into his skin.

"Where is the ghost, Eli?"

Eli snapped his head up to look at Ivas, eyes wide. "My bedroom."

"How long has it been there?"

"Few days. He said…he wouldn't leave until…" His eyes darted to Ruby, then back down. "I'm sorry."

"Who is it?" Ruby asked. "Whose ghost?"

"…Siph." Eli whispered the word as if saying it would summon the spirit.

"Show us."

~

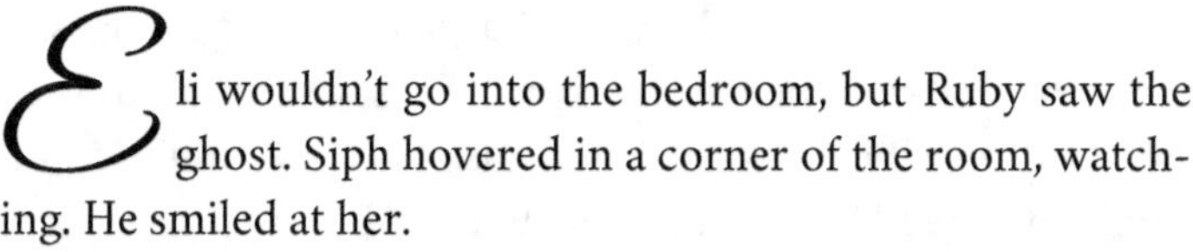

Eli wouldn't go into the bedroom, but Ruby saw the ghost. Siph hovered in a corner of the room, watching. He smiled at her.

"You can see him," Eli breathed. He was shaking again.

"Yes, we can," Ivas said. He stood in the doorway but didn't cross the threshold.

"I thought I had gone mad," Eli said. A tear ran down his cheek and he wiped it away. "He won't leave now. The first night, he went away when the sun came up. But now he's just there all the time."

"How do we do this?" Ruby asked Ivas. "Marlene would probably know."

"Maybe we could get a hold of her. Have your mom lend her a phone."

"In movies there's an exorcism ritual," Ruby mused.

"Mom has books," Eli said, "with old remedies and things like that. She's superstitious. Maybe there's something about ghosts?"

There was no one library, so the three split up to investigate the various corners and shelves of the house containing books. They were stacked on the floor, on chairs and tables, even on the back of the commode. Ruby found old children's books and magazines while Ivas stumbled across yellowing mystery paperbacks. Eli found what they were looking for in the kitchen on top of the refrigerator. There were cookbooks and cleaning guides and thin, hand-written volumes of home remedies. Eli pulled them out.

"Everything okay?" The voice of his father startled him. Eli realized he hadn't even noticed Bram at the stove, cooking beans, sausage, and toast for dinner.

Eli offered only a quick nod as explanation and went to the living room.

They spread the journals over the floor. There were five in total, so they each took one and began to scan the pages.

The door slammed so hard that Eli screamed and Ruby nearly threw the book in her hands. Traverse came scrambling into the living room, screaming for Bram.

"What's going on?" Ivas jumped to his feet.

"Moms in the woods!" Traverse screamed.

Everyone was on their feet now. Ruby felt a lump of fear in her throat at the idea of Connie being taken by Creeping Bones.

"I— I was napping, and I heard a scream out the window. I saw her in the trees!" Traverse was babbling with panic, but Bram was already out the door, holding a kitchen knife in his hand.

"Eli, the gun!" Eli heard his father's order as he ran out the door. He froze.

Ivas and Ruby ran after Bram and Traverse, feet thumping against the night-cooled earth. The older girl led the way to where she had last seen Connie.

"Traverse! Don't go in!" Ruby shouted.

Traverse came to a quick stop at the edge of the trees. Bram kept going, tearing into the brush, shouting Connie's name. Ruby reached Traverse and took her arm.

"I'll draw it away," she whispered in Traverse's ear. "You get your mom."

She didn't give Traverse time to agree or protest as she threw herself into the forest, immediately swallowed by the night.

"No! Ruby, come back!" Ivas's shout went unheeded. "Shit. Stay here. I'll get the dogs and a damn light."

Traverse watched the shepherd change course for his cabin, but she did not stay. Her foot brushed the scythe she had dropped earlier—too exhausted to properly put it away. The blade gleamed invitingly from the grass. She took it in her hands before stepping into the woods.

～

*R*uby called out Connie's name a few times, but otherwise did not announce her presence. She knew Creeping Bones would have no trouble finding her in its domain. Her heart thundered at the notion of how deep she was going into the trees, how dark it was, how impossible it might be to return.

Giving in to her fear, Ruby turned back and sprinted, having no idea if it was the same way she came. Blind and going too fast, she ran into a low branch. It punched her stomach, knocking the air out of her lungs before another slapped her across the face.

Ruby fell, allowing her face to press into the cool, dewing grass. In the darkness, she felt hands on her body, pulling her clothes away. A bark-like texture ran over her skin roughly, yanking and pinching. Ruby yelped at the pain. Then the "hands" released her.

"Where?" the cry of a screech owl demanded.

"Long gone," she rasped.

Something pierced her body, and Ruby screamed. The pain flared in her ribs and then spread like wildfire over her whole body. She felt the presence of Creeping Bones leave, abandoning her in the darkness, the pain pinning her in place like a butterfly to a frame. She couldn't move or make a sound, only breathe haggardly and pray for relief.

～

*T*hough the forest deepened the night with its shadows, Traverse knew how to look in the dark. Years of experience had taught her how to use the silhouettes and the sky to her advantage. Her widened pupils sucked in as much light as they could, and with focus and patience, she was able to make her way through. She kept direction using the sound of babbling creek water and stopped walking when calling Connie's name.

Finally, she heard an answer.

In her rush to answer the call, Traverse almost ran into a waist-high wall of thorn bushes. She came to a stop, just noticing the mass of foliage in time. The long thorns snagged her shirt as she yanked away.

"Connie?"

"I'm here," Connie answered from the other side of the brush. She sounded weak, her breath haggard. "It's like they grew up out of nowhere. I can't find my way past them."

"Hang on." Traverse raised her scythe and brought it down on the plant. In a few swift strokes, she had a way cleared. Connie soon appeared—or at least the shape of her. She was on the ground, holding her arm.

"Are you okay?" Traverse asked, going to her knees and putting her hands on Connie's shoulders. The shorter woman sat up and leaned against her. Traverse felt something warm and wet.

"Are you bleeding?"

"It's part of the spell. I put down my salt."

"It's alright, let's get out of here." One arm went around Connie's waist, the other stayed on the handle of her scythe. Traverse helped Connie to her feet and gently guided her past the thorn bushes.

"Let's go a little faster."

Though cradling her arm, Connie sped up. Leaves and twigs crunched under their feet. Frogs trilled sharply in response. Traverse kept her eyes ahead, listening to the distant creek.

Connie screamed and was suddenly yanked away from Traverse's arm. Roots rose up, tangling her ankles as Traverse tried to turn. She lost her balance and fell.

Traverse whipped her head around in a panic, trying to

keep her eyes on Connie. Her adoptive mother was face-to-face with Creeping Bones. The creature towered over both of them. In the darkness, it appeared to be a mangled tree, and Traverse wouldn't have known any better if it wasn't for the way it moved.

Connie grabbed a bag from inside her pocket and tossed the contents into Creeping Bone's face. It gave no response.

"Herbs are my domain." Its voice was made of frog chirps and the wind.

A great, clawed hand appeared. It pushed Connie aside, right off her feet, and snatched Traverse off the ground. She screamed and thrashed, feeling as if the trunks of trees had closed around her body, bark digging painfully into her arms. Another hand closed around her legs, stopping her frantic kicks, and then a third hand appeared and reached down into her shirt.

Icy sweat broke out over her body, fear plummeted into her stomach like a stone in water. She could feel the dread of the snails along her body as Creeping Bones pulled one from her breast and shoved it eagerly into its mouth.

Traverse retched, tilting her head to throw up. Her body heaved, but nothing came up.

The hand returned. Claws made of sharpened bones brushed over her body as it searched for more.

Then, in the dark, a flash of metal, and Traverse fell. The hand was still clamped around her, but it was separated from the arm. The Creeping Bones screeched in frustration, turning to see that Connie had taken up the scythe.

Traverse flexed her arms and heaved the dead fingers off of herself. She scrambled to her feet, stumbling as Connie grabbed the collar of her shirt and dragged her. Traverse entered a sprint, nearly picking Connie up.

They literally ran into Bram, almost knocking him over

as they rammed into his chest. He shouted in fright but took both women in his hands and guided them out of the woods.

Traverse almost went to her knees, gasping for air as they entered the clearing of the farm, but Bram held her up. Connie was weeping softly at his other side. Bram wasted no time getting them back to the house and the safety of its warm lights. When the door was shut, they both began crying and talking at once.

"It's the curse, Bram…"

"There's a monster—"

"I thought it was going to kill—"

Bram wrapped his arms around them both and pressed them tight to his shoulders until they couldn't speak. Traverse pressed her head down into his neck, his beard becoming wet with tears. Connie put her arms around his waist and dried her face on his shirt.

"It's true," Eli said, stepping into the room. He was holding Bram's rifle but had been unable to leave the house with it. "There is a curse."

Bram looked up, face hard.

"Siph's ghost has been haunting me."

Connie gasped and released Bram to cover her mouth. Traverse lifted her head to stare. Bram released them and stepped up to Eli.

"Show me."

～

*B*ram stepped into the bedroom, stoic, his face blank. He tried the light switch, but it didn't work. The room stayed in darkness. At first, he saw nothing, but as the clock ticked into the witching hour, the shadows shifted. The curtains floated from the window, and in the corner, like a monster hiding in the shape of furniture, he saw Siph, the son he had murdered.

The boy stared back at him, the bags under his eyes growing dark.

Bram stepped forward. Behind him, Eli, Traverse, and Connie watched from the doorway, all clasping hands.

"There's nothing for you here," Bram said. "I'm the one who took your life. If you wish to haunt, then you can haunt me."

At the sight of Bram, tall and unflinching before the ghost, Siph flickered, his fingernails growing long as the flesh pulled back. Eli realized that Siph was afraid.

"You killed him?" Traverse gasped.

"We both did," Connie said. She stepped past the children and into the dark room. "We took him for a walk in the woods. Bram had his pistol."

Siph's eye sockets went black, eyeballs rotting from his head. When he spoke, his voice turned into a high-pitched shriek, like a racing wind. "Stay away!"

Bram took a step forward. "You leave this house, Joseph." Bram's deep baritone rose threateningly, and Eli flinched. He had only heard Bram use that tone a couple of times, and even as an adult, it scared the shit out of him. "Or I'll take you back into the woods."

The hair fell from Siph's scalp and the skin peeled away from his lips, leaving his teeth exposed. The boy backed away, huddling into the dark corner.

The lights flickered, then filled the room with yellow. Siph was gone.

Connie stepped forward, whispering to herself. She sprinkled sage and salt into the four corners of the room. No one spoke while she worked.

"Did you kill him…because he hurt me?" Eli finally asked.

Traverse had both hands clamped over her mouth, eyes bulging with horror.

"Because he hurt everyone, Eli. What he did to the little ones…" Connie covered her mouth and shuddered. Fresh tears sprang from her closed eyes.

"People like that can't be helped," Bram said, heaving a deep sigh. "If we kicked him out, he would have hurt kids in a different house. Grown into a man with deeper appetites. No, we knew what had to be done, knew the price. But if it meant keeping you and the children safe, we were willing to pay it."

Eli and Traverse stared at them, no one emotion able to settle on their faces.

"You don't have to understand, and it's not okay what we did." Bram looked as if he had aged ten years while the lights had been off.

Eli looked at his bedside table where the rusted pocketknife sat. Traverse hugged herself, eyes darting to look at anything but her parents.

Connie shuffled forward weakly. "I need to see to my arm," she whispered.

"I'll help," Bram said.

Traverse rushed from the room, not looking at them. Eli stepped aside so that they could pass. Bram followed Connie but stopped in front of Eli. He took the rifle from his hands.

When the weight of the weapon was gone, mute tears suddenly flooded Eli's eyes. "I'm sorry. I'm so sorry. I'm a fucking coward! I—"

Bram leaned the gun against the wall and grabbed Eli, pulling him into a hug so tight it cut off his breath.

"I don't ever want to see a gun in your hands again, understand? You're better than that. You're a better man than I will ever be."

He left to find his wife. Eli's throat felt so tight he

couldn't breathe. He stumbled after Bram but went the other direction, throwing open Traverse's door. She was sitting on her bed, starting up some music, but looked up as he came in.

Throwing the door shut, Eli stumbled to her bed. Traverse held her arms out and pulled him onto the bed, hugging him tight around the neck.

Eli hugged her back, desperately, like he was drowning, and Traverse was the buoy.

"They killed him," Traverse gasped the words.

Eli trembled, and she squeezed tighter.

"I can't stay here. They're murderers."

"They're not murderers," Eli said weakly, voice muffled by her shoulder. "They were trying to protect us."

"He was a kid. They should have just called the police."

Eli shuddered. "Can we talk about this tomorrow?" he begged.

"Yeah, yes, I'm sorry. Don't go to your room. Sleep in here tonight."

"I don't know if I'll ever sleep again." Eli finally pulled himself from Traverse's arms, head and arms hanging in defeat. Traverse sighed and let her head fall back against the wall, making a hollow *thunk*.

"I hope you can forgive them," Eli said quietly. "Siph really wasn't… He told me what he did. The ghost. If I had known back then…"

Their heads tilted and their eyes met.

"I would have gone into the woods with them."

CHAPTER 19

THE SHEPHERD BRINGS THE LIGHT

It took Ivas longer to get into the woods, but when he entered, he had a lantern and Blanc with him. The Berger Blanc Suisse tore through the brush without fear, her nose filled with the scent of Ruby from a piece of laundry.

"Find," Ivas implored, holding Ruby's shirt to the dog's nose.

Blanc was fast, but Ivas was able to keep up. Her white fur practically glowed in the dark.

Her excited yips told Ivas that she'd found their quarry. A few more steps forward and Ruby appeared in the lantern light. She was on her feet, but barely. She leaned against a tree, her hair sticking to her face, one hand pressed to her side. Blood glinted from between her fingers.

Ivas swore and dashed forward, putting his arm around her. "What happened?"

"It hurts…"

"Okay, okay, hang on." Ivas fumbled with the lantern before hooking it to the belt around his waist. Blanc danced around them worriedly. Ivas picked Ruby up, grunting with effort as she yowled in pain.

"I'm sorry, I know," he muttered in apology as he carried her back toward the farm. The heat from the lamp was sinking through his pants and he picked up the pace. Blanc ran ahead, and he felt reassured by her perked ears and sharp eyes keeping surveillance.

His thigh was getting hot and his head was pounding. He cried in relief when they stepped out of the forest. "We're almost there. It's okay."

"No," Ruby whimpered. "I don't want them to see."

Ivas growled in frustration but heeded her wish, changing direction and going to his cabin instead. He just made it to the door before the hot pain of the lantern built up on his thigh and he dropped Ruby on her feet to pull the light off his belt, hissing in pain.

Ruby didn't seem to notice. She pushed the door open and stumbled inside. Blanc ran in after and Ivas hobbled in last. Ruby laid herself down on his bed, turning onto her uninjured side.

"Is it bad?" she whimpered. Ivas kneeled on his knees next to the bed and lifted her shirt.

"Ouch," he conceded. There was a puncture wound below her ribs, small, leaking blood. Fetching a wet cloth, he cleaned it, and the bleeding quickly stopped. Ivas sighed in relief. "Not deep," he reported. "What happened? Was it Creeping Bones?"

She nodded. "I tricked it. Didn't have the snails."

Ivas gritted his teeth to stay silent as he bandaged the injury. He had Ruby sit up and grabbed iodine and gauze from his human first aid kit. Ruby reached to the window and picked up a soap carving of a bear, rotating it so that her hands had something to do while Ivas sat on his knees, bandaging her. The smooth texture of the soap was soothing.

Once the treatment was complete, Ivas couldn't hold back.

"I thought we talked about this, that you would try to be safer. You threw yourself right into the woods where this monster is trying to kill you. Why are you—?" Ivas pulled back, sighing. Ruby cast her gaze down and pulled her arms around herself, squeezing the bear. Sensing conflict, Blanc went to Ivas and licked his hand.

"I just… How do I make you understand this? Why are you so…? That letter you got from your father, the one the Messenger delivered, that wasn't done without a price, Ruby. Don't you think everyone would be getting letters from their lost loved ones otherwise? Your dad had to pay a heavy price to warn you and save your life. Do you think he'd be okay with how you're putting yourself in jeopardy like this?"

Ruby dug her fingernails into the soft soap body of the bear and stared hard at the ground. She had a million things she wanted to throw back at him, but the words tripped over each other in the rush for her tongue. She wanted to scream at Ivas for scolding her when she was already hurt and scared.

"My grandfather was in the war. When he came home, he got back to work on the farm. When my parents died and I had to live with him, he did the only thing he could think to get me through it—put me to work, the same as he did, cause the only other option was to look into the eyes of the trauma we had faced. I didn't have a childhood. I learned to train dogs, herd sheep, and cry myself to sleep at night because my grief just lived and festered in me. That's what you're doing, trying to work instead of facing your grief, but that cycle has to end, Ruby. It *has* to."

She didn't answer, continuing to glare at the ground. The soap curled under the claw of her nails and fell into her lap.

"I know you don't understand what I'm trying to tell you. Think of Aster, when he attacked that coyote and almost died. Would that have been fair? Would it have been right if he had died trying to fight something like that? A puppy?"

"No…"

"You're just a child, getting to work with a fight like this because it's easier than living through the knowledge that your dad is dead."

Tears were streaming down her cheeks from unblinking eyes. She took the compass pin off her shirt and began carving at the bear with the needle, making deep gouges in its side. Ivas reached forward and placed his hand over hers.

"I'm not trying to scold you, I'm really not. I don't want you to *die*, Ruby."

Ruby looked at him, her hands stilled. "Someone has to do it, Ivas. Someone had to stop the Harvestmen, save the snails, stop Creeping Bones."

Ivas grimaced because he knew it was true. Someone had to fight in wars. Someone had to miss the people who died.

"Okay. But you don't have to do it alone. Please don't do it alone."

"I won't always get that choice."

He winced. He was supposed to be better than this, have answers for this sixteen-year-old girl before him, hurting and in danger. She wasn't supposed to be right. Everything he said suddenly felt empty and useless. His words had only hurt her.

He shook his head. "It should have been me. It's not fair that it's you. You're supposed to have your childhood, safety, adults to fight the monsters for you." His fingers pushed the bear and pin aside so that he could squeeze her hands. He was on his knees, head bowed, arms on her knees.

Ruby looked at him with eyes that were far too wise. "You were supposed to have that too."

They stared at each other, and Ivas finally realized why he had been fighting so hard for Ruby all this time.

"Thank you," she said, "for giving me that. You pulled me out of the fogs, you saved me from the Harvestmen. You gave me this summer, and Aster, and all the things that have actually made me happy."

One more squeeze, then Ivas pulled his hands away, straightening his back. He had a feeling of emptiness in his body, as if all his insides had been pulled out, leaving him weak, like he might blow away in the breeze.

He pushed himself from his knees, wincing at the dig of hardwood, and sat on the bed. "How does it feel?" he motioned to her waist.

"Better, actually. It really hurt before. I thought it had stabbed me through." She shuddered with fear.

"I'm glad you're okay. Let's get back to the house before the others come looking. You good to walk?"

Ruby unsteadily rose to her feet, wincing, then straightening. She breathed deeply and set her face to deception—no pain, nothing to worry about. Taking up his lantern, Ivas opened the door, and they stepped out together.

CHAPTER 20

THE HORNED GIRL FINDS THE HIKER

In the morning, they saw that the forest had grown out again, erasing Traverse's work from the day before. Tall grass, tree sprouts, and weeds tangled the border between the farm and the forest. Traverse rubbed her blistered hands in agitation.

The family moved quietly as they made breakfast. Eli was still sleeping. Despite his declaration of not being able to, he had eventually passed out before the sun rose and slept in Traverse's bed while she took the floor. She left him there to catch up on his lost hours of slumber.

Everyone else had all slept in past the usual time, as was evident when Cherry suddenly walked in the door, making everyone flinch.

"Yesh. You lot look a sight," she said. She attempted to pour a cup of coffee, found the pot empty, and began brewing a new batch.

"Shit, Cherry, I'm sorry," Bram groaned. "We've had a bit of a night…"

"S'alright, Bram," Cherry said. "I can handle a morning by myself. At least the sheep were out."

Ivas waved tiredly from the table, his cheek resting on his arm.

"I take it you were up hunting the poachers?" Cherry prepared a mug with sheep milk and sugar.

"Ah," was the only response Bram gave, not sure of his answer. Finally, he settled on, "Yes."

"Cherry," Connie spoke up, "will you help me load some of the produce into the truck? I want to take it to market today."

"Sure. Got it working again?"

Another long pause from Bram, then, "Yes."

Cherry gave her boss a look of confusion and concern, but the beep of the coffee maker drew her attention and she focused on her drink instead.

After Cherry had her coffee, Bram joined her to finish up the farm chores. Connie gathered Traverse and Ruby to box up the produce from the garden—much of which had been jarred.

The two girls moved slowly, feet shuffling and eyes heavy as they entered the walk-in pantry where rows of jars sat waiting. They each took a shelf and began filling an empty box with the produce. The silence of the tiny room was heavy.

"It took a snail," Traverse said somberly.

Ruby looked at her, eyes widening empathetically.

"It was awful."

The younger girl set aside a jar of tomatoes and hugged Traverse around the waist. Traverse rested her head on top of Ruby's.

"You won't be able to leave," Ruby said quietly. "If Creeping Bones knows you have the snails now, it won't let you leave."

"Then I'll stay," Traverse said. "While you're in town, maybe you can find a way to stop it."

"How?"

"I don't know. Maybe the library? The herbs Connie used didn't work. Maybe if we had something stronger…"

Ruby nodded. "What will you do? You *can't* go near the woods."

"I'll stay close to Ivas and the dogs…if I go outside at all."

Ruby slipped away from the hug and looked up at Traverse's dark eyes. "Are you okay?"

Traverse huffed, smirking slightly. "No."

~

*B*ram backed the truck up to the front porch so they could easily load the boxes of food. While they got everything packed, Ivas pulled Ruby aside.

"This is your chance to escape," he said. "If you're able to leave the farm, this would be your chance to go home."

Ruby frowned. "Would Connie take me to the train station?"

"Just ask. I'll mail your things back to you."

"And Aster?"

"I'll take care of him and get him back to you. Just… Please, Ruby. You don't have to do this, not this time."

Ruby looked down at her foot and started focusing on pushing up a rock half buried in the dirt. "Would that be okay?"

"Of course. Of course it's okay."

The rock came loose, revealing worms and beetles underneath. Ruby carefully put it back in place.

"Just think about it."

"Ruby!" Connie's voice called from the door. They looked up and saw her standing half-in, half-out, holding the telephone. "It's your mom."

Ivas gave her a meaningful look, raising his eyebrows. Ruby jogged to the house and took the phone.

"Hi, Mom. What's up?"

"Nothing, I just wanted to call. Slow day at work. How are you, baby?"

"I'm good. I like the farm. Everyone's really nice." Ruby stepped into the house, following the phone cord into another room where she could talk privately.

"You getting along with their daughter? What was her name?"

"Traverse. Yeah, she's really cool."

"I'm glad. I miss you."

"I miss you too." Ruby pressed her back to the wall and slid down to the floor. "Miss Dad, too."

"I know, baby." She sighed from a hundred miles away. "It really sucks, doesn't it? This is the only thing in your life I can't really help you with. Can't make it better. Has this trip helped at all?"

"It kind of has, yeah," Ruby said honestly. "Having something to do for the summer helps, even if it's waking up early to work on a farm."

Hannah chuckled. "Has Aster been doing better?"

"Yeah, way better. Ivas is really good at training him."

"You like Ivas a lot, huh?"

"What do you mean?" Ruby pulled the phone cord in her hand, wrapping it around her finger then letting it twirl loose.

"It just seems like you guys have some sort of bond. Almost like you're keeping a secret."

"I'm not keeping any secrets, Mom."

"I know that. I just think it's interesting how you've become friends with an old sheep farmer of all people."

"Ivas knows what it's like to lose a parent."

A beat of silence. Ruby coiled the wire around her finger.

"That's good. If Ivas knows to say the things that I don't… then it's good that you're friends."

"I'm sorry." Ruby wasn't sure what she was apologizing for, but it seemed like she needed to.

"There's nothing to be sorry for, baby girl. I don't want you to feel guilty. None of it is your fault."

Ruby felt the sting of tears and winced at the painful lump that suddenly formed in her chest.

"You know that, right?"

"I didn't go with him that day." Her voice caught on the sharp hooks of her tears. She wasn't sure if Hannah had heard her.

"Ruby…"

"When he went out that day, I didn't—"

"He didn't want you to go, Ruby."

"But he—"

"I actually remember talking to him about it before. He was saying that he couldn't take you out on the boat anymore because you didn't follow orders. He—" Hannah laughed. "He said that something was about to hit you, and instead of listening when he told you to get down, you decided to take it full-on."

Ruby smiled. The lump softened. "I remember that. I almost got knocked overboard by the boom."

"He'd yell 'duck' and you'd turn to look instead."

A tear escaped and Ruby wiped it away.

"Please, *please*, Ruby, don't take on that guilt. It's not for you. He wouldn't want you to feel that pain. *I* don't want you to feel that pain, okay?"

"Okay, Mom."

"I love you, baby."

"I love you too."

"Now go on and have some fun. Chase sheep, jump into haybales, whatever you do on farms."

Ruby laughed at that. They made kissing noises at each other until Connie came to check on her, then Ruby hung up.

She was surprised to see that Connie had woken up Eli, making him brush his teeth and get into the truck as well. It was a tight squeeze with four of them in the technically-for-three front seat, but Ruby and Eli shared a seat belt. The older boy dozed against the window. It was quiet except for the sound of Connie cracking her knuckles.

Traverse and Ivas watched them from the gravel drive-way. Ruby watched back, staring at their still postures in the rearview mirror. She held her breath as they came to the edge of the property, where the road slipped from the grasp of the forest.

The truck rumbled through, and they were free.

~

Ivas breathed a sigh of relief when the truck left the border of the farm safely. Ruby was finally able to leave, and with Connie and Bram both gone, he could practice sheep herding without the fear of being caught.

He nodded to Traverse and headed to the field, whistling for Blanc to follow. He wanted to practice something simple, like getting the sheep into a group and moving them to certain spots in the field. Standing at the fence, he sent Blanc to work, calling out orders.

Soon, he was breathless, Blanc was panting and confused, and the sheep kept disbanding. He could put them out to field, and it was easy to get them into the barn at night, but getting beyond that was proving to be futile. They had only been working at it for about fifteen minutes, but he was done, kicking the fence in frustration.

"Why don't you know how to herd the sheep?"

He hadn't even realized that Traverse had been watching him. Ivas jumped, then huffed in anger, stepping toward the barn to get in the shade.

"It's gone. My herding skill was taken from me. I don't know how to command Blanc or move the sheep. I can't even train the pups. My one job, the only thing I've ever been taught to do..."

Traverse followed him and climbed over the fence. "Okay, that's a story you're going to have to tell me another time." She looked out at the field. Blanc was slowly making her way back to them, clearly tired. "You're making it more complicated than it is."

Ivas looked at her.

"You don't have to throw so many commands at Blanc constantly. She's a herding dog, and she's done this a long time. She knows what to do."

"She kept changing direction."

"She's weaving; that's what she's supposed to do. Come on. I've watched you and Bram do this so many times, I can help."

Traverse left the shade and walked through the field, meeting Blanc halfway. Ivas quickly followed.

"That'll do," Traverse said. Blanc laid down at her feet. "You also want to let her rest if she does a lot of running—just let her lay down for a minute to catch her breath."

Ivas nodded.

"Now, watch. Come by."

Blanc took off, running back across the grass. She started at the far end first, where the furthest sheep stood, then made a U around the back of the others. The sheep pulled themselves in.

"Blanc has this in her instincts. She wants the sheep to be all together, so that part she can practically do by herself. Once they're together, then you can tell her where you want them. She's going to want to push them toward you unless you say otherwise."

"So, if I want them over there?" Ivas pointed.

"Hold!" Blanc called. Blanc froze, eyes on the sheep and haunches lowered. "Come by."

Blanc made a clockwise journey around the sheep. They veered the other way.

"Away. Walk on." Blanc doubled back and pushed the sheep forward to the other side of the field.

"Damn," Ivas said. "You know this really well."

"Just years of watching."

"So, if I want them in the other pasture, I can just stand by the gate there and she'll push them to me?"

"Yep. You don't have to stay in one place. Sometimes it's easier to be where you want the sheep to be."

They continued working together, with Traverse imparting what knowledge she had, until Ivas felt confident enough to try it again on his own. She offered tricks to make the process easier.

"You won't win a herding trial, but it gets the job done. And I'll help you, so that Bram doesn't notice."

"Thank you so much." Ivas's voice was hoarse from shouting commands, but he felt at ease as he gave Blanc a well-deserved "That'll do."

"What happened, Ivas? How could you lose...?"

"It's a strange story, and I'll have to go further back, but it also explains where the snails came from. Let's make some lemonade."

"I know where Connie hides the cookies." Traverse smiled impishly.

"Bring the whole box. It's a long story."

～

*R*uby couldn't contain the relief she felt when they entered town, safe from the influence of the forest spirit. They passed the train station—

Your chance to escape...

—and Ruby felt a longing for home.

Their first stop was the food pantry. Everyone made a chain and passed the boxes along, unloading half the stock. The other half went to the market, where a family friend offered to sell the stock from their stall.

"I need to visit the Everharts," Connie said after they had finished unpacking the last of the food.

"Alright, I'll drop you off there while I go to the store," Bram said.

"Could I go to the library?" Ruby asked. "I know I can't check out any books. I just want to look."

"You can check things out on my card," Connie said. "Stay there and we'll pick you up in…?" She looked at Bram.

"About an hour."

"In one hour."

Connie was dropped off, and Ruby was set loose in the library while Bram and Eli continued on to the shops. It was a modest-sized library in a stout stone building. The aisles were narrow and the air was stuffy with the scent of paper. The children's section was the largest, but Ruby found a quiet nonfiction section with a decent selection. With Connie's card in hand, she didn't bother to vet the books, just grabbed anything that sounded remotely useful—books on spirits and the afterlife, home remedies from the garden, local folklore and legends, world mythology.

When her arms were too full to carry more, Ruby made her way to the checkout desk. Setting the books down, she glanced at the newspapers and magazines on display while the librarian went through her selection.

One of the headlines caught her attention: SEARCH CALLED OFF FOR MISSING HIKER.

Ruby recalled that Cherry had been part of a search party when she first arrived. Was this the woman they had been looking for? A black and white picture of a woman in her thirties smiled next to the headline. She had an athletic build, with her long hair pulled into a ponytail underneath a ball cap. On that ball cap, the woman had a collection of pins.

One of the pins was a compass.

Ruby's breath stopped. She pulled the paper out and scanned the article.

Her name was Siobhan, and after a week, officials were canceling the search for the woman who had gone missing in the woods. The disappearance was unusual as Siobhan was an experienced hiker. The family would continue looking on their own.

"Are you ready?" the librarian asked.

"Actually, do you have a newspaper archive?"

"Just a small one," she answered. "Would you like to take a look?"

"Yes, please."

～

*R*uby had never used a microfilm reader before. The librarian was patient and walked her through it, showing her how to slide the small rolls into the machine and blow up the miniaturized newspaper pages. She was soon zooming through black and white frames of print, searching article headlines for stories like Siobhan's.

She only got through a few years of newspapers, but each had what she expected to find—a person camping, hiking, or working in the woods had disappeared and was never found.

One was a toddler who had been playing in a puddle at the edge of camp. The parents had only looked away for a moment.

The other was a man who had been tasked with marking trail trees. Authorities had followed the paint-stained trees he had made until it just suddenly stopped. There was no other trace of him.

There had been a hiker as well, but she had been lucky. They found her a few days later, frost-bitten but alive.

Ruby rubbed the compass pin, wondering how many more awaited in the years prior. How long would it take her to find Siph's article?

The wall clock ceased her search. It was now well past an hour, and when Ruby stepped outside, blinking at the bright sun, Bram was there waiting for her.

"Did they stop you from taking the whole shelf?" Bram teased as Ruby struggled to get her books into the car. Eli—now fully awake—gave her a hand and they continued on to find Connie.

She was waiting for them outside the Everhart's home—an apartment above the local bakery that they owned. Ruby loved the charming white-and-green exterior covered in summer flowers. Instead of getting in the truck, Connie went to the trunk and lifted out a packed duffle bag. She then opened the passenger door and motioned for Eli to get out.

"Mom?" He stepped out, bewildered.

"I talked to the Everharts and they've agreed to open their home to you," Connie said firmly. "Their daughter got married over the spring—you remember Kathleen—so her room is free. Plus, they need help in the bakery. It'll be good to make some money before school starts, yes?"

Eli stared at her. Connie held her gaze, unblinking. "I already packed your bag, but if you need anything, it's no trouble to bring it down next time we're here. The Everharts could really use your help and we have things well taken care of at the farm."

She spoke swiftly and awkwardly, as if she had memorized a script. She put the duffle bag into Eli's hands, but they were shaking, and the strap slipped from his grasp. Bram quickly heaved himself over Ruby and went to his son's side, picking up the bag.

"I got it," he said. He patted Eli's shoulder and took it to the front door.

Ruby couldn't hear what was said next. Eli went to his knees before his mother and melted as she put her arms around his neck. They spoke softly into each other's ears, and Ruby could tell by the tremble of Eli's shoulders that he was crying. She looked away.

"You don't deserve any ghosts," she heard Connie say.

Bram returned and helped Eli to his feet, guiding him to the bakery where the smell of sugar and yeast bellowed from the doorway. They left their arms around each other for a long time before Bram gave Eli several hard pats on the back and gently pushed him on.

The car doors slammed shut, the engine rumbled to life, and the truck began its journey back to the farm.

"Is there anywhere else we need to stop?" Connie asked. Her voice was strained.

Ruby glanced at the train station as they drove by. "No."

CHAPTER 21

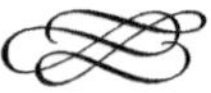

THE SHEPHERD GETS A LETTER

*R*uby could see the disappointment in Ivas's eyes when she stepped out of the truck. He marched up to her, but she distracted him by putting the tall stack of books in his arms, then she fled to the house.

"Ivas, you got some mail," Connie said, holding out a letter separate from the rest of the envelopes she had collected on their return trip. With a frown, Ivas accepted, and was surprised to see Archibald's name in the sender's portion.

He set the books down on the porch and sat next to them on the stairs. Blanc laid down at his side. Her tail thumped the wood a few times, then settled. Ivas tore open the envelope and pulled out the letter.

Archibald's handwriting was clear and legible, but the thickness of the stack made Ivas sigh, knowing he was in for a long read.

Dear Ivas,

I'm writing this letter for two reasons. The first to thank you for introducing me to Mr. Poppermill. He has agreed to come to the university with me, and we have spent the last few days selecting which stories from his collection to bring with us. I am very excited for this opportunity. I believe his contributions will—

Ivas skipped the next two paragraphs that pertained to Archibald's project, seeking out the second point to the letter.

I was thinking about our last conversation, and since we won't be able to call each other, I decided to write to you with the details of the story I told you about. Mr. Poppermill actually had references to similar tales, and it invigorated my memory. Here is the story of The Monster of Mnt. HaAri:

Once upon a time, there was a small village at the base of a mountain called HaAri. It was occupied by desert dwellers—farmers and shepherds. Poor folk who lived off the well. Up in the mountain was a family that lived isolated from the village. They were goat farmers and would only come down to the village twice a year to sell milk and meat, buy supplies, then go back up into the mountain. Everyone was suspicious of the man and his family. Rumors spread that they were occultists, witches, worshipers of the dark arts.

One winter, a large blizzard hit the small village. It was odd to get snow in the desert, and many people died. The snow filled the mountain pass, trapping the mountain family. The snow was so deep that it didn't fully clear until summer.

When the pass was clear, only the husband/father came back down, taunt and starving. He was ill and rambled madly about a monster that had killed his family—his wife and two children. The village gathered together and went up the mountain to hunt this man-eating beast, but they found no trace of it. No tracks, fur, or burrow. Only three graves and dead goats.

Believing the goat farmer to be crazy, the villagers returned home, but one woman stayed. She was an old shaman and medicine woman, and she feared that the creature the farmer described was a monster that was called a "Mala Sort" (a word meaning "bad luck"). This was a traveling monster that would bring despair in its wake—unusual weather, sickness, famine, etc. The shaman was already seeing the beginnings of sickness in the village and knew that if there was a monster, their population would not survive it.

She began working on a charm that would banish the monster. She took a branch from the hardy acacia tree and worked it into a loop so that it made a perfect circle. She then communed with a silkworm to procure fine red thread to weave into the circle like a spider's web.

This all took several days, and during that time, the goat farmer slowly fell to madness. He wailed and cried for the loss of his family and went into the desert at night to hunt the beast. The shaman would hear gun shots throughout the night, but the farmer could not kill his target. On the day she finished the charm the farmer did not return. She found his body in the desert. His head was gone.

She buried the body and sang a song over the grave. Hearing the music, the Mala Sort hunted the shaman down. When it tried to attack her, she held her charm aloft and trapped it for a hundred years.

Eventually, the Mala Sort would escape—you might recall the famous, deadly blizzard that hit the desert several decades ago—and continue its journey of misfortune, but for the end of the story, the shaman's village was at least safe.

There was more, but Ivas took a break from the letter to rest his eyes. Blanc raised her head and licked his hand. He looked out to the field where the sheep were peacefully grazing. Magnus was back on duty as well, laying in the grass, quietly watching his charges. With a heavy sigh he folded the letter back into its envelope and stood up. Blanc eagerly followed suit.

"Well, let's see if we can find an acacia tree."

The screen door creaked and he turned. Ruby stepped outside and spotted the books. She bent down, touching the stack.

"Research," she said, "to stop Creeping Bones."

Ivas knelt next to her, putting a hand out gently over her own to stop her from standing again.

"Why didn't you get on the train?" he asked. His tone was curious, no rebuke behind the question.

Ruby squeezed the fabric of her shirt. "My dad didn't send his message to make me run away," she said. "He knew better."

Ivas didn't fully understand, but he didn't press. Instead, he handed Ruby the letter from Archibald, then picked up the top book from her stack. "Let's get to reading."

They stayed on the porch since the weather was nice, rocking and reading. Inside, Ruby could hear Traverse's voice, demanding to know why they didn't tell her that Eli wasn't coming back.

"I didn't want to give him room to protest," Connie explained. Huffs and slammed doors answered her. Bram's voice gave a warning rumble.

"Is this what you do?" Traverse's voice rose several octaves, making Ruby and Ivas flinch. "When you get tired of your kids you just send them away? *Murder* them?"

Connie cried out and began to sob.

"Don't talk to her like that!" Bram shouted, deep and terrifying. Ruby actively rushed to the other side of Ivas's chair, grabbing his arm.

"You don't scare me!" Traverse screamed back.

"Eli couldn't stay here, Trav. It was dangerous." Bram tried to lower his voice. Connie was sobbing.

"I didn't even get so say goodbye!"

"He's just in town. You can see him anytime you want. We both know what you're really upset about, and if you're really that scared of me, if you really think I'd *ever* hurt you, then we'll find a place for you off this farm too." Bram's high angry voice morphed into sadness when he reached the end of his sentence.

"Good!" Traverse's voice was also tear-filled.

The screen door flew open and Traverse stomped outside, but seeing Ivas and Ruby there, she released an exasperated screech.

"Cheesus Christ, is there any place on this farm I can be alone?" With that she stormed through the house the other way, to the back door.

A tense silence followed, except for Connie's weeps. Bram gently shushed her, speaking softly. Then the house was quiet.

Ruby looked at Ivas, eyes wide. "Should I go after her?"

"Don't ask me," he said, having not looked up from his book.

The door opened again. Bram stepped out.

"I think Connie and I are going to go visit the Stewarts," he said, eyes staying firmly on the horizon. "Traverse needs some space, and Connie likes them. They got five kids that'll keep her busy."

"*Five?*" Ruby raised her eyebrows. Bram smirked.

"Tell 'em I said hi," Ivas said. "Stay as long as you need. I'll keep an eye on everyone over here."

"I appreciate that," Bram sighed. "We probably won't be back until late. Specially if they pull out the wine."

Bram went back inside and returned a few minutes later with Connie under his arm. Her face was still red. Ruby rose, inflated with sympathy, and gave Connie a quick hug around the neck. The smaller woman returned it tightly.

"I'll talk to her," Ruby promised.

Connie gave her a grateful smile and they loaded up into the truck, waving goodbye out the window. Ruby and Ivas finally felt their shoulders relax.

After a moment of contemplation, Ruby took Archibald's

letter and declared that she would go find Traverse. Ivas waved her on, returning to his book. She left through the back door and passed the garden. In the open field she was easily able to spot Traverse sitting next to the lake. Ruby jogged after her.

Traverse was sitting on an overturned pail, looking at the water. She didn't break her gaze when Ruby arrived. Ruby kneeled beside her, balancing on the balls of her feet. When Traverse didn't acknowledge her, she handed over the letter, waving it under her nose.

"Read this story. Ivas thinks it might help."

Traverse snatched the paper from her, making Ruby flinch. Traverse's shoulders relaxed as she read, her mind greedily taking in the distraction from her absent brother.

"A charm… We can make that, right? I don't know what an acacia tree is, but we can find something."

Ruby nodded eagerly. Her legs began to cramp, so she allowed herself to fall back on her rear and sit in the grass.

"I don't know if it'll be enough though. Connie's salts didn't work, and that was *before* it took another snail. And if it's made of wood, then…"

"Your house is made of wood. If we take it and reform it to our purpose, I think it counts. Maybe it'll hold it off long enough for you to escape."

"Maybe," Traverse murmured. "I have some girlfriends in town. I could stay with them for a few days and cast the snails off. At least then I can remove them safely."

"Do you really want to leave? I mean, like, for real?" Ruby asked. "Are you scared about what they did to Siph?"

"Of course I'm scared." Traverse crossed her arms. "How would you feel if your mom had…" She shuddered and lowered her head. "Connie and Bram were supposed to be different. Everyone who comes here already has parents who are awful or dead. They were supposed to be safe, normal. I've been on walks with Bram, just us, alone in the woods."

"He loves you, though."

"I know, but this… I don't know if I can accept this."

Ruby wrapped her arms around her knees. "I mean, you don't have to, right? You don't have to accept it or agree with it. But you can still love him without loving what he did."

Traverse shook her head. "They're supposed to be the people I can always trust, and I don't know if I can anymore."

Ruby hesitated, trying to think of wise words that could fix the rift that had been formed, but all she could say was, "I'm sorry."

She leaned her head on Traverse's knee. Traverse slowly unfolded from herself and touched Ruby's hair. "Thank you."

They let the silence linger, watching the lake water sparkle in the afternoon light. Traverse breathed deeply, switching to the problem at hand.

"It's been watching," Traverse said solemnly. She folded the letter up and ran the pads of her fingers over the thick texture of the paper. "I can feel Creeping Bones staring from the woods. It's stronger, and all the more hungry. It's waiting for its opening."

Ruby hugged her forearms and rubbed away the goosebumps that had appeared there. "I won't let it get you."

Traverse smiled and gave her a soft punch to the shoulder. "Thanks."

"So, if there aren't any acacia trees, what kind of branch can we use to make a circle?"

Traverse rubbed her fingers against her mouth thoughtfully. "A grapevine, or a willow."

"Any around here?"

"Yeah, down the creek, not far from the treehouse actually. But—"

"We'd have to go into the woods."

Traverse nodded.

"Could we try going in with the dogs? It doesn't like the dogs, and it's only really attacked people that had the snails."

Traverse exhaled loudly, fluttering her lips and pulling at her hair. "That's such a dangerous risk though."

"Let's see what Ivas thinks," Ruby suggested. "If he takes Blanc and Magnus and maybe one of the puppies…"

"Maybe." Traverse pushed herself up, wincing and popping her knees. Ruby hopped up with ease.

"I found out some stuff at the library," Ruby said as they walked back, "about people who have gone missing in the woods."

"Yeah?"

"Do you think Creeping Bones took them?"

"That's the story. It finds people in the woods, gets them lost, then…"

A tense silence fell over them. Stomach tightening, Ruby suddenly grabbed Traverse's hand, like a child afraid to cross the street. She kept her eyes on the ground and only relaxed when Traverse gave her palm a tight squeeze.

~

*I*vas was still on the porch, and when they revealed their plan, he tensed. "I don't think any of us should go back in there."

"Do you think it's too dangerous? Even with the dogs?"

"It let us leave last night," Ruby reminded him, "because we didn't have the snails."

"Not before stabbing you," Ivas said icily. Ruby shrank, and Traverse's head whipped around.

"It hurt you? Where?"

"It wasn't bad," Ruby said, raising her shirt so Traverse could see the patch of gauze taped over her ribs.

"Cheesus, Ruby. No one is going back into those woods."

"Half of your idea might work," Ivas said before Ruby could argue.

"Which half?"

Ivas looked out to the fields, where patches of white floated in the green. "Magnus."

~

Ruby and Traverse climbed up on top of the fence, legs dangling, while Ivas called to the Great Pyrenees. Blanc stayed at the fence as well, following an order from Ivas, though she eagerly watched, tongue hanging out, ready to herd. Magnus dutifully approached, picking up speed as Ivas lowered down to his knee. Ivas looked around, checking that the girls were the only witnesses.

"What's going on?" Traverse asked.

"You'll see," Ruby said.

Ivas spoke quietly to Magnus, touching his head, then standing. He ran his hands up his body, inviting Magnus to join him.

Magnus lowered his head, and then from beneath his white fur, the limbs of a man appeared, and Magnus rose to his now human feet.

Traverse almost screamed, slamming her hands against her mouth to stop sound from escaping. She started to fall backward from the fence, but Ruby caught her.

"M-magnus…"

"I know."

"How?"

"The same way that Creeping Bones exists," Ruby whispered.

They couldn't hear what Ivas was saying, but Magnus

turned to look at the woods, his dog ears twitching. Ivas reached into his pocket and pulled out a pocketknife. He presented it to Magnus, who took it gingerly. Ivas turned and walked to the fence. Magnus followed.

Traverse jumped off the fence and backed away, her eyes full of fright as she stared at the dog-man. Seeing her trepidation, Ivas changed course and led Magnus a few yards away. They crossed the fence—Ivas climbing over the top while Magnus crawled underneath. Ruby and Traverse followed at a distance with Blanc at their side.

They went to the forest's edge, where the grass was as tall as their knees. From there, they could hear the babble of the creek.

"He doesn't know what a willow tree is," Ivas said to Ruby. He pointed at the trunk of a random tree. "Tree."

Magnus narrowed his eyes.

Ruby stepped forward. "Willow tree looks like this." She flipped her head over so that her hair hung down over her face. "It has branches hanging down."

Ivas took the pocketknife back and took a lock of Ruby's hair. He mimed cutting it with the knife. "We need one of its branches." He pointed at Ruby, then at a tree. He handed the knife back to Magnus. "Follow the water and you'll find the tree."

Magnus gritted his teeth, making an unsatisfying growl with his human throat. He turned away from them and ran into the woods.

Traverse finally stepped forward, hugging her arms. "It's like in fairytales," she murmured, staring after the white of Magnus's retreating back. "Animal-human things." She jumped, realizing something. "What about the other dogs?"

"They're all normal dogs, as far as I know," Ivas said. He kneeled down and pulled Blanc gratefully into his arms.

"Magnus has gone up against Creeping Bones before,"

Ruby said. "He told us about a little girl that went missing."

Traverse's eyes widened. "Emily?"

"Who's that?" Ivas asked.

"She's the daughter of the people who own Magnus," Traverse explained, "I remember… Yeah, a few years ago, she got lost. Her parents called us asking to keep an eye out. She had been playing in the woods and hadn't come home all night. It was awful. Her parents were so scared. They were putting together a search party, then that afternoon she came home, holding on to Magnus." Traverse's mouth dropped. "Oh my god! I remember Emily saying that a man had been there. Her parents asked if we had seen anybody. I had totally forgotten."

"I wonder if she still remembers," Ruby wondered.

They grew quiet and stared at the forest worriedly. Blanc paced and sniffed at the ground. Ruby sat down. Traverse picked a tick off her pants. She pinched it between her fingers, watching its tiny legs twitch and flail.

~

The last time Magnus had entered the woods, his girl-pup had been lost inside them. He stayed in the fields, guarding his charges from the things that came from the forest. One night, a group of them had come to his fence, desperate and hungry, and he had slaughtered them.

They had called him cousin, and Magnus saw a resemblance, but he felt no comradery toward the creatures from the woods. He was dedicated to man, who petted and cooed and fed. He slept near their fire. He did not know hunger or desperation.

Walking through the creek water, he looked for the tree that had hair, fingers wrapped hard around the tool he had been given. In his human form, he was able to understand their words better, even some of their concepts—but it was still tricky. With humans, a tree wasn't just "tree." There were so many names.

This one turned out to be simple, at least. The tree was clearly the one they had described—its long branches hanging down just like hair. Magnus focused on using his fingers to unfold the tool Ivas had given him. His first instinct was to use his teeth, but the tool produced a long, sharp claw that would do the trick. He picked a branch and began to cut at the bark.

"Hear me, sweet earth."

The voice Magnus heard was that of the two-leg-hunter, but it did not speak the way humans spoke or dogs barked. His ears laid back against his head in agitation, and he kept cutting.

"You of many names: Barmanau, Coco, Bunyip, Shaitan. I take the belief, the stories, the rumors, and I make you real."

The tree branch was stubborn with green tree meat. Magnus put his weight behind the blade and finally tore the branch free from the body of the tree.

"You who haunt the corners of their vision, who may cross their borders—boot-trodden, plant-cut, and soil-tilled. I make you solid, visible, dangerous."

Goal completed, Magnus headed back the way he came. The air shifted around him, the leaves pulled by the wind, and the voice continued its strange incantation.

"Take form, take their rules—shadow-dweller, child-stealer. Enter the home and bring the snail-bearer into the woods."

The rocks lining the edge of the creek shuddered and tumbled into the water as the earth trembled. Magnus broke into a run, splashing through the water as he fled from the voice and the wrongness of the woods.

"Get rid of the Guardian first."

CHAPTER 22

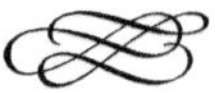

A MONSTER COMES

Ivas focused on turning the branch Magnus had brought them into a hoop that was as close to a perfect circle as he could manage. Traverse and Ruby stood at each of his shoulders, watching intently. Blanc sat at his feet. Ivas felt completely surrounded and struggled to keep his mind on task. He had carved one end into a wedge and attempted to fit it into the other end by carving out a gap.

"Are you going to carve out the edges?" Traverse whispered.

"Mmhmm."

"We only have one, what if you mess up?" Ruby worried.

"I won't."

"Do you want me to do it?"

"No."

"Have you carved things before?"

"Yes."

Blanc thumped her tail on the porch. Ivas fit the wood into place. The flexible willow branch turned nicely and didn't break. He breathed a sigh of relief. The girls echoed the exhale. Blanc looked up and panted.

"How do we even know this thing will work?" Ivas wondered aloud, turning it in his hands like a steering wheel. He had smoothed it out and removed the leaves. With the flimsy end removed, it had reached the circumference of a dinner plate. "Sounds like a hooky dreamcatcher."

Ruby slouched. "It does feel pretty weak. What's a circle of wood going to do?"

Traverse took the hoop and ran her hand over it. "Magnus can turn into a human. A ghost is haunting the house. There's a monster in the woods. Those are all things from stories, yet they're really happening. This is from a story, too. If we give it some belief, then it'll work." She looked at them firmly. "I'm going to get some red yarn. It has to be red, right?"

Ivas nodded. "That's what the story says."

"Then it has to be red."

"Dab on some wood glue, too, so it doesn't slip," Ivas advised.

Ruby followed Traverse to the craft room. Ivas leaned back in his chair, feeling very tired. His thoughts went to Magnus and the cryptic message he had tried to give them after leaving the woods.

"Something's coming," Magnus had said.

"We know, Creeping Bones."

Magnus shook his head. "No, it called something."

He was unable to explain more, perhaps lacking the skills to describe what he knew with human words. Instead, he had handed over the branch and knife and returned to his dog form, jogging back to his post in the field.

It called something...

Ivas looked to the trees. They were going to have another sleepless night ahead. Precautions would need to be taken. Perhaps he could stand guard outside Traverse's window, or place Magnus in the bedroom with her. Creeping Bones couldn't leave the woods, but if—

It called something...

—then there might be something that could.

"Keep your eyes peeled, girl," he said, rubbing one of Blanc's ears. She looked at him lovingly and leaned into his hand. "Come on, let's gather the sheep."

At the word "sheep," Blanc jumped up eagerly.

"Come by."

CHAPTER 23

THE REAPER AND THE CHILD-THIEF

Traverse wanted to make a fire.

"It doesn't feel right," she said, staring at the unraveled yarn tangled on the floor. "Not…mystical enough."

"Does it need to be mystical?" Ruby asked.

"It needs to feel right." Traverse stood up and gathered the supplies. Ruby picked up the hoop, avoiding the spot where fresh glue had been applied. She followed after Traverse, but as they passed the kitchen, her stomach gave a low rumble. Traverse stopped and chuckled.

"Why don't we have dinner first?"

"We can do the fire after. I'll help."

Traverse looked down at the yarn, then nodded. "Yeah, okay. I don't want you to starve. Connie would have my head."

"She might even take you into the woods and shoot you."

Traverse froze and stared at her, eyes widening, then a laugh cracked out from her throat. Her whole body trembled with it and she had to bend over as tears built up in her eyes. Ruby laughed at Traverse, joining in with mad cackles.

"Oh my God, I can't believe you said that."

Ruby only grinned pridefully.

"You are so messed up."

They changed course for the kitchen and Traverse started pulling out fixings for dinner. Ruby noted rice and different vegetables.

"We doing stir fry?"

"Eli would be happy to know we're keeping meat off the table," Traverse said, a touch of sadness in her voice. "Plus, it's easy." She passed the package of rice to Ruby, who scanned the instructions. Traverse started chopping with a skill that Ruby didn't realize could be applied to vegetables.

"You like cooking?"

"I'm indifferent, but it's an 'essential skill,' as Connie says."

"Did she teach you?"

"Yep. Every kid who came here had a job and learned a skill, especially cooking. Connie has this weird thing about the kids leaving and being able to cook for themselves when they go to college or whatever, which, you know, is a good point."

"The jobs thing sounds sucky, though." Ruby poured water into a pot and stared at it, waiting for the tale-tell bubbles of boiling.

"They were, but it makes sense now that I'm older. It can get really boring out here really fast, and bored teenagers get into trouble. One day, the lawn mower broke and I saw Bram using the scythe to cut the grass. I thought it looked cool, so I asked him to teach me. The lawn mower was retired and that became my job. I could just plug my ears with music and swipe back and forth for hours. It was really soothing, actually calmed me down."

"Calmed you down?" The water began to roll. Ruby poured in the rice and covered it with a pot lid.

"Ugh, I was angry all the time. We all were. Except Eli, the freak."

Ruby stared at Traverse as she finished cutting and putting the vegetables into a skillet. She thought about being a young kid without parents, going to live with strangers. Maybe lots of different strangers.

Traverse stirred the vegetables as they began to sizzle.

Ruby thought of her mom, alone back at home, and her father, with whom she had only fifteen years. She felt homesick and wished she had gotten on the train when she had the chance.

"Ruby?"

"What?"

"How long has the rice been boiling?"

"Oh, shoot, I forgot to put on a timer. How long have we been talking?"

"Don't worry about it. I'll watch the rice; you get the plates."

After the meal was completed, they ravished their plates, hungry from the lunchless afternoon.

"Trauma's a real calorie burner," Ruby said, earning another fit of laughter from Traverse. The meal was done quickly, and they put away the leftovers before grabbing the yarn and resuming the journey to the backyard.

It was closer to nightfall now, the sky a mix of red and purple as the sun pulled the horizon up over itself like a blanket. A firepit was set up away from the house, surrounded by a circle of mismatched chairs. Traverse forwent a chair and sat in the grass, so Ruby joined her.

"Know how to start a fire?" Traverse quizzed.

"Kerosine and matches."

Traverse chuckled. There was a basket full of old newspapers underneath one of the chairs. She made strips of paper into a small pile, followed by twigs and sticks. "Go grab a couple of logs. They're under the tarp on the side of the house."

Ruby found the firewood—years of it stacked and dried—and took a few pieces. When she returned, Traverse had a tiny fire going. The logs were added, and the flames grew, pushing the growing shadows back.

Traverse started to weave the yarn, then paused and put it down again. She reached into her pocket and pulled out her portable music player. She pressed play but left the head-phones unplugged so that the music played out of the tiny speaker. Haunting female voices sang forth in a strangely operatic rock and roll.

"Okay, *now* it feels right," Traverse smiled. The light shined off her face, and the wood crackled along with the low music. Ruby smiled back and nodded. Traverse picked up the willow branch and the yarn and finally began putting them together.

The sound of a dog's scream ripped through the night, freezing their spines. Even the fire shrank—as if in fear.

~

*T*vas didn't go into the main house for dinner. He was tired and done with human interaction for the day. The sheep were put away, the dogs were fed, and he was ready for a can of beans and sausage.

He ate his meal, slipping a couple of sausages to Blanc while watching one of the two black and white channels his little TV managed to pick up. It was relaxing, and he didn't have to pay attention to the story, just take in the staticky noise while he sat back in his bed, carefully spooning beans into his mouth. Drops of gravy dripped onto his chin.

Blanc silently rose from her bed and tread carefully

across the floor, her triangle ears pointed straight up, eyes unblinking.

"What's wrong?" Ivas asked, pushing himself up.

Blanc didn't answer. She went to the door, head lowered. Then, a soft growl rumbled from her chest, and Ivas's heartbeat doubled.

He put his bowl down and got to his feet, scrambling into his boots. Blanc didn't take her eyes off the door. She seemed to be staring past it, as if she could see what was on the other side. Ivas imagined that, with her powerful ears and nose, she could, in a way.

Boots on, he grabbed his shepherd staff and opened the door.

As if inviting in horror, an awful scream hit him like a bolt of lightning, and if it weren't for his staff, he might have fallen to his knees. Blanc immediately took off, disappearing in the dark, ignoring his order to stop.

Ivas chased after her, realized how dark it was, and doubled back for his lantern. He lit it as he jogged from his cabin, hand trembling on the knob. The scream hadn't been human. It had bolted itself through his ears and burrowed down into his stomach, twisting it up painfully. He heard Blanc's yips and followed the sound to the barn. The white of her fur caught his eye at the edge of his lantern light, and he ran up to her.

Then he saw the blood, coating white fur and green grass. Inside the barn, the sheep were screaming and banging their bodies against the walls.

Magnus was panting too fast, drool pooling around his mouth. He stayed on the ground, not looking up even as Ivas said his name. He was shaped like a dog, but he raised a human hand from under his leg. Ivas went to his knee and took it, squeezing tight.

"Monster," Magnus spoke with a human tongue. "Pup-stealer."

Ivas wanted to stay with Magnus, to save him. His heart broke as he stood up. New screams echoed over the farm, full of fight and terror. Ivas heard Ruby's voice. So did Blanc. The Burger Blanc Suisse turned her head to the sound and jolted forward like a gust of wind. Ivas followed. The shadows bobbed and danced, the lantern swinging as he ran.

The light of a fire appeared ahead, with figures silhouetted by its light. Two were familiar, human, but the third wasn't shaped like anything Ivas had ever seen before.

He caught glimpses of it in the swing of the lantern and flow of the campfire. Fingers like the straps of a straitjacket. A face with a kind smile that made him sick to his stomach. Empty eyes that didn't reflect the firelight. Feet that were cloven hooves.

And that smile... Wide yet soft, promising sweets and safety, but sending ice cubes down his back.

The girls were screaming each other's names. Ivas recognized Traverse's hair as she was dragged away by an arm that was too long for the creature's body. It dragged along the ground with the girl in its grasp.

Ruby had a hold of Traverse's ankle, trying to pull her free.

Blanc zoomed into the fight, her fur spiked straight up, and her voice transformed by a snarl. She sank her teeth into the thing.

It stopped and turned its empty eyes on the ones opposing it. Ivas shouted in fear and urged his legs to go faster. He raised his shepherd's staff, but instead of hitting the thing, he hooked Ruby's stomach and yanked her back. She released Traverse and fell at Ivas's feet. The thing had been raising its other hand—this one different from the one entwining Traverse.

It wasn't a hand but a stump from which thin branches hung, the kind grandmothers used to whip disobedient children.

One to bind, one to harm...

With Ruby out of its way, it turned its gaze to Blanc.

"That'll do!" Ivas screamed, hoping the desperation in his voice reached his dog. Blanc released the monster and stepped away but kept barking and snarling.

The thing raised the whipped claw over its head.

"Blanc!"

The dog yelped in fear as the whips came down, darting to the side and dodging the blow. It struck the ground instead, creating a burst of soil. Blanc backed away and Ivas was able to jump forward and grab her collar, pulling her back.

The thing turned away and continued its walk. Traverse was carried beside it, dragged along the ground, screaming and crying.

Ruby's scream echoed as she pushed herself up and made to chase after them. Ivas grabbed her around the waist and held her back, one arm around the girl, the other around Blanc. They both fought against him.

"Let go, let go! It's got Trav!" Ruby punched at Ivas's shoulder. "You bastard! Coward!"

Ivas forced Blanc's collar into Ruby's hand. "I'm going after them. There's an address book next to the phone. Call the Stewarts and get Bram back here as fast as he can."

Ruby stopped punching and stared at him, tears streaming down her face like perpendicular rivers.

"I'll get her back, but you need to get help and get Blanc in the house. She'll kill herself trying to stop that thing."

You will too...

He let go of Ruby and stood up. Blanc fought against her hold, desperately wanting to follow Ivas, but Ruby held on.

"Stay," he said firmly. Shepherd staff clutched in his hands, Ivas ran to the forest, following the upturned soil— the path of the monster.

Ruby stared after him, his instructions ringing in her ears. She stood up, arms shaking so badly she wasn't sure if she would be able to hold Blanc much longer. She looked toward the house, took a step, then stopped. Her own inner voice spoke over Ivas's.

Bram's gun wouldn't stop that thing. Ivas alone couldn't stop them.

She remembered what it was like to have horns, to be taller than the trees and facedown the things that would swallow her whole. She looked down at Blanc and said, "Stay," her voice deep and hard.

Blanc obeyed and stopped pulling. Ruby released her collar and went back to the fire. In the dirt, close enough that part of the wood had been singed, was the willow branch, dropped by Traverse when the monster had come out of the shadows right behind them and scooped her up.

Guns never stopped the monsters in stories, but things like this did.

Ruby picked up the yarn and wove it between her fingers. Muscle memory took over and she began to loom it into a tangible shape that Traverse had taught her. A Jacob's Ladder appeared in her hands, intricate as a spider's web, and she tied it into the circle of wood.

Clutching the makeshift charm in both hands, Ruby stood up and looked to the woods. Blanc pressed herself against her leg anxiously.

"Let's go."

The trees embraced them with darkness and cool, wet air. Ruby maneuvered between the branches and bushes swiftly, holding the charm against her chest, both protecting it and hoping it would protect her.

Blanc stayed at her side. Ruby wished there had been time to get her to safety, to get help from anyone, but Creeping Bones was the woods. The minute Traverse crossed the threshold, she was at its mercy.

There was a fleeting bit of clearing, and Ruby realized they were passing the treehouse. She wasn't sure where to go at this point. She thought they would have caught up to Ivas by now, but the woods were not on their side. Blanc pressed her nose to the ground and sniffed about urgently.

Once upon a time, Blanc had found Ruby, who had been lost in something otherworldly. Ruby's hand went to the compass pin on her shirt, and she slipped the needle free.

"Blanc," she called, holding out the trinket. Blanc went to her and sniffed at her hand. "Can you find her? Can you smell it?"

Blanc sniffed loudly, then turned away and resumed smelling the earth. Ruby had no idea how to command her to follow the scent. Ivas knew all those special code words for the dogs.

"Come on, Blanc. Find them. Creeping Bones wants Traverse. And Siobhan is with Creeping Bones. If we find her, then…"

Blanc suddenly whipped her body around and started to trot. Ruby jumped up and followed at a steady jog. Blanc was swift and undeterred by the tangled forest, but Ruby easily tripped and stumbled, falling behind. Blanc didn't stop, becoming a ghostly flash of white as she got out of range.

"Blanc! Slow down!" Ruby panted, sticky sweat bursting along her skin in the warm night. She doubled over to catch her breath.

The sound of growling gave her a second wind.

Her head shot up, and Ruby saw the silhouette of the monster, its whipping hand resting on the ground. Its head turned to look over its shoulder to stare at her.

She had almost run right into it, thinking the thing was a tree.

Blanc was glaring it down, pointed ears flattened, growling warningly. A feminine whimper told Ruby that Traverse was still there, in the thing's hand.

Swallowing, Ruby held her yarn and willow charm aloft. She was ashamed to see her hand was trembling, and she couldn't stop it.

The creature turned toward her. Ruby took a step back, then willed herself to hold her ground.

It was just yarn and a stick. How could it stop this thing?

You were just a little girl...

If we give it some belief, then it'll work...

Ruby pulled in a deep breath, practically wrangling it into her lungs.

She took her step back.

The creature slowly raised its arm, a warning of the pain to come if she didn't behave.

She could feel the willow branch grow warm in her hand. In the spot where it had burned, a spark shot out. Ruby put both her hands on the charm and took another step forward.

Hotter now, the red of the yarn seeped into the wood, almost glowing with the vibrant color.

The switches came down, and Ruby tilted the charm to meet it.

There was a burst of fire, a scattering of sparks. Ruby winced and turned her head away to protect her eyes. Blanc barked wildly, running circles between the trees.

Ruby opened her eyes, and the monster was gone.

In her hands, the yarn of the charm was burning. It was alight with fire, but the string did not burn away. Slowly, the fire dimmed and disappeared, leaving only smoke behind. The yarn was completely intact.

Traverse's moan forced her eyes off the charm. The older

girl shakily pushed herself up. Ruby went to her knees and wrapped her arms around Traverse.

"Oh God! Oh my God, are you okay?"

Traverse's body was trembling like the last leaf of fall. She looked at Ruby with lost, bewildered eyes. They began to fill with tears and her face cracked like broken glass.

"It's okay. I got you. It's okay." Ruby put her arms around Traverse's chest and pulled her to her feet. "Come on, you can do this. We need to get somewhere safe."

Traverse walked, but in stumbling, faltering steps. Ruby had to keep her upright as they made their way too slowly back through the trees. Every snap and creek made her tense, waiting for Creeping Bones to appear.

When it did, she screamed. The cry jolted Traverse, who started to run.

Its eyes were everywhere. Ruby could see the flash of night creatures watching them, guiding Creeping Bones to them as they fled. Tree branches slapped their faces, thorns tore their pants and sliced their skin.

It was toying with them. It was more powerful now, and it had time to play.

Ruby found the treehouse. It was in the woods, but manmade. Would it protect them? She pushed Traverse to the ladder, shoving her upward. The older girl still had enough sense to start climbing. Ruby held the charm in front of her, covering their retreat. Once she was sure Traverse was up, she began to climb as well.

"I was just going to kill him," a voice said, "but if you want your shepherd alive, you'll have to hand over the snails."

Ruby heaved, a cold sweat bursting painfully across her skin from the sound. Creeping Bones wasn't using the forest to talk. The second snail had given it its own voice. Turning, she saw it standing there in front of the tree house. In its hand of branches and dirt, it clutched Ivas around the neck, forcing him to his knees. The shepherd's face was screwed up in pain, eyes shut and teeth clenched.

Blanc was staring at them, soundless.

Jumping down from the ladder, Ruby held out her charm and stormed forward, face set in an expression of determination. She walked right up to Creeping Bones and shoved the charm into its chest.

The crack of the willow branch was like a gunshot. Splinters buried themselves into her hands, making Ruby yelp in pain. She jumped back, the red yarn unraveling and falling to the ground. The charm had split in two, the branches fell uselessly, and Creeping Bones still stood before her.

It laughed.

Back, back, Ruby scrambled back, mouth open in fear, her breaths coming in short and sharp. Creeping Bones squeezed Ivas's neck, turning his face purple. Blanc began to bark hysterically.

"Stop!" Ruby screamed.

"Give me the snails, you insufferable wretch!" Creeping Bones screamed back. The whole forest seemed to scream with him. Birds flew, leaves shook, insects shrieked. Ruby screamed in fear, hands shooting up to cover her ears.

Creeping Bones threw Ivas aside, his body limp as he rolled across the ground. Blanc ran to him.

He's dead, he's dead...

The forest spirit stormed to her, drawing leaves and dirt into itself to grow taller. Ruby screamed and collapsed into a ball, covering her head with her arms. She waited for pain.

She heard Creeping Bones growl in frustration and looked up. Ivas was on his feet, his shepherd's staff hooked around Creeping Bone's arm and pulling him back. He wasn't strong enough to physically stop it by any means, but it was enough of a distraction for Ruby to get to her feet and run.

Something struck her in the back so hard that her feet left the ground. Her breath stopped as she briefly became airborne, then was returned to the ground with painful consequences. She rolled through the leaves, spine pounding. A flash of red caught her eye as she came to a stop—the broken charm.

With two snails consumed, Creeping Bones was too powerful for such things. Maybe it always had been.

Her hands wrapped around the thin willow branch, now broken in two.

She remembered what it was like to have horns. To take them from the fog.

She looked up at Ivas and Blanc, trying to fight off a creature that stood a whole man higher than them.

She remembered what it was like to be that size.

Ruby picked up the two broken branches, red yarn dangling, and pressed them against her head. She dug them into her flesh, wincing in pain as the skin broke. Blood bloomed where wood met bone. Tears of pain fell down her freckled cheeks.

Give me horns and claws and fangs...

Make me scarier than the things that scare me...

Roots crawled from the branches, following the trail of her blood. They buried themselves down beneath Ruby's skin, and now she was screaming, falling to her knees as the amputated tree became a part of her, drank her in.

Both Ivas and Creeping Bones ceased their attack to look at Ruby. Ivas thought that what he was seeing was a hallucination brought on by his strangulation. The branches solidified themselves on Ruby's head, standing up like a set of antlers. Buds and small leaves appeared over them as they grew.

Panting, gasping, sobbing, Ruby looked up and shakily pushed herself to her knees. Ivas saw engorged veins pulsing beneath the skin of her forehead, and realized they weren't veins, but roots.

She lifted her eyes, found Creeping Bones, and charged.

The two became locked in—the branches that were part of their bodies tangled together. Creeping Bones roared in anger, making the whole forest tremble. Ruby pressed it to the ground, having grown to match its size. Her eyes slid up and found Ivas. A green tinge marred her skin. Her hair hung in bloody mats around her face.

"Leave," she said through her teeth. "Take Traverse and *get out*." Her expression and tone were so angry, they frightened Ivas. She was bigger now, getting larger than her opponent.

Ivas looked to the treehouse and saw Traverse staring out from the door. He ran to the ladder and motioned for her to come down. "Come on, hurry!"

"No!" Creeping Bones screeched and thrashed. Ruby wrapped her arms and legs around it and pinned it down.

Traverse scrambled down the ladder, and Ivas took her hand. With an order to Blanc, they ran. The forest reached out to try and stop them—rocks jutted upward, branches reached out, but they ducked and dodged, Creeping Bones too distracted to stop them.

They found the trail worn down between the farm and treehouse, feet pounding against the dirt. When they found the edge and broke free into the field, they both collapsed, gasping for air.

Traverse stared at the ground, sweat dripping from her chin, her irises ringed by the whites of her eyes, and her fingertips digging into the grass. "We left her. We left Ruby…"

Ivas couldn't answer. He could barely hear her over his

pounding heart. Blanc licked at his cheek sympathetically. "We need…help…" he panted.

"From who?"

"We'll get your dad and—"

"No! Connie and Bram can't go in there. They'll get killed. What can they do that we haven't tried?"

Ivas managed to push himself to his knees. He met Traverse's eyes. "The only thing we haven't tried is just giving it the snails."

Traverse wrapped a hand around her arm, squeezing tightly.

"If we give it what it wants, it'll let Ruby go."

"But Ruby won't let *it* go." Traverse looked back at the trees. "Only one of them is coming out of this."

Ivas groaned, lowering his head. Blanc slipped in with another lick. "How do we stop it then? How do we give Ruby the edge?"

A memory presented itself in Traverse's mind, and she perked her head up. She stood and started walking to the barn. Ivas scrambled to follow her.

"What? What is it?"

"When Creeping Bones found me in the woods, there was something that stopped it." She was running again, a light jog this time. They reached the barn and opened the doors. The eyes of the sheep all shot up, staring at them unblinkingly.

Traverse found the scythe on the wall where the tools were kept and took it from its spot on the wall. "When Connie used this on Creeping Bones, it actually hurt it…and that was after it had eaten the second snail." She turned, clutching the tool tightly in both hands. "I'll cut it to pieces."

Ivas's eyes widened. "It can't cross human borders, not even the treehouse."

Traverse nodded.

Ivas looked at the tools on the wall. A sheathed axe hung there, retired for the summer from cutting firewood. He took it down.

"What else?" He wondered, looking around the barn. Traverse was already walking away. "Wait a minute. Is this enough?"

"It has to be. I don't want to waste any time."

Ivas grabbed her arm. "Let's get a light at least. My cabin."

She nodded and they changed course, going to Ivas's room. Walking across the field, they were noticed by the dogs, who started barking from their pen. Ivas opened the door to his home and found another lantern, along with an emergency flashlight, which he passed to Traverse.

The dogs barked louder, as if demanding to know what was going on.

Ivas stopped and looked in the direction of the pen.

"What is it?"

"The dogs... Magnus entered the woods without being harmed." His stomach ached, remembering Magnus. Was he still alive? Left alone in pain this whole time?

"You're right." Traverse changed direction again and jogged to the dog pen. When she opened the door, the puppies lined up eagerly to see who would be leaving.

"Aster," Ivas said.

"Just him?"

"Ruby is his." Ivas didn't finish his thought aloud—that Aster might be the motivation Ruby needed to leave the woods. She might not do it for him or Traverse.

Aster hopped forward excitedly, first circling Ivas and Traverse, then licking his mother's mouth. Ivas gave a sharp order, and the two dogs came to attention, following as the humans walked back to the woods. They found the trail that would take them to the treehouse.

Their steps slowed again, becoming unsure as the trees

swallowed them, even their lights not giving any comfort. The dogs stayed by their sides, Aster's ears laid back against his head.

When they reached the treehouse, the woods were not the same. Both of them gasped with sharp intakes of air.

The trees were bent, as if they had been warped by years of harsh winds. A wall of thorns and brambles had grown up from the earth, tangled and impassible, hanging from the twisted branches of the bowed trees like the curtains of a stage. Even the ground had changed, the soil heaved into a hill with the grass and stones broken and cracked.

"Jesus," Traverse whispered. Blanc concurred the sentiment with a whine. "They're in there."

Ivas stepped forward, set down his lantern, and raised the axe. Traverse mimicked him, swiping the scythe through the thorns, cutting the bottom. They still hung in place, so she did the same to the vines above.

A small piece of the barrier fell away, but the wall was deep. Ivas hacked, his tool too short to spare him the sting of the thorns. Traverse had better luck, swiping across and pulling the barbed vines away with the curve of her blade. With each hit, the thorns seemed to lash out at them, leaving thin red lines across their faces.

The deeper they went, the larger the thorns became, until the scratches became welts. Traverse cried with each swing, and Ivas kept his head down, protecting his eyes. The debris tangled into his hair instead. Pieces of the plant snagged into their clothes, burrowing down to pierce their skin, even through their shoes.

When they made it to the other side, they were panting in pain, covered in sweat and blood. Traverse grabbed a thorn the size of a pencil that had dug itself into her shoulder and yanked it out.

Lifting his lantern, Ivas stepped forward to see what they had uncovered.

A large mass lay before them at the base of the treehouse. It almost looked like a giant, gnarled tree in the darkness, but then Ivas saw that it was breathing, heaving in and out with incredible difficulty.

It wasn't a tree. It was the giant forms of Ruby and Creeping Bones, twisted together like two snakes in battle, both trying to swallow the other.

Traverse couldn't stop the sound of horror that left her mouth. She had to turn away. The two dogs stepped forward, growling, fur spiking up.

"Ruby, can you hear me?" Ivas asked, scared to raise his voice too loudly.

One of the masses shifted, and they heard a sound, like a rush of air. Ivas realized it was sniffing the air.

"The snails..." the voice of Creeping Bones rumbled from the entanglement.

Traverse looked back, eyebrows drawn together, scythe raised. "Ruby!" was her battle cry as she ran forward and sliced the blade downward into a mass of bark and bone.

Dual screams shattered the night. The twisted trees writhed and lashed, their leaves kicking up in a nonexistent wind. The two creatures before them moved, pulling away from each other. Teeth appeared, unsheathed from flesh. Claws flashed. Bugs crawled in mass, skittering from the bodies where they had buried themselves. One of them lifted their head and howled like something unnatural.

Traverse yanked her scythe free and struck again.

Creeping Bones and Ruby pulled away from each other entirely. The snap of breaking wood made Ivas flinch. He felt wet drops hit his shoulders like rain. Looking up, he realized tears were falling from Ruby's eyes as she returned to herself.

She yanked her hands from where they had dug themselves inside Creeping Bones. Her adversary grabbed her shoulders and pushed her away. Their ribs had become encased. Bones cracked when they pulled apart.

Ruby threw her head back and screamed.

Ivas and Traverse covered their ears, wincing in pain. The dogs yelped and whimpered.

Finally free, Ruby and Creeping Bones collapsed away from each other, moaning and snarling. Ruby dug her nails into the ground, dragging herself away. Creeping Bones turned its sniffing snout toward Traverse.

The girl didn't hesitate. Raising her scythe again, she swung with all her might. The blade passed through the plant matter of Creeping Bone's wrist, separating the hand. Creeping Bones fell forward onto its elbow.

Ivas went to Ruby. She was big, fallen forward with her head bowed, back heaving as she focused on breathing.

The willow branches protruded from her head. They had wept into arches, hanging down from her like hair, gleaming with green leaves.

Ivas raised the axe, stepping up to Ruby and aiming for the base where the tree fused into her skull. He remained frozen there, remembering the last time he had broken her antlers, remembering his promise never to do it again.

His arms trembled with the exertion of holding the axe aloft. He had to break these. They were killing her.

But he had promised.

Slowly, with the agony of indecision, Ivas lowered the axe.

As the tool came down, Ruby's eyes lifted. She gazed at him with eyes the color of fresh soil, her skin green and wet. She reached for him with a hand the size of his torso and gently grasped his shoulders.

"I can see them, Ivas," she said, tone sad and so, so tired.

"Who?"

"The ones Creeping Bones has taken. Look. Remember the fogs and *see*."

Ivas turned to look at the monster. Traverse was as good as her word, hacking at it, removing its limbs. She shaved it down bit by bit, removing the armor of vine, tree, and dirt.

Beneath it all were bones.

It was completely made up of the bones of humans and animals alike, stacked and plated together. Some parts still had rotting organic parts that pulsed. The top half of its head was a human skull, but the bottom half was the jaw of a deer. Different kinds of sharp teeth jutted from the tooth sockets.

Tied into those bones, in the darkness of its body, were the ghosts.

They hung off Creeping Bones like a mist, their faces staring out with horrible sadness and fear. They were caged inside, or shackled by the wrist around a femur, or simply dragged along the ground, clutching its ankle, unable to let go.

There was a child, a couple of men, a woman. Their hair floated ethereally, eyes blank.

"Siph…" Traverse stopped cutting. Only the bones remained, and she could see the spirits trapped within it. Siph hung by his neck between two ribs, staring out at the world without emotion.

Her hesitation was enough. Creeping Bones seized her by the neck with a hand made of phalanges of different sizes and colors and shoved her to the ground. The scythe was cast aside so that Traverse could use both hands to push the creature away, allowing her to still breathe.

Its other hand began to grope for her, seeking out the snails. Traverse screamed as her clothes were torn.

Ruby rushed forward, launching herself with her arms. She grabbed Creeping Bone's wrist and put an arm around its neck, trying to pull it away. Traverse wiggled her neck free, but Creeping Bones grabbed her shirt instead. The snails shimmered against her skin, leaving trails behind as they slowly moved to hide.

"Mine... Mine..."

Ruby put her fingers into its eye sockets and twisted its head backward. Ivas brought his axe forward and used it to cut Traverse's shirt down the middle. The girl scrambled backward on her forearms, away from Creeping Bone's grasping hands.

Ruby kept the creature in place, her eyes squeezed shut with effort as Creeping Bones fought against her, thrashing wildly.

Traverse pushed herself up and went forward. Ivas choked and tried to grab her, but her shirt slipped away, hanging from his hand.

Back in Creeping Bone's reach, Traverse took a snail from her stomach, holding it carefully between her fingers. Creeping Bone's gaze locked onto the snail, and its tongue lashed out desperately.

Traverse grabbed its collarbone, hooking her fingers and locking her elbow. She glared up into its empty sockets.

"Those bones don't belong to you."

She dropped the snail, and it fell into the ghostly hands of the woman locked inside its ribcage. Her ponytail swung as she brought the snail to her mouth and wrapped her lips around it.

Creeping Bones froze, one of its reaching hands pulled away as if by an invisible puppet string. Traverse took another snail and gave it to the toddler that had hooked itself onto one of Creeping Bone's legs. Another she fed to the man whose wrists were stuck in the space between the arm bones.

Siph held a hand out to Traverse, eyes widening with

desperation. But she did not give him a snail, pointedly turning away to serve the other ghosts instead.

With each snail given, Creeping Bones lost control. The bones rattled and shifted, yanked away, until Ruby was able to release it without repercussion.

Creeping Bones screamed and howled, but the ghosts were breaking free, slipping from their bonds and pushing it back. Traverse watched in horror as the man took hold of Creeping Bone's collarbone and broke it away. The woman pulled the ribs until they snapped. Each ghost took their bones back, watching as what remained began to crumble away.

Ivas grabbed both girls by an arm and tugged. "Let's get out of here."

Traverse nodded, but her eyes didn't leave Creeping Bones, watching as its skull was taken, different pieces of the spine, all pulled away. The ghosts that retrieved their bones began to drift away into the trees, becoming only a mist in the darkness.

They slowly retreated, back through the thorns, onto the path. With each step, Ruby came back to the size she was when she had first entered the woods. Ivas kept his arm around her as she began to stumble.

She resisted him as they came to the edge.

"Come on, Ruby, we're there. We're back."

She shook her head.

Traverse went to her side and took her hand. Ivas squeezed the other, and together, they pulled her forward, out of the trees and into the open air.

Ruby swayed and fell to her knees. Leaves fell from her hair.

"What do you need?" Ivas asked.

"Lay down…" she murmured.

With Traverse on one side and Ivas on the other, they

half carried Ruby to Ivas's cabin. Inside, she collapsed onto the cot. Traverse kneeled by the bed, squeezing her hand.

"It's going to be okay," the older girl said. "I'm right here. Aster's here too."

As if to confirm, the puppy stepped forward and licked Ruby's hand. Tears welled in her eyes.

"My good boy."

Ivas came to her side with a cup of water. He lifted her up and pressed the rim of the mug to her lips. Ruby sipped it tentatively.

"What hurts?" he asked.

"Everything," she whimpered.

Traverse lifted Ruby's shirt and winced at the sight of purple splashed across her ribs.

"Cut them off..." Ruby gasped.

Ivas bit his lip. "Are you sure?"

She nodded.

Ivas pulled out his pocketknife. With one hand, he grabbed a branch, and in the other he began to saw at the wood. Traverse pressed her hands together nervously. "Is that safe?"

Ivas wasn't sure and hesitated as Ruby started crying. "I was ready... I was going to..." Her voice cracked on her tears.

"What, Ruby?" Traverse asked, leaning closer.

Ruby sniffed and tried to regain control. "I...I locked myself in with Creeping Bones. I thought I would hold it there forever."

"Forever?"

"I couldn't let it go...not ever... And it's still out there. You should have left me! I had accepted it. Then it couldn't take anyone else."

With a slash, Ivas cut through the branch and tossed it aside. Ruby cried.

"We would have *never* left you, Ruby," Traverse said harshly.

"I had accepted it…"

Ivas went to work on the other branch, pushing himself into the blade to quickly remove it. With a *snap*, it broke away. Traverse took Ruby's face in her hands and kissed her forehead tenderly.

"It's not happening. You're free. We came back for you."

Ruby put her arms around Traverse's neck and squeezed her tight. Traverse pulled her up so that she could rock her. Ivas took the branches and stepped out of the cabin. He let them fall from his hand next to the wood pile. The red yarn stood out in the shadows.

Legs giving out, Ivas slid down against the wall until he hit the cold earth. He wrapped his arms around his knees and lowered his head. He couldn't stop himself from shaking.

CHAPTER 24

SICKNESS AND FORGIVENESS

Traverse and Ruby dozed off on Ivas's bed together, though not really sleeping. Traverse found herself drifting in and out of consciousness. At one point, she heard the rumble of the truck and wondered what time it was. She let herself pass out again, then came too when Ivas entered the room. A hint of blue sunlight shined in the open door behind him.

"Are you hurt anywhere?" he whispered.

Traverse shook her head.

"Use my bathroom and get cleaned up. Then we'll get you two back to the house."

Traverse pushed herself up, but Ruby didn't move. Her stomach dropped with fear, but the girl was only asleep. She went to the bathroom and studied herself in the mirror. She was shirtless, her hair was filled with twigs and leaves, and thorns marred her skin. She slowly pulled them out, then used a washcloth to wipe away the blood and the dirt.

When she was done, she and Ivas tried to wake Ruby, but she only made protesting groans. The two of them half-carried her to the house, and Ruby didn't even seem to realize that she was being moved.

The truck was parked in the driveway, but the house was dark and quiet. Traverse could hear her adoptive father's snores through their bedroom door.

"What time did they get in?" she whispered.

"It was late. I watched them, but they didn't see me," Ivas whispered back.

They put Ruby in the guest room, and Ivas left to let Traverse change Ruby's clothes and clean her face. Ruby didn't react to any of it, returning to full unconsciousness when her head hit the pillow.

Ivas had cut off the branches, but the stumps and roots still remained. Getting a pair of plyers from a toolbox, Traverse went to work pulling them out.

This finally woke Ruby.

Traverse covered Ruby's mouth to keep the scream from waking her parents, pressing her down into the bed. The branch came free with a firm yank, the roots slipping out from under the skin, shining with blood.

Ruby's eyes rolled back, and she passed out again.

Keeping her hand in place, Traverse took out the second one.

Ruby stared up at her pitifully, her eyes overflowing as she stared at the mangled roots that had been inside her. Traverse pressed a cloth to her forehead, catching the blood that wept from the wounds.

"You're okay. It's all done," Traverse promised. She stroked her hair and hummed deep in the back of her throat so that Ruby's eyes would close again. The younger girl followed the sound into sleep, tears still wet on her face.

Traverse took the roots and went outside.

True morning was still hours away, with the farm dark and quiet on the edge of dawn. She went to the fire pit, where the embers of their fire still glowed. Traverse dropped the remnants of the horns on top of the embers, deciding to burn them, lest they find a way into the ground.

The roots popped and crackled as fire burst up from the embers, eagerly consuming them. Traverse felt relief as they became ash.

Something cold touched her neck, like a breeze in the shape of a hand. She turned and saw Siph standing in the shadows, at the edge of the firelight, a vague white outline easily lost by those not knowing how to see.

He held out a hand.

Traverse shook her head. "You hurt my brother."

His fingers curled back menacingly, his form shifting from young boy to rotting corpse. "If you don't give it to me, I will stay here and haunt them."

Traverse stood up and glared down at the dead boy. "They're already haunted. It's what all of you deserve."

~

*I*vas stared down at Magnus. Despite the injuries, despite the blood, and the length of time he had been left alone, his breaths continued to flow, shallow and brief.

In all his years working with them, he had seen dogs remain resilient against things that should have killed them, sometimes lasting for days. His grandfather had taught him that letting them linger was cruel. That dogs were so loyal, it was up to their owners to set them free. Otherwise, they would just hang on, dealing with the pain to make sure their human was okay.

Ivas stroked Magnus's head, thinking about where Bram kept his gun. At his touch, Magnus shifted his eyes, looking up at the shepherd.

"We got her back, Magnus," Ivas said, swallowing around the rock-like lump in his throat. "You did good. You did so good. You kept everyone safe."

Pink foam formed around Magnus's mouth as he panted. He whimpered from the pain. Ivas winced.

"What can I do, Magnus? I can stop the pain. I can end it for you. What do you want?"

Magnus's breaths came and left more quickly. He whined and dragged his paws through the dirt. Ivas withdrew his hand, begging Magnus not to get up. Instead, the dog turned to him, now possessing the mouth of a man.

"I want…to live."

~

Only Traverse noticed when Ivas entered the house, then left again. She paused at Bram and Connie's bedroom door, listening as the truck was started, the sound of its engine fading as it was driven away.

"Connie…" Traverse pushed her parent's door open. Their bodies shifted in the bed at the disturbance.

She shook Connie, who slowly blinked awake and removed her earplugs. "Trav? What time is it?"

"It's early. Ruby's really sick."

~

Connie had dealt with many sick children in her life, and she knew what to do. Illnesses always seemed to happen late at night, but at least this time, there was no vomit to clean up or sheets to change. Ruby had a fever and complained of bodily pains. Medicine was given, a wet towel was placed on her head, and onion-garlic soup was prepared.

The sun rose fully, and Traverse stayed with Ruby, fighting off her own desire for sleep by adding blankets to Ruby's bed as she shivered. Her skin was sickly and grey, with a sheen of sweat.

"It's still there!" Ruby cried, suddenly sitting up.

Traverse pushed her back down. "It doesn't have a body anymore. It can't hurt us."

"You gave the snails to the spirits…" Ruby said.

"It's what they wanted. I could feel it from them, they wanted to go to the ghosts that were there."

"All of them?"

Traverse smiled and pushed off her shoe. She took a snail from her ankle and showed it to Ruby. "There's one more."

Ruby reached her hand out and touched its shell. The girls held hands, watching as the snail made a slow journey from Traverse to Ruby.

"You hang on to this one until it's ready," Traverse said softly.

Ruby smiled and finally relaxed back against her pillow. She studied the snail as it crawled across her knuckles.

When Connie came back, Traverse took the food she had prepared and fed Ruby herself. She stroked her red hair and spoke softly until the younger girl fell asleep again, her face looking more peaceful this time.

Connie watched them from the chair in the corner, silent as Traverse put Ruby to sleep. She stood up and took the empty bowl back but paused as she turned to leave.

"Do you hate me?" Connie whispered.

Traverse blinked in surprise. She felt her stomach flip, nervous at the prospect of having this conversation. She would have been happy to never speak of it again.

"No, I don't hate you." She kept her voice low, smoothing the blanket over Ruby's chest. "Learning what happened… It scared me."

"You don't have to stay," Connie said. "The Stewarts said they would be happy to have you for the rest of the summer if you need to get away. We would understand."

Connie's head was down, and it was clear that she was fighting back the urge to cry. Traverse sighed so hard her shoulders heaved.

"I don't have to like what you did, but…that doesn't mean I don't love you. School starts in the fall, so let's have this summer together, okay?"

Connie turned to her, tears falling, lips rising. She nodded eagerly.

"Love you, Mom."

CHAPTER 25

THE FOREST WATCHES

The summer became heavy with heat, the air alive with moisture and the thrum of bug noise. Ruby spent the final tolerable weeks of the season bedridden, plagued by nightmares and fever.

When she woke in the night, convinced that Creeping Bones was coming, Traverse was there, soothing her back to sleep. Ruby would find the snail on her body to remind herself they were safe.

When her fever finally broke, she was weak, and her body ached more deeply than she had ever experienced. Traverse put balm on her bruised ribs and helped her take short walks around the bedroom. When she was too tired to hold up a book, Connie would read to her.

Mostly, she slept and ate.

She dreamed of being locked together with Creeping Bones, their bones and limbs entwined. She would wake up hurting, clutching at herself and panting in pain. She had only spent a short time as its warden, but she knew that if they had stayed together much longer, she would not have been able to break away and live.

Her walks around the room turned to walks in the house, mostly trips to the craft room to watch TV. Bram even moved furniture around, dragging a couch into the room so that they could all sit comfortably.

Soon, Ruby was able to go outside and sit on the porch, but the heat made that unbearable, so they moved to the lake instead. Traverse carried Ruby on her back and acted as her steed, carrying her into the water.

Warmed by the afternoon sun, the lake had become heaven. She stood neck-deep, then laid down in the grass to dry off before returning to the cool embrace of the water. The lake helped return her strength.

~

"What time is your mom going to be here tomorrow?" Traverse asked. The afternoon was waning, and supper would be ready soon, which was good because they had been swimming all day and Ruby was starving. They were sitting together on the lakeside with their feet in the water, letting the sun warm their bare backs.

"Later in the morning, not too early," Ruby said.

"You happy to be going home?"

"Yes and no. I want to see my mom again, but I'm going to miss you guys."

"Just a couple of years before you start university. Come find me when you do."

"I will," Ruby promised. "Write me when you get to school."

"I will."

Ruby leaned into Traverse's shoulder, her skin hot yet soothing. She rubbed her cheek against it, then looked up at Traverse. "Could I try something with you?"

Traverse looked down at her. "What do you want to try?"

"I was just…thinking…" Ruby stared at her lips, her face filled with terror.

Traverse smiled and leaned forward. The kiss was quick, but tender. Ruby stared up at Traverse with wide eyes, face red, heart pounding.

"I'll miss you too, Ruby." Then Traverse turned away, unable to hide her own shyness.

The humming of bugs filled the air. Their cheeks turned as hot as the afternoon sun.

~

When Ivas drove onto the property the next day, he had three passengers. Hannah sat at the passenger window, admiring the landscape as they passed. He had picked her up at the train station, and the ride back was silent after he had answered her questions about Ruby.

Yes, she's feeling much better. She had a great summer. She's very excited to see you.

Sitting between them was Magnus. He was so big that both Ivas and Hannah were pressed up against their respective doors so that the dog could curl up comfortably. Ivas had one hand on the wheel and the other on Magnus's head. The Great Pyrenees was still bandaged but had been given the all-clear to go home to finish his recuperation.

In the back of the truck, Eli was already jumping out before Ivas could come to a full stop. Eli ran past the driver-side window to the house, where Connie's scream of happiness echoed over the property.

Ivas picked Magnus up himself to carry him out of the truck and set him down. Magnus immediately found himself a shady spot on the porch to curl up.

Ruby came running out through the door, nearly tackling

her mom in a hug. The two squeezed and spun each other, and Ivas was relieved to see that Hannah's hug was neck-based, not pressuring Ruby's ribs.

"I missed you so much! I can't believe I haven't given you a hug all summer." Hannah peppered kisses over Ruby's face. Ivas touched the top of her head as he passed. It comforted him to feel a smooth skull and hair under his hand.

"Mom, you're not going to believe how Aster is now. It's like he's a whole new dog. Come on!" Ruby took Hannah's hand and led her to the pen.

Ivas stepped onto the porch and sat on a chair next to Magnus, whose long pink tongue hung out of his mouth, attesting to the heat. The door opened and Traverse stepped outside, stopping next to Ivas's chair. She watched Ruby and Aster give Hannah a tour.

"I was always jealous of the kids who got to leave here with their actual parents," Traverse said. "Sometimes, the parents would actually get their act together and get to take their kids home. It was nice when I finally realized that I was already home."

"You're such a sap," Eli said, lightly punching her shoulder.

"Don't hit your sister!" Connie scolded.

"So glad I was at the bakery so I didn't have to deal with all this mushiness." Eli shook his head.

"Did you make mad cash?"

"Might have got a little something-something," Eli said nonchalantly. "Not that I would spend any of it on you."

Traverse pounced, searching through Eli's pockets until she came up with a brand-new CD. With a happy squeal, she gave Eli a hug. "I take back all the mean things I said about you."

Bram stepped outside next, carrying Ruby's bags, which

went into the back of the truck. Eli sighed. "Sucks that she has to leave. It was like having a foster again."

"Let's have her back for sheering season," Connie said.

Hannah and Ruby eventually made their way back to the house. Aster jumped into the back of the truck with the bags, and Bram started the engine to get the air conditioning going.

When the rest of the family had said their goodbyes, Ivas and Ruby stepped aside.

"Mom says we're moving," she said.

"Really? Where?"

"Don't know. We're looking into towns inland, places with good schools."

"Hmm."

"If you go back to Loch Lamond… I just… I don't know when I'll see you again. If ever."

"We'll see each other again," Ivas said, a promise in his voice. "And if you need help picking out schools, I know a university with a promising new literature teacher."

He touched her shoulder, but Ruby brushed it away to rush into a tight hug, pushing the air out of his lungs.

"I love you, Ivas."

"I love you too, Ruby. Take care of yourself, okay?"

Final goodbyes were given, with Traverse lingering the longest in a farewell hug. By the time they finally got in the truck, the AC was at full blast, granting them a chilly relief from the day.

When the farm was out of sight, Ruby turned her gaze to the snail that rested itself in the curve of her palm.

～

When the truck was gone, Eli and Connie went inside to escape the heat, but Traverse and Ivas stayed until the dust settled back onto the road. Traverse leaned her head against Ivas's shoulder, heaving a deep sigh.

"Guess we'd better get back to work," Ivas said. "I thought we could see about training the puppies together. I've been reading up on those books you got me from the library."

"I don't know as much about training, only what I've seen you do. But I'll help as much as I can," Traverse said.

"It's more than I have. Let's start with Shiro; she was showing a lot of promise."

Traverse nodded. "You go ahead and get started. I have some reaping to do, then I'll meet you at the corral."

They went their separate ways, but Ivas kept Traverse in his sight as she worked her scythe over the tall grass, even as he picked up the puppy's training.

The woods stood at her back, quiet, and waiting.

ABOUT THE AUTHOR

Breanna Bright lives in Missouri, working as a technical writer by day and a fiction author by night. When she's not writing she's traveling the world and going on adventures, looking for her next story. You can learn more about her and her other works by visiting her website, breannabr.wixsite. com/website

Make sure you never miss a new release. Subscribe to our newsletter, http://redempresspublishing.com/subscribe/

f facebook.com/authorbreannabright

ABOUT THE PUBLISHER

VISIT OUR WEBSITE
TO SEE ALL OF OUR HIGH QUALITY BOOKS:

http://www.redempresspublishing.com

Quality trade paperbacks, downloads, audio books, and books in foreign languages in genres such as historical, romance, mystery, and fantasy.

www.ingramcontent.com/pod-product-compliance
Lightning Source LLC
Chambersburg PA
CBHW072101300726
48975CB00003B/664